B

TERENCE MUNSEY

RETRIBUTION

MUNSEY MUSIC
Toronto Los Angeles London

This book is entirely a work of fiction. Any resemblance or similarity or likeness to actual people living or dead, places, events, names, incidents, is totally coincidental. This work is entirely the product of the author's imagination.

RETRIBUTION

published by:

MUNSEY MUSIC

Box 511, Richmond Hill, Ontario, Canada, L4C 4Y8

Fax: 905 737 0208

E-mail: info@MunseyMusic.com

WEBSITE: www.MunseyMusic.com

National Library of Canada Cataloguing in Publication Data

Munsey, Terence, 1953-

Retribution

ISBN 0-9685152-1-5

I. Title.

PS8576.U5753R47 2001 C813'.54 C2001-930761-6

PR9199.3.M87R47 2001

Library of Congress Control Number 2001117063

First MUNSEY MUSIC original soft cover printing August 01

Manufactured in Canada

Acknowledgments

Thanks to everyone who helped make this a better book.

Books by Terence Munsey

The best-selling Stoneman Series™

The Flight of the Stoneman's Son

ISBN 0-9697066-0-X LCCN 93-93660

Book 1

The Keeper of Three

ISBN 0-9697066-1-8 LCCN 93-86550

Book 2

Labyrinths of Light

ISBN 0-9697066-2-6 LCCN 95-94007

Book 3

Marks of Stone

ISBN 0-9697066-3-4 LCCN 96-94015

Book 4

They of Old

ISBN 0-9697066-4-2

Book 5

MYSTERY

Obsession

ISBN 0-9697066-5-0 LCCN 97-92895

Emerald City

ISBN 0-9697066-6-9 LCCN 98-65102

Dive Master

ISBN 0-9697066-7-7 LCCN 99-70052

L A

ISBN 0-9697066-9-3 LCCN 00-190468

Retribution

ISBN 0-9685152-1-5 LCCN 2001117063

Tatoo

ISBN 0-9685152-2-3

NON-FICTION

How To: be a Published Author

ISBN 0-9685152-0-7 LCCN 99-90327

Author's Note

RETRIBUTION is a chilling, murder-mystery uncovering the darkest schemes of powerful men in powerful places. The many twists and turns make the story a compelling read.

The next mystery book is entitled TATOO.

Thank you for reading Monika Queller Mystery™ novels.

For late-breaking information visit the website:
www.MunseyMusic.com

Can you get even in an odd world?

for Rita Goulding

Prologue

The St. Lawrence Seaway during January in Québec City would be completely ice-bound if it were not for the fast-moving current caused by the rising and lowering tides. In the middle of the river, slowly breaking its way through the ice flows, the 11:45 am Québec-Lévis ferry was making its way across to the Lévis side. The Alphonse-Desjardins was sixty-six meters long, twenty-two meters wide and fifteen meters high. It was a large craft. It could carry seven hundred passengers and fifty-five vehicles on its ten-minute trip across the river, but this was the slow time of the day. The Alphonse-Desjardins was busiest during the rush hours carrying the residents of Lévis to their jobs in Québec City on the north shore and back. At this hour of the late morning there was only a handful of passengers making the crossing.

In its large forward passenger area on the main deck two women were sitting with their children listening to the music that was playing over the PA system. The only other passenger in this section was a man in his late thirties dressed in a light colored trench coat over a dark suit with a gray shirt and a dark matching tie. His blond hair was wind-blown and he was nervously playing with a package of cigarettes. He looked tired and unkempt. He was sitting on the port side of the ferry looking through the window at the panoramic view of the hilltop fortress city from the Citadel on the west, past the Château Frontenac to the Old City and the port of Québec City in the east. It was a beautiful sight even in the overcast, snow covered, bitter chill of January.

Coming up the stairs from the lower deck where the vehicular passengers waited in their cars, was a man wearing a midnight blue parka with fox trimmed hood. His weathered face was just visible beneath a black toque. The man walked out onto the main deck and checked his watch. It was almost 12:00 pm. The glass on his watch was cracked diagonally from eleven o'clock to five.

He went along the starboard promenade of the boat to the forward passenger section and paused to examine the passengers. Seeing the blonde man sitting on the port side bench against the window, he nonchalantly came over and sat down beside him. Neither man looked at the other, nor made contact, but there was a knowing familiarity between them.

The Alphonse-Desjardins continued its journey across the river. It was not a long trip but in the late January ice flows of the rapid St. Lawrence River it was a tricky passage. The boat determinedly made its way through the ice and fast current and five minutes later was making its approach to the dock on the Lévis side.

Suddenly the man in the parka got up from the bench and walked away. He had to return to his car and get ready to disembark. He did not look at or acknowledge the blonde-haired man beside him on the bench. He simply got up and, as nonchalantly as he could, left a large Kraft envelope on the bench and walked away. Without saying a word, the blond-haired man picked up the envelope and put it into his coat pocket. He would examine its contents later. He cautiously looked around to see if anyone had noticed his action but no one was paying attention to him. The other passengers were busy readying themselves to disembark. He remained seated. The first stage of his mission was completed. He was now anxious to get back to the Québec City side and complete the second stage.

The blonde man sat nervously in place watching

as a deckhand lowered the gangplank on the starboard side of the boat and allowed the passengers to leave.

The ferry remained stationary for five minutes waiting for its new passengers. Only vehicular passengers were waiting to make this trip. When the last car was aboard below decks, the deckhand raised the gangplank, locked it in place and signaled the all clear. The powerful diesel engines of the ferry groaned. The boat shuddered and pulled away from the dock, beginning the journey back across the river. No pedestrian passengers were on this trip. The blonde man was relieved to be alone.

- - - - - - - - - - - - - - - -

Later that afternoon the blonde man from the ferry was dressed in the hotel's white housekeeping uniform. He was pushing a large cart along the corridor of the seventeenth floor of the Château Frontenac. To any outside observer it looked as if he was there for the daily set-up of the rooms. He appeared nervous despite the fact there was no one other than himself in the corridor at this time of the afternoon. He kept his head down trying not to be identified. He was not regular housekeeping staff and was not really there to clean up the rooms.

Cautiously he pushed the cart along the corridor. The hotel was old with narrower, more decorated halls than new modern ones. The ceiling was sculpted in an intricately designed cream-colored plaster. The upper half of the walls was covered with beautiful rose-colored brocade wallpaper and the lower half was wainscoted in a dark mahogany. The fixtures were fifties in style and the floor was covered with a slightly worn but impeccably maintained plush dark maroon carpet. The hotel was very luxuriously laid out. In its day it must have been a grand old dame.

As he pushed the cart, he checked the brass room numbers that stood out on the sturdy wood doors that matched the wainscoting. Not finding the room he wanted, he continued down the hall.

He soon came to the end of the corridor, where a large picture window that overlooked the frozen St. Lawrence River and La Terrasse Dufferin stood next to one last room. He stopped in front of the door—1720. He carefully leaned forward and put his ear against the door listening for any noise coming from the inside. Hearing nothing, he got out a pass card and put it in the door lock. A green light glowed indicating that the pass card had been accepted. He removed the card, twisted the handle down and opened the door.

The room was of standard size and comfortably styled in warm colors. To his immediate left was the bathroom. He walked into the room allowing the door to gently close. He scanned the closet for any sign of occupancy. Nothing was hanging up and there were no bags in the closet. It appeared that the room was vacant. More confident, he went further into the room.

A king size bed took up most of the living space. Opposite the bed was a large cupboard that contained a chest of drawers and a television set. Next to the cupboard on the wall to his right was a large mirror. The mirror was hanging like a valuable painting in a heavy ornate gold frame. At the far end of the room a set of ceiling to floor drapes in a warm off-white patterned cotton fabric framed a large window. A small desk with a high back wood chair neatly tucked under it, was kitty corner to the right of the window.

The man did not waste time. He was worried that someone might walk in on him before he could complete his secret task. He pulled out a large Kraft envelope from inside his uniform. Attached to the envelope was a short piece of transparent fishing line. He quickly crossed over to the mirror, reached along its top edge and pulled it an inch from the wall. He took the envelope in one hand and placed it centrally behind the mirror. Taking a small gold flat-head tack that matched the color of the frame from his pocket, he wrapped the line around the pin, then firmly pressed it behind the frame where it could not be seen, securing the envelope in place. Satisfied with the job, he let go of the mirror and adjusted it, making sure it appeared normal and undisturbed and then returned to the room door.

Twisting the door handle, he took one last look around the room to be certain everything was in its place. Everything was perfect. Now more composed, he slowly opened the door and peeked into the corridor. The coast was clear. He stepped into the corridor allowing the door to firmly snap closed behind him. His job done, he grabbed the cart and began to push it back the way he had come. In moments he had disappeared down the corridor and into the service elevator.

Chapter 1

A flash of flame engulfed the kitchen grill but it was a normal occurrence and went unnoticed. Several chefs of various ages and sizes, all wearing their professional whites, were feverishly preparing the dishes that had been ordered by the patrons waiting inside the restaurant. Their minds were too focused on their own gastronomic delights to give much attention to the fire. The sound of the sizzling fat on the grill as the flame peaked, overpowered all of the questions that were being shouted between the kitchen staff as to the status of their preparations. Many different exotic smells and aromas emanated from the variety of foods being prepared: Caribou, grilled salmon, sautéed mushrooms, fiddleheads, sauces and much more. Everyone was paying attention to their assigned tasks, concerned about meeting the restaurant's demanding standards. The stress and pressure in the room was reaching the boiling point as the rotund chef standing in front of the grill backed away from the sudden flame. He was using the edge of his spatula to dice and flip two small rabbits in an attempt to control any damaging effect from the unanticipated fire. A bead of perspiration dripped down his forehead and splashed onto the piping hot grill next to the frying game, instantly hissing and popping as it mixed-in and burnt with the fat before evaporating. Slowly the flame came under control.

- - - - - - - - - - - - - - - -

"James!" Craig Jeneau, standing outside the Empire Grille on the north side of Clarence Street, called out to James Anstey who was just about to cross the street.

"Over here." Craig, a young French Canadian RCMP undercover officer in his mid-thirties had known James Anstey for several years. They had met on a case in Toronto that had involved James' fiancée Monika Queller.

"Damn," James cursed to himself as he stepped off the sidewalk into the slush of the street soaking his right foot. He wasn't used to this Canadian winter. He never experienced snow like this in Los Angeles and would be happy if he never saw it again after this trip. Hearing Craig's call, James looked up and waved acknowledging him. Looking both ways he tried to avoid the slush as he crossed the busy street over to the entrance of the restaurant.

"How are you my old friend?" Craig looked more haggard compared to the last time James saw him. He was nervously smoking a cigarette and like an insecure drug addict negotiating a deal out in the open, was constantly checking the street and area around them.

"Fine. I didn't know you smoked." James was a little surprised. He noted Craig's nervousness but did not comment. As a CIA agent he paid attention to these details. Craig had lost weight and looked fatigued. His face was drawn and there were large bags under his eyes. His once full blonde hair seemed thinner. He was not as well groomed as he used to be. He was wearing a tan trench coat over a dark suit with a gray shirt and dark matching tie. The coat was unbuttoned. The clothes were wrinkled and had a slept in appearance. It was not what James had expected.

"Oh this," Craig took the cigarette from his mouth as he spoke. His hand shook. "Once in awhile. That's all." He wasn't convincing. "Come on. Let's go inside. It's cold out here." He quickly changed the subject and put his arm around James to both greet and guide him up the stairs from the sidewalk to the large glass doors of the

Empire Grille.

Though concerned, James was happy to see his old friend. Beside Craig, James looked very svelte and debonair. He kept his dark hair shortly trimmed. The only change from their last meeting was his neatly trimmed dark moustache. He wore a new midnight-blue overcoat that Monika had picked out for him and a black suit with a black polo neck shirt. Everything was zipped up. He did not appreciate this cold weather.

- - - - - - - - - - - - - - - -

At this late hour of the evening in the Byward Market area to the immediate east of the Château Laurier and the Parliament buildings, Ottawa was busy for a Monday night. There were many people milling about on the street. Mostly the crowd was made up of affluent young college students but there was also the odd tourist trying to take in the wintry nightlife. In this part of the market there were mostly bars. It was a livcly area at this time of year with all sorts of loud and colorful clubs filled to the brim, but the Empire Grille was the only restaurant that served a good meal late at night.

Amongst this crowd of students, following just out of sight behind James, were two very clean-cut, svelte looking men, wearing casual pants and midnight blue parkas with fox trimmed hoods. One was in his late thirties and the other his late forties. They both wore dark toques, which were pulled over their ears. Their faces were chiseled and their skin was leathery from years of exposure to the elements. They were large men in excellent physical condition. They were keeping a watchful eye on James. Though they had done nothing sinister, they had a menacing military or police air about them. They stuck to the shadows and were careful not to be seen by James or to let him get out of their sight. As James crossed the street and met Craig the two men instantly stopped and stood to one side of the sidewalk concealed in the dark alcove of a building's entrance about fifty feet away.

- - - - - - - - - - - - - - -

"Good evening, gentlemen. Two for dinner?" The maître d' was a small man in his thirties with longish auburn hair and a thin face, wearing dark flannel pants, dress shoes and a perfectly pressed white shirt. He greeted them with a patronizing tone. The noise of the conversation of the people at the bar just behind him forced him to call out his greeting in a loud voice. The Empire Grille was hopping.

"Yes," Craig answered. He was still nervously checking out everything around him and continued to smoke his cigarette.

"Smoking or non-smoking?" the maître d' asked in a disapproving manner.

"Oh." Craig took the cigarette from his mouth and butted it out in an ashtray placed at the small lectern in front of the maître d'. "No. Non-smoking. Have you got anything?" Preoccupied, he had not taken offense at the maître d's churlish manner.

"Yes. This way. You can leave your coats there." The maître d' turned, indicated the coat rack, picked up two menus and walked off into the restaurant expecting his two new patrons to follow.

"I see you have the same odd types as we have," James privately directed his comment to Craig. He did not like the maître d's attitude. They quickly removed their coats and hung them on the rack to the right of the maître d's station.

"I know. It's the new religion." Craig smiled. "After you." He ushered James after the maître d' who by now was well ahead of them.

The Empire Grille was a very new and trendy 'fusion' restaurant. After entering its main doors a large bar was immediately to the left. The decor of the bar was as chic and modern as its young clientele. James noticed how well dressed everyone was. Subdued modern light fixtures, adding softness to its atmosphere, dimly lit the bar. It was standing room only.

The restaurant section of the Grille was down a short flight of stairs that created a split-level effect. A long balustrade ran the length of the room separating the upper level bar from the lower level restaurant. Small tables with white tablecloths were scattered along the large rectangular space of the restaurant that ran the full eastern length of the building. Ceiling to floor windows looked out over the market and the street.

The restaurant was very full but, unlike its bar side, the mixture of its patrons varied from students nicely but casually dressed, to middle-aged people in semi-formal attire. It was an eclectic combination. There was no wall separating the bar from the restaurant and the conversation from both sides of the Empire Grille intermingled, making it a loud and lively place.

"Here we are gentlemen. Your waiter will be right with you." Their table was cozily situated in front of the window.

"Thank you," Craig said. "James." He took the seat facing the entrance and indicated that James should sit opposite him.

"Thanks." James acknowledged him and smiled. As he and Craig sat down, the maître d' gave them each a menu and walked away.

"It's a nice place," James said to fill in the time while they started to look over their menus. Though it was good to see Craig, he wasn't sure why he had been asked to come from Los Angeles and meet him here in Ottawa. Craig had been unwilling to say much over the phone.

"Yes. There are very few places where you can eat in Ottawa at this hour of the night. They have very good food and it's very popular." Craig leaned forward and spoke a little louder than usual because of the level of noise in the restaurant. He was still very agitated and constantly checked the room.

An awkward silence fell between them. Just as James was about to say something and become more direct, their waiter interrupted them.

"Good evening, gentlemen." He was a husky well-groomed man in his twenties with close cropped red hair. He wore the simple uniform of the restaurant: gray flannel pants and a pressed, open-collared white shirt with Empire Grille monogrammed on its pocket. There was a slight lilt to his voice as he greeted them. Both James and Craig glanced at one another but made no comment. The waiter, pen and pad in hand, waited to take their drink orders.

"How about a bottle of red wine?" Craig asked James.

"Sure. Sound's good," James agreed.

"A bottle of your dry red house wine, please," Craig ordered.

"Will you be dinning, sir?" The waiter wrote the order on his pad.

"Yes. Craig answered.

The waiter seemed pleased by their decision, turned and went away to get the wine.

There was another awkward silence between them as they looked over the menus and James waited for Craig to continue the conversation, but

Craig only fidgeted with his cutlery and nervously scanned the restaurant after he finished glancing at the menu. James remained calm and observed him. It was obvious that Craig needed a little more time to relax. It was unlike him to be so unnerved. James realized whatever the reason he was here, it was important. He hoped Craig would say something soon and when he did, he also hoped he would be able to help.

- - - - - - - - - - - - - - - -

Outside the Empire Grille the two men who had followed James waited and watched the entrance of the restaurant. They had their orders. It was a freezing cold January night. The air was crisp and biting. Their breaths lingered on the breeze like small clouds. One of the men adjusted his parka as they waited, making sure it was zipped up and keeping the cold air out and the other checked his watch. The time was 12:45 am. They settled in for a long uncomfortable wait. Their feet were cold and their bodies chilled. This was the aspect of their job that they disliked.

- - - - - - - - - - - - - - -

"Here you are." The waiter returned with a bottle of red wine and presented it to Craig for inspection.

"That's fine." Craig recognized the brand. It would be a pleasant drink.

The waiter proceeded to uncork the bottle. James and Craig watched silently as he expertly removed the wrapper, uncorked the bottle and poured a small sample into Craig's wine glass.

Craig smirked, picked up his glass and went through the tasting procedure. Though he was distracted, his French Canadian background had prepared him well. Like a connoisseur he swilled the wine gently in the glass and brought it closer to his face. He observed its color, smelled its bouquet, noticed how the ruby liquid clung to the inside of the glass and then took a sip. The waiter stood holding the bottle awaiting Craig's comments.

"Perfect," Craig said without looking at him and placed the glass back on the table.

The waiter acknowledged Craig's approval, and satisfied with his good taste, filled both their glasses, placing the bottle on the table after he finished. "Have you decided?"

"Almost," Craig said and opened his menu again.

"The specials tonight are Caribou and Salmon. I'll give you a couple of minutes." The waiter turned and scurried off into the restaurant to tend his other tables.

"So what do you feel like?" Craig asked James. He seemed a little more relaxed.

"I'll have the fish." James hoped that after they ordered they could get down to business. He was tired. It had been a long flight from Los Angeles to Toronto and then on to Ottawa. He had only had time to quickly check into the hotel that Craig had pre-booked, the Château Laurier, and drop off his baggage before making his meeting with him. It had been a wearing journey. He wanted to call Monika and let her know he had had a safe journey and arrived, before it was too late.

"I think I will too." Craig picked up his glass and took another sip of wine. Though he seemed to be relaxing more, he was keeping an eye on the street outside in between his scanning glances around the restaurant. Noticing the waiter, he put his glass down and signaled him over so they could order. The waiter responded.

"We're both going to have the salmon," Craig said curtly.

"Yes sir." The waiter wrote down the order, collected the menus and left. James and Craig were again alone and again an awkward silence grew between them.

"Craig. What's wrong? You didn't bring me all this way for dinner, now did you?" James decided it was time to take the first step. It was clear to him Craig wouldn't.

"No you're right. Sorry. I've stumbled onto something big and I'm not sure what to do," Craig's voice took on more intensity.

"What is it? How can I help?"

"I don't know if you can. I don't know who to trust." He picked up his glass and took another sip of wine. His agitation was clearly growing.

"You can trust me. What's up? You look a

mess."

"Thanks," Craig chuckled.

"You know what I mean. I've never seen you this way," James' concern showed.

"I've never been this way before. This is very, very big. I don't know if you can help." He took another larger sip and put the glass down. He seemed to be building up courage.

"Try me." James realized that whatever was wrong it was much more serious than he had anticipated. He prepared himself for Craig's answer.

"You know all these years living in Canada and being a French Canadian I had certain understandings, uhm...beliefs." Craig began to tell his story. Though he did not understand where he was coming from, James did not interrupt.

"In school I was always taught how Canada was formed and as a French Canadian I always had been taught to remember. Je me souviens. First it was the English and French, and then the English—Canadians and the Americans, but it was always the English element, the British, that we have distrusted. We always believed that the enemy was out there—out there somewhere outside of Québec. It has helped to unite us. But I think now that it was wrong. It is a lie. It's all a lie." Craig stopped and took another drink and put his glass down. It was almost empty. He played with the stem of the glass and fell silent.

"I'm not sure I understand." James was a little lost. He picked up the bottle and refilled Craig's glass.

"I know. I'm still not sure I understand. We have all been distracted," he started up again.

"Distracted?" James put the wine bottle back on the table and sat back into his chair trying to comprehend what Craig was trying to tell him.

"It has all been a game. We have been nothing but puppets." Craig's anger continued to rise. He glanced around the restaurant to the street outside.

"Puppets?" James couldn't follow any of this and he was concerned about Craig's mounting paranoia.

- - - - - - - - - - - - - - - -

Outside the Empire Grille the two men who were following James separated. It had been about twenty minutes since they had seen James and Craig go inside the restaurant. They did not want to take the chance of losing them through the back door of the restaurant. They decided that one of them should go along the street and try to reestablish a visual contact while the other remained and watched the front entrance. The traffic on the street was dying down. The older one of the two hurried across Clarence Street en route to the street bounding the southeast side of the restaurant. As he walked he tried to see James and Craig through the restaurant's windows.

- - - - - - - - - - - - - - - -

"Look. There." Just as Craig was about to explain what he meant, he noted a man in a dark parka slowly walking up the street. The man was paying more attention to the patrons in the restaurant than his trek along the snow covered sidewalk. Craig's police instincts knew there was something out of the ordinary about him.

"At what?" James hadn't noticed.

"Him." He carefully drew James' attention to the man outside.

"What about him?" James didn't see any danger.

"We aren't safe here. I'm sorry that I got you involved." Craig became more unnerved and focused all his attention on the man outside.

"Involved in what? Who is he?" James looked to Craig for an explanation while he scrutinized the man outside making contact with his eyes.

- - - - - - - - - - - - - - - -

Realizing he had been spotted, the man outside pulled out a small two-way radio from his jacket pocket and alerted his partner at the front of the building. He could not quite make out what James and Craig were doing inside the restaurant but he assumed that now he had been seen, they would know they were being followed and he expected they would try to escape before they could be trapped by him.

According to plan, his partner was watching the front of the restaurant. It was up to him to get to and watch the rear and make sure they didn't give them the slip before he could intercept them. Now that he had been spotted, catching them unawares would be difficult to accomplish. He chastised himself for not being more careful. He did not know this part of town well. He looked up the street and saw the side street that the restaurant backed onto. It was a fair distance away. He was not as quick as he used to be. He was not prepared for a foot chase through the back streets of Ottawa, but now he had no choice. He started to panic. Craig and James might get away. If he lost them his superiors would be unforgiving.

Without checking the traffic, he hurried across the street to the back of the restaurant, putting his radio back into his jacket pocket. He had to get there before they could escape.

- - - - - - - - - - - - - - -

"Damn. He's seen us. We've got to get out of here—now!" Craig abruptly got up.

"Now? What about dinner? What's going on?" James was annoyed, but he sensed Craig's fight or flight reaction and stood up with him.

Seeing the commotion at his table, the waiter rushed over to find out what was going on.

"Is something wrong, gentlemen?" he asked as he came up to them.

Craig was fixated on the man outside and had not heard the waiter's question. James shuffled closer to Craig and grabbed onto his arm.

"Craig. Craig," he said shaking him and trying to get his attention. "What's going on?"

"We have to get out of here. Now." James had no choice except to leave. Craig was not going to explain. "Just trust me. This is bigger than both of us. I'll explain later." He turned, oblivious to the waiter and the other patrons' stares, and said, "If anything happens."

"If what happens?" James was confused. Craig was acting unusually paranoid. If he did not already know him, he would have thought him crazy, but he knew better. "What about our coats?"

"There's no time. Trust me." Craig used a more sober tone. "If anything happens...I sent an envelope to you at your hotel. Now stay close and let's get out of here."

Not waiting for a response Craig twisted around and hurried to the back of the restaurant. James pulled some money out from his pants pocket and threw it on the table.

"Sorry. We've got to go. That should cover it," he apologized to the waiter.

The waiter was flabbergasted and stood speechless as James ran and caught up with Craig who was at the door at the back of the restaurant. Craig opened it and they found themselves in the kitchen amongst the chaos that was usual at this time of the evening. No one bothered to remark on their intrusion.

"Where's the back door?" Craig shouted out to the dishwasher just in front of him.

The dishwasher pointed across to a steel door about twenty feet away.

"Come on." He turned to James behind him. "I know a place where we can go." Craig reached into his jacket holster and drew out his revolver. The sight of the weapon caused only a mild reaction amongst the otherwise preoccupied kitchen staff. It almost appeared they were used to armed men rushing through their space. With James in tow, Craig made his way across the kitchen to the back door. The kitchen staff kept out of their way, not wanting any confrontation.

Craig carefully opened the door. He tentatively peeked outside. The back door opened onto a narrow side street that was lined on both sides by a series of two and three-story stone heritage buildings. Though the side street was dimly lit by one lone lamp perched atop the opposite building, Craig could see that the coast was clear. Their pursuer hadn't managed to make his way from the other side yet. There was no time to lose. He threw the door wide open and leapt down seven icy steps onto the street. Once off the steps of the restaurant, Craig's feet sank up to his ankles into the recently plowed snow. The street had a lot of snow piled up alongside it.

"Hurry. No one's here," he called out to James, his breath billowing out on the frosty night air.

James made his way through the door and down the steps to Craig. It was freezing outside. He wished he had been able to get his coat. He would not last long exposed to these temperatures. They stood together for a moment.

"Which way?" James asked as he rubbed his hands and watched his breath cloud around him.

Craig was unperturbed by the cold. His concern was elsewhere. He reconnoitered the side street. The street ran east and west. At both ends, about a block away, it opened onto a main road.

"That way." He pointed westward away from the direction their pursuer would be coming. "You go ahead. I'll cover the rear."

- - - - - - - - - - - - - - - -

After being alerted, the man watching the front of the Empire Grille darted wildly through the traffic and across the street. He understood the need to stop James and Craig getting away. There were several near misses as cars screeched and honked their horns at him as he careened through the traffic.

Once across the street and in front of the restaurant, he leapt up the short flight of steps, opened the front door and stood in the maître d's area. He was out of breath and trying to figure out where James and Craig were. He wasn't paying attention to the maître d'.

"Good evening, sir. Are you here for dinner or drinks?" The maître d' begrudgingly greeted the man. He did not like the look of this new patron nor did he appreciate being ignored.

"Where's the back door?" the man spoke gruffly. He continued scanning the restaurant as he barked out his words.

"Back door? I..." The maître d' was taken aback by this rudeness.

The man was impatient and shoved his right hand into his parka pocket and pulled out a revolver. The gun was freshly oiled and glistened.

"The door. Where is it?" He waved the weapon at the maître d' threateningly. He did not have any time to waste and the effeminate manner of the maître d' irritated him.

"Back there." The maître d' froze, meekly lifted his arm and pointed down the steps through the restaurant to the back door. No one else had noticed the commotion or the gun. Though he was frightened and didn't want to tangle with this brute, the maître d' also wanted to avoid any trouble. He didn't want his restaurant to get a bad reputation. The sooner the man left the better.

With his revolver held out, the man pushed past the maître d' and crossed through the restaurant to the back door as directed. He shoved aside any one who got in his way as he rushed through the crowded aisle. There was an uproar as patrons were distracted from their meals. They boldly complained about the man's boorish intrusion into their otherwise perfect evening until they saw his gun. After they saw it, they recoiled in fear.

Arriving at the back of the restaurant, the man pulled open the kitchen door and stepped inside. Compared to the restaurant, the kitchen was utilitarian and spartan in design. Everything there had its purpose and place. It reminded him of an institution. There was an abundance of stainless steel fixtures and glaring fluorescent lights lining the gloss white painted ceiling. Three chefs dressed in their white tunics and wearing matching stovepipe hats, were busy at the grill. The dishwasher was standing to the right in front of the sink three feet away.

"Where's the back door?" The man's voice was menacing. He pointed his gun at the dishwasher, not wanting to squander anymore time. He feared he might already be too late. James and Craig might already have far too great a lead on him.

The dishwasher backed away but was stopped by the stainless steel sink. Realizing he was trapped, he pointed to the same door that James and Craig had gone through only moments before. By the time the other kitchen staff became fully aware of the threat of this intruder, he was already across the room and opening the back door.

- - - - - - - - - - - - - - -

"Okay," James reluctantly agreed with Craig. He started to make his way along the sidewalk but found it too difficult in the deep snow. Though he was worried about being exposed, he jumped over the snow-covered sidewalk into the openness of the street, which was plowed of snow making it easier for him to move faster. James knew they had to get to the next street as fast as they could. There was nowhere they could hide. They were thirty yards away from the intersection and sitting ducks. Their only hope of escape was to mingle with the crowd on the main street.

Craig waited a few seconds, providing cover while James made his way up the side street. Once he was ten yards ahead, Craig followed him. As they ran on the slippery street, they kept looking over their shoulders, checking for their pursuer. Just as they thought they might be able to get to safety, the back door of the restaurant opened and one of their pursuers stepped out. James was about ten yards from the main street and Craig was about ten yards behind him.

"Go. I'll cover." Craig seeing the threat called out to James. He hoped he could hold their pursuer off long enough for James to escape. He felt responsible for putting James in jeopardy.

James did not like the idea but he knew it was the only way. There was no time to waste arguing.

The man at the restaurant door quickly sized up the situation. There was no way he would be able to catch up to them on the slippery side street. They were getting away. He checked for his partner but could not see him. It was up to him to stop them. He aimed his revolver at the closer of the two men rushing up the street and fired two shots.

Everything happened in seconds. Neither Craig nor James were able to react as two shots rang out. With nowhere to take cover, James and Craig continued their escape down the street.

"Ugh. James," Craig gasped then let out a cry of pain as the second bullet sliced through his jacket. He stumbled forward and though his pace slowed, he did not fall.

Hearing the shots and Craig's cry, James, who was almost at the main street, stopped and looked back for his friend.

"Craig?" he called out fearing the worst. His eyes caught Craig's strained expression. He saw death in his eyes.

"Go on. Go!" Craig insisted while he clutched his chest, his breathing becoming more strained.

To leave a downed man went against all of James' training. He had to try and save Craig. He pulled out his revolver, took aim and shot at the man at the rear door of the restaurant. Without regard to his own safety, he rushed back to Craig who, though still standing, was loose-kneed. The man at the restaurant anticipating James' shot, took cover, allowing James to get to Craig unharmed.

"Craig?" Craig fell forward into him. James grabbed hold of him wrapping his arms around his dead weight. He felt the warm blood that saturated Craig's jacket on his cold hands. Not certain of what to do, he fired off a couple of covering shots and dropped to one knee while trying to support his friend.

"Go. I'm hit bad." Craig knew the extent of his injury. A trickle of blood oozed from the corner of his mouth, causing him to gag.

"But I…" James didn't know what to say. It was clear Craig wouldn't survive.

"Get…outa here," it was difficult for Craig to talk. "The envelope. It's all…" He forced the words out but did not finish. His head slumped down into James' polo shirt.

James hugged him. A wave of emotion rose up within him making it difficult for him to speak.

"God bless you, my old friend." James managed to whisper his good bye. Craig closed his eyes and was gone. It was more than James could bear but his own instinct to survive now stepped in.

Refocusing on the danger he was in, James fired off a round in the direction of Craig's assassin. He did not want to leave Craig there in the middle of this cold street but he knew he had to. Gently he lowered Craig's body to the street. He fired off another round. So far this had kept the pursuer at bay but he knew it would not last. Keeping a lookout he got up and darted up the street not looking back.

Suddenly the second man appeared at the far end of the side street. He could just make out

James at the other end getting away. Having heard the shooting he had stopped and carefully peeked around the corner of the brick building. He saw his partner hiding behind the restaurant door. He was unharmed. He wondered what had happened. He checked the side street and saw Craig's motionless body three quarters of the way up the street and smiled. Pulling out his revolver he took aim at James who was a good sixty yards away. It was an impossible shot to make but he fired all the same.

James was out in the open. He was only a few feet from the main street. Out of instinct he ducked as he heard the shot whiz harmlessly above his head. He turned and saw the dark image of the man who had fired at the far end of the side street. James took aim and let go his fourth shot. He was a better marksman than the man at the far end of the street. The man took cover as the bullet ricocheted off the wall about a foot away from him. Firing off two more shots, James turned and sprinted as fast as he could. It was his only chance. It was now or never. He was outnumbered, in the open and low on ammunition.

The two pursuers remained concealed. Though they did not want James to get away, they also did not want to get killed. They each waited a few seconds longer after James' gunfire before looking out. Everything happened quickly. The man at the end of the street was first to appear from behind the protection of the restaurant's brick wall. He understood the situation in a glance. Craig was lying in the middle of the street. The snow was blood stained around him. James was only a few feet from escaping. The man took careful aim and fired a series of five shots, hoping that one would find its target.

Unlike the side street, the main street was busy. There were many cars and pedestrians even at this late hour of the night. By the time James heard the rapid gunfire, it was too late to take cover. He was only a couple of feet from safety. He instinctively ducked as he ran. Suddenly he felt a burning impact in the center of his back. He was hit. The force of the bullet in striking him pushed him forward as he ran. He lost control, twisted around and stumbled into the oncoming traffic. He heard the screeching sound of brakes being applied followed by the crushing impact of a speeding vehicle against his leg. He was pushed down to the hard pavement and heard the crack of his bones as they broke. His head was spinning. Everything was chaos. He felt so much pain he could not single out any one source. But the pain did not last long. The last thing he was conscious of was a woman's blood curdling scream.

- - - - - - - - - - - - - - - -

A large crowd had gathered by the time the ambulance left from the scene of Sussex Drive to the east bank of the Rideau Canal. The area of the side street to Sussex Drive was cordoned off with yellow police tape. Traffic was jammed and was being diverted from this portion of Sussex Drive. There were several police officers minding the crowd at the site on Sussex Drive where James had been hit and fallen. A couple of plainclothes officers were examining the scene.

It had not taken the police long to discover Craig's body. After they had arrived on the scene at Sussex Drive and spoken to witnesses, they immediately went down the side street to investigate and found Craig. The area had become a major crime scene. Camera crews from the local media arrived not long after the police and were all vying for the best position behind the police line for their stories.

"What do you make of this?" one of the plainclothes detectives at the scene asked his partner. They were both standing a couple of feet from where James had been hit.

"I don't know, Jack. There's much more involved here. What's the CIA doing in Ottawa?" He indicated the wallet in Jack's hand.

"Maybe it's just a coincidence, Jean-Paul?" Detective Jack Callot, an English Canadian of French origin was flipping through James' wallet examining each piece of identification. As the detective in charge it would be his duty to call any next of kin. He did not like that part of his job. "He's from California."

"Maybe. How do you explain the gun? This isn't an accident. And what about the other guy?" Jean-Paul was matter-of-fact. Not being in charge, this was just another homicide to him.

"I think they were together. This was done by someone else," Jack guessed. He was a thirty-year veteran of the Ottawa Police force, and had investigated many homicides in his time. This was not the usual homicide, though. He was wearing a navy blue three-quarter length police-issue parka and black gloves. He was a clean-shaven heavy-set man, with a large double chin, who exuded gentleness. Despite his balding head, he chose not to wear a hat even in this frigid weather.

"Seems logical," Jean-Paul casually agreed. He sipped from a steaming cup of coffee as he spoke. "Their bullet wounds both enter from behind. But who is he?" Jean-Paul meant Craig. They had not found any identification on him.

Jean-Paul Ferisse, Jack's partner, was in his late thirties. He was also wearing the typical parka most of the authorities in Ottawa wore at this time of year. His hair was dark and cut short framing his lively hazel eyes and welcoming smile. Though a proud French Canadian, he worked for the Ottawa police but lived across the river in Hull, Québec. He spoke with only a slight accent.

"I don't know. Run his prints. I'm going back to the station. Join me after you've finished. I've got to get this..." Jack held up James' wallet between his thumb and forefinger, "...taken care of."

"Sure. I won't be long." Jean-Paul understood what Jack meant.

- - - - - - - - - - - - - - - -

The two men who had been chasing James and Craig mingled with the crowd behind the police line. They watched as the ambulance took both bodies away. Though they felt certain that Craig was dead, they weren't as confident about James.

Before the police had arrived the two men had hurried up the side street to Craig and rifled through his jacket looking for something. They took Craig's wallet and a few other loose papers they found in his pockets but were unable to search James, who was lying farther away in the middle of Sussex Drive. A small crowd was already gathered around him. They hoped he was dead. It would solve a lot of problems.

They quickly finished searching Craig, made their way back down the side street and hid behind the restaurant. They did not want to be seen by the crowd around James' body at the other end of the street. After a brief discussion, they decided to go the longer way along Clarence and mix in with the crowd on Sussex Drive. By doing this they would be able to safely check on James from the security of the crowd and not arouse any suspicions. They would merely be curious bystanders. But by the time the two men made their way to Sussex Drive from the restaurant, there was a huge crowd gathered. Three police cars were on the scene. Two policemen were controlling the crowd and putting up yellow police tape while a third tended to James. Two plainclothes detectives stood near the scene talking. The two men waited quietly and observed.

- - - - - - - - - - - - - - - -

Fifteen minutes later Detective Callot was sitting at his desk at the police station. James' wallet was open and in front of him. Detective Callot had found an 'in case of emergency' notification card. The card contained a woman's name and phone number. This would be his first call. Though he would be making several calls, this first call to family and loved ones was the most difficult. He picked up the phone and punched in the Los Angeles phone number. He checked the clock on the wall of his cubicle and subtracted three hours. It was 12:30 in the morning there. No matter what the time he would have to make this call.

- - - - - - - - - - - - - - - -

Monika's phone rang. She was sitting in bed reading with her bedside lamp on. She had not yet gone to sleep as she was expecting to hear from James. Excited, she put down her book and reached for the receiver.

"Hello, James?"

"Hi. I'm Detective Jack Callot of the Ottawa Police Department. Monika Queller please." Jack was formal.

Monika's heart dropped. She had a sudden cold feeling of fear.

"Speaking." There was a nervous tremble in her voice.

"I have some bad news," Jack said and then paused.

Monika's heart skipped a beat. She began to shake in anticipation of something terrible. She swallowed, took in a deep breath and held it for a second.

"Is it James?" her voice cracked as she said his name. She wondered if he was dead. She searched her feelings for any trace of him. She had had no emotional warning. Certainly, she believed, if anything had happened she would have felt something.

"Yes. He's been in an accident."

Monika was afraid to ask. She waited, expecting the worst. Tears welled in her eyes.

"He's alive…"

"Oh. Thank. Thank you…" Monika interrupted the Detective mid-sentence, sobbing out her words.

"Ms. Queller. It's serious, but he's alive," Jack continued, not wanting to raise false hopes.

"Where is he? What happened?" Monika interrupted again. Though relieved, she was still upset by the shock of the news.

"We're not sure yet. How soon can you come up

here?" There was no question in Jack's mind that Monika would want to come and be at James' side. It was his experience in these cases.

"I'll be on the next flight. Probably tomorrow sometime."

"That would be good. When you know all your details let me know and I'll meet you." This was not the usual routine but Jack felt an instant liking for Monika. She sounded very nice and something moved him to offer.

"Thank you. That's very kind of you." She was grateful and relieved.

"Let me give you my number."

"Hold on. I need a pen." Monika opened the bedside table drawer and found a pen. "Go ahead."

Chapter 2

The two men in midnight blue parkas from the previous night made their way along the south side of Sparks Street about a block south of Parliament Hill. It was rush hour. There were many people hurrying to work, most of them civil servants of one sort or another. The major business in Ottawa was government. Everyone was warmly bundled up. It was a cold but clear winter day. The breaths of the pedestrians as they bustled along lingered in the frosty sub zero air. The street was freshly cleared of snow and clouds of steam were rising from the sewers. It was so cold that the steam clouds ran horizontal to the ground instead of rising straight up.

There was a fresh bite to the air as the two men made their way to a coffee shop at the corner of Kent and the Sparks Street Mall. At one time Sparks Street was a regular roadway. But nowadays cars were not permitted to drive its length. It was a pedestrian right of way.

Sparks Street was lined on both sides with restaurants and stores of every description. The area was a major tourist attraction, particularly in the summer months when tourists from all over Canada and the world could slowly ambulate along its length admiring its park-like atmosphere, enhanced by large potted trees and planters of brightly colored flowers. In the winter months during the workweek however, the majority of people walking along were government workers and local employees of other businesses and they did not care about the picturesqueness of Sparks Street Mall.

Thirty feet before the coffee shop, in the same building it rented space from, was a doorway to another business. There were no windows or signs indicating who occupied the space other than a solid wood door painted in black with the slightly tarnished brass number 119A . The coffee shop was 119. It was a very plain, slightly battered door. It appeared to the average passerby that it might be the entry to an apartment above the coffee shop.

Before the two men entered through 119A, they

waited a moment, giving the people around them a thorough check-over, then went inside. The door opened into a narrow hallway with a long narrow stairway rising up to a second story. Closing the door behind them, they walked up the stairs in single file to the second story landing which was equally as narrow as the stairwell. The whole place was run down. At the far end of the landing was another solid wood door.

The men went over and paused in front of it. Canadian International Institute, or C2 as they called it, was hand painted in black letters similar to the numbers outside, on the door. They seemed apprehensive about entering. Finally, the older of the two men opened the door and they entered into a tiny twelve by twelve foot reception area that was in need of a new coat of paint. The room was dirty and smelled of stale cigarettes. The only thing it had going for it was the fact that it was nice and warm. Directly in front of them a woman sat behind a gray metal desk. There were no windows in the room only a closed door adjacent to her desk on the other side of the room from where they entered.

"You're late," the woman said curtly as she looked up from her work. It was unclear if she was just a secretary or someone in a position of power. "He was expecting you half an hour ago." Her tone of voice was definitely scolding.

"We got held up," one of the men answered.

"How is he, Marylyn?" The man felt as if a schoolteacher was reprimanding him.

"You should know better than that, Hackett." Marylyn was a hard woman in her early forties. She wore a conservatively cut brown tweed suit. Her heavy out of style dark rimmed glasses gave her a matronly appearance.

Hackett didn't like Marylyn. He glanced over to his partner, trying to solicit his assistance.

"It took longer than we thought. We tried…" the other man started but was cut short.

"Save it for him, Stone. He's waiting inside." Marylyn picked up a green folder and walked across to the door that led to the inner office. Without prompting, Hackett and Stone followed her. She stopped in front of the door and knocked twice.

A man inside gruffly called out, "Yeah."

"You wait here." She opened the door and went inside closing the door behind her. A few moments later the door re-opened and she returned without the green folder.

"You can go in now," she smirked at them.

Hackett and Stone said nothing. They were nervous. Marylyn sat back behind her desk and saw them take in fortifying breaths in preparation for what they thought was about to happen to them. As they entered the inner office she chuckled and returned to her paperwork.

The inner office was marginally larger than the

reception area. Its warm brown, industrial grade carpet was the highlight of its decoration. In front of them on an old wood desk that had seen better days, were a telephone and a computer. The desk took up most of the office and was centrally located in front of a small window that had a set of dirty venetian blinds half open and half pulled up the window. The window looked out over Sparks Street Mall. There were no pictures on the walls and only a large circular clock adorned the wall space between the door and the ceiling. Two yellowed fluorescent light fixtures illuminated the otherwise dim room.

"Did you see that?" Morgan Skinner, a man in his middle fifties of average build and wearing a simple gray suit, spoke abruptly startling the two men. He was standing with his back to them looking out the small window. It was clear from the tone in his voice he was not happy. He had both his hands in his pockets and was tapping them against his thighs. He was angry.

Hackett and Stone weren't sure what their superior meant. They scanned the desktop but all they saw was the morning's edition of the *Ottawa Citizen* newspaper.

"See what, sir?" Hackett responded. It was the safest answer he could think of under the circumstances. Something was wrong that neither he nor Stone understood. He shrugged as he answered. From their experience they had learnt to be cautious with Morgan Skinner.

Skinner turned around. He was not an attractive man. He had thinning brown hair and dark brown eyes set a little too closely together around a bulbous nose. Clean-shaven, his face was pitted by what must have been a bad case of acne during his younger years. His glare was penetrating and menacing. He turned and stepped toward his desk and picked up the paper. He read from the front page.

"Murder on Sussex," Skinner read the headline then paused to see the reaction of the two men standing nervously in front of him. "Last night one unidentified man was shot in the back and killed and another injured on Sussex Drive." Skinner stopped reading and again glared at the two men in disgust.

"I shot them both, sir. And..."

"Shut up Hackett. I'll let you know when it's your turn." Morgan hadn't made his point yet. He picked up the paper and continued to read.

"The injured man has not yet been identified, pending notification of next of kin. He was taken to Ottawa Civic Hospital where he remains in critical condition."

Skinner threw the paper down on his desk. His face became redder, showing the extreme level of his rage. He walked from behind his desk and stopped directly in front of Stone and Hackett who were now standing at attention. He reined in his temper and continued.

"Remains in critical condition," he repeated and glared at them. He looked like he was going to explode.

"We thought they were both dead," Stone replied as he and Hackett prepared themselves for Skinner's berating.

"You thought? It isn't your job to think, that's mine. RIGHT! It's your job to do your job and you didn't do your job, did you?" Skinner vented his anger on them.

"No sir." Hackett and Stone answered in unison. Skinner was right and even if he were wrong they would not talk back to him. He was their superior.

Skinner walked back to his desk and picked up the green folder that Marylyn had brought him. He opened the folder and turned again to face the men.

"I don't see it in here. Have I overlooked something?" He indicated the material in the folder.

"No, sir. That was all we found on Jeneau, sir. We didn't get a chance to search Anstey, sir." Hackett replied formally and in military-style.

"Your orders were to retrieve all, I repeat, all documentation and then dispose of any loose ends. I don't see the list here. Where is the list?" he sarcastically demanded.

"I don't know sir," Hackett said, speaking for both of them. He had dropped off the package of documents in the early hours of the morning. He had not checked them thoroughly. He had falsely assumed that everything they found on Craig Jeneau was complete.

"*I don't know, sir*. What's that meant to mean? Do either of you morons know how important that list is?" Skinner was not impressed with Hackett's weak answer.

"Yes. I mean no, sir," Hackett said weakly.

"Well... Which is it?" Skinner eyeballed him.

"I...ah..." Hackett didn't know what to say next. Everything he had said so far had only gotten them into deeper trouble.

"And what about you, Stone?" Skinner stepped into Stone's face. "Cat got your tongue?"

"I'm not sure, sir." Stone remained at attention, staring forward as he blurted out his response as respectfully as he could, paying no attention to the proximity of his superior. He hated Skinner but would not allow his feelings to show no matter how mad Skinner got.

"Exactly. This operation has been running smoothly since the sixties. Until now only the highest level in Washington has been aware of our activities. Now because of your sloppiness the whole operation is jeopardized. We have spent years placing the right people and creating the right circumstances and now you two 'professionals' have screwed up. Do either of you know what is on that list?" Skinner stared at both men, not expecting an answer. Hackett and Stone remained silent. "I didn't think so. But then it's my job to think, not yours. Your job is to do. And you haven't done your job—have you?"

"No sir," both men answered reflexively.

"That list contains the names of all our operatives in Québec and we don't want anyone else to see that list. Especially now. Do we?" Skinner began to lecture them.

"No sir," both men agreed.

"You are going to retrieve the list and dispose of anyone who has seen it. Do you understand? First the list, then disposal. It's that simple." Skinner began to shout.

"Yes, sir," both men answered standing more rigidly to attention hoping that Skinner's tirade would soon be over.

"I want you to get over to that hospital and find out who else might know about this and take care of them. Find the list before everything goes up in smoke. Do you understand? Is it clear enough this time for you?" Skinner looked threateningly into both men's eyes without blinking, awaiting their response.

"Yes, sir—say it!" Skinner barked.

"Yes, sir," Hackett and Stone replied.

"Good. Make sure there aren't any copies of the list lying around. Now get out of here and do your job. I have to make my report." There was an implied 'or else' in his voice. Both men knew what would happen to them if they failed again in their duties.

Hackett and Stone turned together. They were dismissed. Stone opened the door and they hurried out of the office. Once they had shut the door behind them, they both breathed sighs of relief.

"See you two later. Try not to screw up this time," Marylyn mocked them.

Hackett and Stone did not respond to her. They grimaced and continued through her office to the main door. Once outside of C2 they began to argue.

"Why did you shoot?" Stone reprimanded his partner for acting prematurely.

"They were getting away. What do you think would have happened if they got away?" Hackett made a good point. If James and Craig had gotten away it might have been worse. Stone knew Hackett was correct in his analysis. He remained quiet. There was no need to answer.

Hackett and Stone made their way down the narrow stairway, opened the door and disappeared among the crowd. They had their orders. This time they would not fail.

- - - - - - - - - - - - - - - -

Skinner opened his office door and stepped into the small reception room. He had on his overcoat and was buttoning it up.

"Marylyn. I'm going out for coffee. You want anything?" he asked. He seemed completely recovered from his show of anger.

"No thank you sir," she replied amiably. "Will you be long?"

"No. Just a couple of minutes. I'm going downstairs."

Skinner walked through the office and opened the door. He went out onto the landing and as he walked down the stairs he adjusted his overcoat. He was not happy. He did not like having to go outside in this cold weather. He had grown up in Florida. He blamed Hackett and Stone's incompetence for this chilling aggravation.

He stepped out onto Sparks Street Mall and stood a moment to check the area. He always followed this procedure. Next he checked his wristwatch. It was almost nine. He continued past the coffee shop to the corner, where a public telephone was situated in the double-doored entrance. He walked into the entrance alcove to the payphone and picked up the receiver.

Taking a credit card from his jacket pocket he ran it through the card reader. The phone display accepted the card for payment. He punched in the Washington, DC phone number for the CIA. This was all part of C2's security system. No calls were to be made from the C2 office to his superiors in Washington. The phone rang three times.

"Executive Director Crane's office," a woman with a Southern accent answered.

"Morgan Skinner C2 for the EXDIR, please,"

Skinner said in a businesslike tone. It was not often he called the Executive Director of Central Intelligence.

"Certainly, Mr. Skinner." The secretary knew to put any calls from Skinner directly through to her boss without delay.

"Jon Crane," the EXDIR answered.

Skinner got right to the point. "Sir. Everything is under control. It will take a couple of days. There's nothing to be worried about,"

"That's what I wanted to hear. The Summit starts next week and we can't afford any indiscretions. Don't screw up. You've got forty-eight hours. After that I'm pulling the plug on the whole section." Crane hung up the phone.

Skinner put the receiver back down. He hoped this was the last time he would have to call Crane under such circumstances. Jon Crane was a vindictive, powerful man and he didn't want to cross or disappoint him again. He knew the price of failure. He knew his government would disavow any connection or knowledge of his mission if anything went wrong and he would be left to face the consequences alone.

He picked up the phone and made another call. This time the number was a 418 area code—Québec City. The phone rang twice.

"Bureau du président de l'Assemblée nationale," a woman answered formally. It was the secretary of the Président of the National

Assembly. The Président's job was to run the National Assembly for the duration of a legislature. He was a very influential man.

"Morgan Skinner for the Président, please." Skinner did not attempt to speak French.

"Please wait," the secretary replied in perfect English.

"Hello Morgan. How are you?" Claude Bonneau, the Président, answered without a hint of a French accent.

"It's still out there." Skinner didn't waste time on small talk. Bonneau worked for him.

"How did Jeneau get hold of it?" Bonneau was worried.

"It might be an inside job. We might have a leak." It was the only way Skinner believed Jeneau could have gotten the information.

"Who?" Bonneau wondered who had betrayed them but he knew Skinner would find out. Skinner always knew how to ferret out and deal with anyone who crossed C2. The way he had forced the recent Premier back in line and eventually to resign by infecting him with a rare disease and turning his own party against him, came to mind. It was an ingenious plan. It had been easily and secretly accomplished after the Premier had begun to push more radically for a sovereign Québec than C2 wanted. That action had sent a strong warning to any others in their service who were faltering in their PQ, Parti Québécois,/C2 platform. By the time the dust had settled, C2 had managed, through their moles, to install a more suitable leader who would continue the turmoil in Québec without raising suspicions and without actually separating from the rest of Canada. C2's purpose was to maintain a constant turmoil that never resulted in any political finality. Those moles were on the list. It was imperative the list was recovered. "What do you want me to do?"

"I don't know. Just be careful. It should all be cleared up in the next couple of days. Until then trust no one. By the beginning of the Summit this will be behind us and forgotten. I'll be up tomorrow on the usual flight. Send a car to meet me." Skinner hung up the phone. He was now relying on Hackett and Stone to complete their mission and secure the list. All he could do now was wait. The next forty-eight hours were going to be long.

He opened the inner door to the coffee shop and went in to get a hot drink. He hated this Canadian winter.

- - - - - - - - - - - - - - -

In a room on the second floor of the building opposite the coffee shop, a casually dressed man was spying on Skinner through the large telephoto lens of his camera. As he watched, he snapped pictures. The room was a small ten by ten foot vacant office. The camera was set up on a large tripod looking down directly on the public telephone at the coffee shop. Both the man and the camera were hidden behind the mirrored office window which provided a clear view of the coffee shop and the C2 entrance. A reel-to-reel tape recorder sat on a small table next to the tri pod. Its twelve-inch reels turned very slowly. Skinner's voice could be heard talking on the bugged public telephone.

"Here we go again. You guys are up to no good." The man, with a black goatee, was in his late twenties and spoke with an accent. It was his first undercover assignment and he was being very thorough. He was keeping tabs on the Canadian International Institute. The last twenty-four hours had been busier than his first two months. He kept snapping pictures while he listened to Skinner's conversation. His superiors would find his daily report unusually interesting.

Chapter 3

"Wait here. I won't be that long." Hackett ordered Stone to remain with the car. There was no need for both of them to go inside. They were at the main entrance of the Ottawa Civic Hospital.

"I'll park over there." Stone indicated the short-term visitor parking to the left of the main entrance. They had come to the hospital directly after their meeting with Skinner.

Ottawa was not a very large city. Though it was the political seat of Canada, everything was accessible within a fifteen or twenty minute drive. Hackett checked his watch. It was almost ten in the morning—a good time for him to find out about James and see if he had the list.

"Okay," Hackett replied. He got out of the car and crossed to the short flight of concrete steps that led from the road to the hospital entrance.

Like most hospitals of its age, the Ottawa Civic was very institutional in design. Its red bricks were sooty and old. The entrance was part of the original wing of the building, which was comprised of ten stories. Hackett made his way up the steps and opened one of the heavy wood double doors. He knew the hospital well, having visited it many times in the past. He entered the center lobby and approached a small information kiosk. A young candy-striper filling in for the usual Woman's Auxiliary volunteer, was on duty. He crossed over to the kiosk. Other than the candy-striper, he was the only one there. The hospital was not busy.

"Good morning," Hackett began his act. He was very calm and convincing.

"Good morning. Can I help you?" The girl, a new volunteer, was in her late teens. She was pretty with dark, straight red hair. Her candy-striped dress, along with her youthful face, made her look younger than she actually was.

Hackett pulled out a fake police badge from his pocket and flashed it quickly, pretending to be incognito.

"I'm investigating a case. I need to know where a patient is." He smiled at her as he looked right into her gray eyes.

The girl was excited and intimidated at the same time. She had never met a real police detective at the hospital.

"How can I help?" she asked, eagerly offering her assistance.

"I'm looking for a James Anstey. He was brought here earlier this morning." Hackett turned on the charm and took advantage of the situation.

"Anstey?" The girl picked up a list from behind the counter and thumbed through it. "Here it is."

"Great." Hackett was pleased. Everything was going as expected.

"He's in intensive care. That's directly above us on the second floor. You can take the elevator over there or go up the stairs. The stairs would be faster." She was very friendly.

"Thanks. You've been extremely helpful." Hackett winked and walked away.

"You're welcome," the girl answered and watched him as he went to the stairs, wondering what exciting case the detective was on.

About five minutes later Hackett opened the second level door and stepped out into a brightly lit corridor. There was a little more activity here on the second floor. He stood a moment in the corridor just in front of the door to the stairwell. To his left, the corridor ran about fifty feet. There was a gurney and some staff members dressed in hospital scrubs, going about their duties. They paid no attention to him. To his right, about fifteen feet away, were a set of double glass doors. The left door had the letters ICU painted on it. He walked down the hall and went through the ICU doors.

The Intensive Care Unit was set up like a ward. The patients were lying in beds with all sorts of tubes running in and out of them. There was medical equipment and machines placed around their beds to monitor their vital statistics. Three nurses in the room were taking care of the patients. Hackett searched the room for James but was not able to identify him. He stood for a moment, considering his next move. He realized there was no way he would be able to search through James' belongings once he found him. There was not enough privacy. His eye caught one of the nurses in the room who had seen him come in. She put down a tray she was carrying and came over to see what he wanted.

"Can I help?" she said pleasantly. She had a lovely smile.

"Yes. Sorry to bother you. I'm Detective Philips. Nurse…?" Hackett went through the routine with the fake detective's badge. The nurse, a petite Filipina in her late thirties, was suitably impressed and accepted his credentials without question.

"Geena." She felt more comfortable now that she knew he was a police officer.

"I'm following up on a James Anstey. I understand he was brought here this morning. How is he?" Hackett bluffed.

"Oh yes. He was pretty bad when he came. He was in surgery a long time. He's stable now but still on the critical list. You won't be able to speak with him. He's over there." She turned and pointed to him. He was four beds away on the right side. He looked very ill.

"That's too bad. Maybe you can help?" Hackett saw his opportunity.

"How?" She didn't understand.

"Did he have any personal effects when he came in? They might give me a lead." he asked.

The nurse thought a moment. "All he had were his clothes, watch and money. You guys took his wallet." Geena found it odd that the detective wasn't aware of these facts.

"That's the night shift for you. Too bad they didn't tell me." He shook his head and feigned disapproval trying to cover up his faux-pas. "Sorry. I'll check back at the station for the wallet."

"That's okay detective. It's not your fault." She understood the problems that could occur between changing shifts.

"Thanks anyway." Hackett turned and started to walk away. He was disappointed. He wondered if the list had already fallen into the hands of the authorities.

"Detective Philips," Geena called out just as he

was reaching the double doors.

"Yes, Geena?" He turned to face her.

"I understand that his fiancée is arriving later today. Maybe she could be of help?" She sensed Detective Philips' disappointment and wanted to be of assistance.

"Yes. She could be. Thank you. I'll check back later. Thanks again." Hackett's mind went into high gear. He cheered up. This could be a lucky break. He made his way through the double doors en route to his partner outside with a quicker pace.

Hackett was smiling as he exited the hospital. Stone was waiting with the car running, in the short-term parking area. He had seen his partner exit and was trying to determine if he had been successful in his mission. Hackett had only been gone a short time. Hackett opened the front passenger door and got into the warm car next to Stone.

"Was it there?" Stone asked, expecting a positive reply.

"No. I don't think he has it." Hackett seemed happy with this bad news.

"What you mean? Then who has it? Skinner's not gonna be happy about this." Stone struck the steering wheel with his hands in frustration.

"I don't think Jeneau had it on him last night and that's why he didn't give it to Anstey. I think it's hidden somewhere. That would be just like the RCMP. Jeneau was scared. He didn't bring it with him in case something went wrong. He was trained well. He wouldn't know who to trust." Hackett started to reason out the scenario of the previous night.

"So how does that help us?" Stone didn't understand. He wasn't as quick as his partner.

"What would you have done?" Hackett posed the question.

"I'd be careful. I would of called someone I knew…someone I could trust. Hidden the list but left a clue in case something happened." Stone began to see Hackett's point.

"Exactly. The list is still out there somewhere, hidden. Jeneau trusted Anstey, but before he could do anything, we came along. Skinner was right. We blew it."

"So you're on Skinner's side now?"

"No. All it means is the list is still out there and we have to figure out where he hid it before someone else does." Both of them knew what 'someone else' meant.

"Yeah. So."

"Anstey's fiancée is on her way here," Hackett began.

"The one in California?"

"The same one. She'll probably stay at the Château Laurier like her fiancé." They both remembered reading James' file days ago when they had discovered that Jeneau had contacted him. Skinner had done a background check. It had alarmed them to discover that James also worked for the CIA. The connection was too close for comfort. It had made them nervous, wondering if C2 was being secretly investigated. Why else would Jeneau contact a CIA agent? They did not know that James and Craig were just friends—that the California CIA Bureau was not involved officially with James' trip to Ottawa.

"So you think she might know something?" Stone asked.

"Maybe. Maybe not. But it's the best lead we've got. I want you to go over to the Château Laurier and hang around the lobby. Let me know when she shows up." Hackett was in command. He had a strong feeling about the case.

"What about you?" Stone didn't fully trust his partner. The operatives who worked for C2 had questionable backgrounds. As a result, he wondered if there was some ulterior motive for Hackett leaving him.

"I'm going back to C2 and see what else I can dig up on his fiancée. Drop me on the way."

"Okay." Stone was satisfied with Hackett's answer.

It was their best plan under the circumstances. It was their only lead. They stopped talking. Stone put the car into gear and backed out of the parking space. Hackett was deep in thought. For the first time that day they felt optimistic about their future.

Chapter 4

By 3:15 Tuesday afternoon Monika's plane had touched down at the Ottawa airport. It had been a very long flight. First she had flown from Los Angeles to Toronto, where she changed planes for the flight to Ottawa. With her one suitcase in hand, she was making her way out to the arrivals area of the Ottawa airport. She was very eye-catching in her fur hat and three quarter length black coat, black stockings and tight knee-high patent leather boots. She had a trendy sixties look. As she walked, she kept an eye out for Detective Jack Callot. He had told her he would meet her at the airport. She was anxious to get to the hospital and see James.

The Ottawa airport was small and not crowded.

The flight from Toronto had taken an hour.

"Ms. Queller. Monika Queller?" A rather large man wearing a dark overcoat about six feet away from her, called out as she entered the arrivals area.

Monika focused on the man. "Detective Callot?" she asked, stopping in front of him.

"Yes. Call me Jack. Let me take your bag. How was your flight?" Jack noted how pretty Monika was. She exuded warmth and friendliness. Though she was tired and worried about James, her blue eyes still sparkled as she spoke. He took her small suitcase and led the way through the other arriving passengers to the exit about twenty-five feet away.

"Thank you. How is James?" She walked beside him. Though the arrivals area was heated, the draft of cold air that wafted in through the opening and closing sliding doors of the exit gave her a chill. She was not used to this type of cold weather. She noted how the cold didn't seem to bother the detective, who was wearing a very thin overcoat compared to her thick winter coat.

"He's stable now. There's been no change. We'll be there in about twenty minutes." Jack understood her concern, and wished he had given her better news.

As they walked through the exit, Monika felt the sudden impact of the cold on her face. It was similar to the shock of walking into the hot

California summer, from a wall of cold air-conditioned air in a mall. It must have been zero degrees Fahrenheit outside and she had just come from eighty-five degree weather in LA. It was quite an adjustment for her to make.

"Whew. It's cold here," she commented. Though the sun was out and the sky was blue, it was freezing. Snow was piled everywhere. In some places it stood as tall as her.

"You get used to it." Jack was amused by her complaint. "I'm over here," he pointed to his late model car parked about fifteen feet from the exit along the sidewalk of the arrivals section. The car was running.

"Don't you worry about it being stolen?" She was surprised that Jack would leave his car unattended in such a busy place.

"No. It's very cold here and lots of people do it. We're still small enough to get away with it. Besides, we aren't that bad yet and I am with the police department. It wouldn't be a smart choice." Jack realized in Los Angeles his car would have been stolen in seconds if left running and unattended, but this was Ottawa in the wintertime and leaving a car running here was a fairly common occurrence.

Jack opened the passenger door and ushered Monika into the warm car. He then opened the back door, put her suitcase on the back seat, went around and got into the driver's side. He put the car in gear and pulled out into the street en route to the hospital.

"I hope you don't mind me asking," Jack started.

"No, go ahead." Monika expected the detective to ask her some questions. She was fascinated by the white winterworld she saw through her window despite her concern about James.

"Why was your fiancé in Ottawa?" he asked as he concentrated on the road.

"He was visiting a friend. It was personal." Monika was not privy to the real reason James had made his trip. Though she had found the notice unusually short, she had not questioned him about it. He was only going to be gone a day or two.

"What was his friend's name?" Jack pressed.

"Craig Jeneau. He works for the RCMP. They've known each other a long time." She did not find his questions bothersome. She was still being distracted by the snowy world around her outside.

"I see." Though Jack was happy to identify the dead man from the side street last night, he had not realized the connection to James, or for that matter, Monika. His death would be another blow for her. He wasn't sure if he should say anything until after she had seen James.

"Why?" her concern increased and she pushed for more information.

"He was with James last night. He was killed." Jack decided to tell Monika straight out and wait for her reaction. He always found it wiser to get to the point and not cause any more agony than necessary. He likened his belief to that of pulling off a band-aid—the faster it was pulled, the better.

"Oh. No..." Monika gasped bringing her hand to her mouth.

"Should I pull over?" Jack wasn't sure if she was going to be sick. He would understand if she was. It was a common reaction to such news.

"No. No. I'm okay. Just give me some time." Monika was upset. She had been very fond of Craig. She fell silent and began to reminisce. She blanked out the ride with Jack to Ottawa Civic Hospital and allowed herself to recall her first encounter with Craig in Toronto several years ago.

Jack understood her silence and decided not to disturb her. He said nothing. He concentrated on the drive to the hospital. He felt sorry for Monika. It had been an horrendous twenty-four hours for her.

- - - - - - - - - - - - - - -

Hackett had returned to the C2 office and briefed Skinner. They had gone online and checked more thoroughly into James' file with the CIA. They were shocked to discover that James' fiancée, Monika Queller, had quite an extensive CIA file.

"This is a little coincidental." Skinner was alarmed at what he read on the computer screen.

"Maybe she's involved as well?" Hackett suggested.

"It seems that way. She has quite a history. We'd better keep a tail on her." Skinner sat back in his chair and considered all this new information.

"It's already taken care of. I sent Stone to the Château Laurier. She'll be staying in her fiancé's room." Hackett was correct. Monika would feel closer to James by staying in his room at the hotel.

"You're right. Maybe she can lead us to the list. And when she does..." Skinner didn't have to finish his sentence.

"Yes, sir. It'll be taken care of." Hackett understood. He had redeemed himself in Skinner's eyes. The two men continued to read Monika's file online.

- - - - - - - - - - - - - - - -

"Here we are." Jack's words brought Monika back from her remembrances. He parked the car in the short-term parking to the east of the hospital's main entrance. They got out of the car. Monika continued to be amazed at the quantity of snow that fell in Ottawa. It was very cold and she clasped the collar of her jacket to cover up her neck.

"James is in the Intensive Care Unit on the second floor." Jack walked around the car to her.

Monika was silent. She looked up at the huge red brick building before her to the second floor wondering behind which window James was. She tried to sense his presence and his condition but was unable to make any connection. Jack was sympathetic. He put his arm around her and comforted her. "Come on. He'll be okay. I know it," he reassured.

"Thank you." She smiled. She was grateful for Jack's paternal comforting. She hugged him. His body was much more firm than his roundness suggested. Together they crossed to the hospital's double-doored entrance.

They soon arrived on the second floor. Monika felt a chill of fear run through her as she looked down the second floor corridor to the double doors of the Intensive Care Unit. She did not like the antiseptic smell of hospitals. It always reminded her of pain and suffering.

The corridor was busy. Two attendants were talking to a nurse a few feet away in a small waiting area. They were both dressed in hospital scrubs. A trolley full of covered food trays sat next to the elevators opposite the stairwell.

Monika and Jack walked down the corridor to the Intensive Care Unit where the same Filipina nurse, Geena, who had spoken with Detective Philips that morning, instantly greeted them. The room was full of activity. There were two rows of four beds in the unit. Each bed was separated from the other by a white curtain that ran along tracks in the ceiling. In each 'room' there was a patient. Two or three of the conscious patients were curious and watched them as they entered the unit and spoke to Geena but the majority were unconscious or out of view behind drawn curtains. The sound of oxygen pumping through tubing to the patients in the ward, the beep of cardiac monitors and other equipment set a steady, rhythmic background of white noise. Monika's heart pounded in her chest. She did not like the ominous feel of the room, nor the mixture of medicinal smells that wafted throughout the unit. She tried to take shallower breaths while she scanned the ward looking for James.

"Good afternoon. Can I help you?" Geena asked.

"Yes. I'm Jack Callot of the Ottawa Police. This is Monika Queller," he introduced her. "She's here to see her fiancé James Anstey. How is he?"

"There's been no change. He's still on the critical list. But I think he's going to be okay," Geena tried to soften the bad news. She really wasn't certain if James would survive or not and there was no point in being negative and expressing the worst. James needed all the positive energy they could muster.

"Can I see him?" Monika felt emotional but in control. She tried to steady her voice and keep it from breaking. She needed to be strong for James.

She fought against her natural emotional reaction. She had to be strong. James needed her strength now more than ever.

"Certainly. You'll have to wait here, Detective Callot. This way Ms. Queller." Geena was very kind and compassionate. She turned and escorted Monika into the unit. Jack stood and watched. He thought James lucky to have such a loving, loyal fiancée.

"Here he is." Geena stopped at the fourth bed of the right hand row.

"Oh. James." Monika was momentarily deflated at the sight of James lying there. He was horribly hurt. His left leg and right arm were in casts. His chest was wrapped in a bandage that was stained red at his sternum. His face was terribly bruised and his right eye swollen shut. She could not see his hair as his head was completely wrapped in a turban-like dressing.

"It's okay." Geena noted Monika's trepidation. "You can touch him. Go ahead. I'll be back in a few minutes." She gently squeezed Monika's arm to reassure her.

"Thank you." Monika stared at James while Geena walked back to Detective Callot. She slowly moved closer to him then very carefully leaned over to give him a kiss. She brushed her hand across his forehead and gingerly sat on the edge of the bed. James was much worse than she had expected. Dismayed, she regarded the oxygen tubing going in his nose, the I V drip in his arm and the variety of wires that sent a continuous signal of his vital statistics to an array of monitors situated behind the bed. She felt her heart drop. She did not want to lose him but she didn't know what she could do other than be at his side. She felt helpless. She hoped that he could sense her presence though he gave no indication he was aware of her being there. He was obviously in a deep coma. She leaned down and, putting her arms delicately around his wrapped body, hugged him. Tears filled her eyes.

"Oh James," she whispered into his ear. "Please don't leave me."

Detective Callot and Geena stood by the entrance and watched the scene. It was difficult for them. By the way Monika held James, she was obviously passionately in love with him.

"It is such a bad thing to happen." Geena broke their silence.

"Yes," Jack agreed, without taking his eyes off Monika and James.

"Who would do such a thing?" Geena couldn't comprehend how someone could be so cruel.

"I don't know, but I'll do my best to find out." Jack was determined to find an answer. "Is he going to be okay?" He wanted the truth. He sensed that she had not been completely honest with Monika.

"We'll know in the next twenty-four to forty-eight hours. Right now, he seems stable. Did Detective Philips speak with you?" Geena suddenly remembering the other detective's earlier visit, asked.

"Detective Philips?" Jack's interest perked.

"Yes. He was here this morning." Geena was surprised by Jack's reaction. "Is something wrong?"

"What did he want?" He turned, giving Geena a questioning glance.

"The usual. He also asked about any personal effects. I told him what we had and he said he would check back later but he hasn't come back." Geena found it strange that Detective Callot was not aware of Philips having been there. She privately wondered at the inefficiency of the Ottawa Police.

"Really. What did he look like?" Jack was the lead detective on this case and he hadn't sent anyone over to the hospital. He wondered who this 'detective' might really be?

"He was big with brush cut dark hair. Leathery skin. In his forties. Very nice. Why?" Geena remembered him well.

"No reason," Jack caught himself. He did not want to give his surprise away. He didn't know any Detective Philips on the force, particularly one matching Geena's description. He contemplated this new information. It was obvious to him that Philips, if that was his real name, was an impostor. It was an unusual occurrence. It added a new dimension to the case. His initial instincts on Sussex Drive had been correct. There was something much more sinister going on than the regular homicide he was used to investigating in Ottawa.

"Detective Callot?" Geena interrupted Jack's thoughts.

"Oh. I'm sorry. I don't know him. He must be new to the department. I'll catch up with him later. Thanks." Jack was happy to have his first big lead.

"You're welcome. Please excuse me. I have to get back to work." Geena changed the subject. Detective Callot had become distracted and since it was almost dinner, she had a lot to do.

"Is it okay for me to stay?" Jack asked. Geena was walking away to the nurses station, adjacent to the ICU doors.

"Yes," she called out as she went into the station.

Jack returned his attention to Monika who was still desperately clinging to her fiancé. He checked his watch and noted the time. He had to get back to the station but he didn't want to leave Monika this way. He decided to go over and speak with her.

"Monika?" Jack came up beside her. She did not respond. He leaned down next to her and placed his hand on her shoulder. "He'll be okay. I promise." She was quietly weeping.

"Do you really think so?" Monika sat up. Her eyes were puffy, red rimmed and her mascara running. She looked like a sad rag doll.

"Yes. Here," his tone was confident, as he gave her a clean white handkerchief.

"Thank you." She was grateful for his strength and handkerchief. She needed something to bolster her. His confidence helped to lift her spirits.

"I have to get back to the station. Why don't I take you to your hotel?" He did not want to leave her alone and felt compelled to ask.

"No. I couldn't leave now." Though she wanted to freshen up, she also felt a need to be with James.

"I understand. Then, why don't I take you to your hotel so you can drop your bag, freshen up and then I'll bring you right back here. You would be back within the hour." Jack knew the break would be good for her.

"I don't know." It was a good idea but Monika was fearful about leaving James in his condition. He was far worse than she had expected him to be. If anything happened she would never forgive herself for leaving.

"I understand but it wouldn't hurt. The nurse says he's stable. It's going to be a long couple of days before we see any change and you may not get another chance. The hospital doesn't have very good accommodations for guests. I don't want to force you but it's only an hour. I'll tell you what. I'll take you and drop you back here within the hour and then get you some take-out to eat. What do you say?" Jack's kindness was winning Monika over.

"Only an hour?" She would feel better to get settled at the hotel. If she could quickly freshen up, it would help her get through the next couple of days. It would also give her a chance to catch her breath and come back stronger.

"Less." Jack hoped for her acceptance. Though he realized her need to remain, he also knew that she needed a small break to rekindle her emotional stability. The shock of finding her fiancé this way had been a terrible one. The fresh air would do her good.

"Okay. But I want to be back here within the hour. You promise?" She wasn't sure if this was the right decision but James was stable right now and it might be a good opportunity.

"Yes. Probably less," Jack encouraged.

Monika turned away from Jack, leaned down and whispered, "James. I won't be long. I'm going to the hotel. I'll be right back. Don't go anywhere." Of course there was no response. She got up from the bed.

"Who could have done this?" she demanded of Jack.

"I don't know. But I'm going to do my best to find out. They won't get away with it," he assured her.

"I hope not." She took one last look at James to be sure she had made the right choice in leaving. Something inside told her he would be okay. Jack put his arm around her and they walked away en route to his car and the hotel.

Chapter 5

The Château Laurier, resembling a medieval castle from the north of France, was perched east of Parliament Hill on the east side of the Rideau Canal a stone's throw away from the Byward Market and the Empire Grille. It rose majestically into the Ottawa skyline. Its green oxidized copper turreted roof and gray stonework blended in well with the Parliament buildings, which stood a block to the west. The hotel had been built at the turn of the last century and had weathered a great deal of Canadian history. Originally part of the Canadian Pacific Railway, the hotel had recently changed hands but was still a proud Canadian landmark in this city. Once one entered through its canopied entry into the lobby, you were instantly transported to a traditional five star hotel setting.

To the left of the lobby entrance was the concierge and the front desk. To the right was an alluring dining room that looked out over the grounds of the hotel. The furnishings in the lobby as well as the restaurant were formal but comfortable.

The uniform of the bellhops and the various other staff was reminiscent of a glamorous 1920's New York hotel. The lobby floor was made from a highly polished marble. The off white walls set off a series of landscape oil paintings of the Ottawa area that hung strategically between the sheer draped windows of the lobby. The windows overlooked the hotel driveway that meandered from Wellington Street in the south to the lobby entrance. It was a magnificent place.

Stone was sitting with his back to the restaurant at the right of the lobby entrance. He had been waiting there since before lunch. No one had bothered him. Only a waiter had spoken to him as he took his order for lunch and then again during the course of the afternoon to refill his coffee cup. He was growing tired of the wait and wondered if Hackett had been correct in his assumption that Ms. Queller would come to the hotel.

Looking up from the late edition of the *Ottawa Citizen*, Stone watched at the opposite side of the lobby across from the front desk, the three polished brass doors that housed the elevators that led up through the ten floors of the hotel to the various rooms. He had a clear view of the front desk and the lobby entrance about thirty feet away. It was almost 5:30 pm, and getting dark outside. Stone hated the early evening darkness in the winter.

"I'll wait for you here." Detective Callot pulled in front of the lobby entrance to let Monika out. Immediately the doorman came over and opened the passenger door. A blast of cold air filled the car.

"I won't be long. I'll drop my things and be right back," she said as she got out of the car.

Jack popped open the trunk and the doorman, without being asked, helped Monika to the sidewalk, then went to the rear of the car and pulled out her suitcase. Monika carefully crossed the sidewalk to escape the cold and feel the warmth of the lobby. The doorman followed, carrying her suitcase.

Monika paused to get her bearings in the lobby. She was very impressed by the opulence of the Château Laurier. She noted the ornate lobby door handles that tastefully incorporated the hotel's initials, CL, into their design.

"This way, ma'am." The doorman handed off her suitcase to the bellhop inside the lobby and ushered her toward the front desk.

"Thank you. " She felt spoiled and a little

underdressed.

Monika followed the bellhop to the front desk and walked up to the counter to check-in. The bellhop remained with her suitcase, standing to the side.

Stone was elated. It was perfect. Hackett was right. He saw Ms. Queller enter into the lobby. He recognized her from Anstey's CIA file photographs. Putting down his paper he kept his eyes glued to her as she crossed to the front desk. Though he could not hear the conversation, he carefully watched everything that transpired at the counter.

"Hi. My name is Monika Queller..." she began.

"Yes, Ms. Queller. We've been expecting you. Detective Callot has already spoken to the hotel manager. Everything is arranged. I'll get your key. Do have any identification?" The man behind the desk interrupted her. He was in his early thirties, clean cut and physically fit. He wore the dark sports jacket of the hotel with its ornate gold crest on the breast pocket. Whatever Detective Callot had said to the manager, it had put the front desk clerk on his best behavior.

"Yes." Monika opened her purse and presented the clerk with her passport.

"That's fine. Thank you, Ms. Queller. One moment please." He quickly checked and handed back her passport. He then sidestepped over to the row of letterboxes in the wall directly behind the front desk. He found the box for 828, pulled out a card key and a small Kraft envelope that was folded in half. 828 was handwritten on the envelope in dark blue magic marker.

"Here you are. It's room 828 on the eighth floor. This came last night." He handed the card key and envelope to her.

"Thank you. I wasn't expecting anything." She put the envelope directly into her purse without opening it and kept the key in hand.

"Paul. Show Ms. Queller to room 828," the clerk directed the bellhop.

"Yes sir." The bellhop graciously accepted his charge.

"I hope you have a wonderful stay at the Château Laurier. If there is anything you need, please call. My name is Anthony." Anthony smiled pleasantly.

"Thank you." Monika turned and followed the bellhop to the elevators.

Stone watched Monika's every move as she conversed with the front desk clerk. He wasn't expecting anything out of the ordinary but when he saw the clerk hand her the Kraft envelope, he became curious. He instantly assumed that something important was in the envelope. He couldn't wait to report this discovery. After Monika disappeared into the elevator, Stone stood up and crossed over to the hotel courtesy phones adjacent to the concierge's table. He picked up a phone and pressed zero for the hotel operator.

"Château Laurier," the woman operator answered.

"Can you tell me which room Monika Queller is in?" he asked.

"Just a minute, please." The line went blank. Stone checked out the lobby once more while he waited.

"Sorry to keep you sir. That's room 828. Would you like me to ring you through?"

"No, thank you." He disconnected and dialed a local number. The phone rang once.

"Hackett," his partner answered his cell phone.

"She's here. Staying in the same room that we followed Anstey to. Just arrived," Stone spoke quietly into the phone being careful not to be overheard.

"I knew she would show." Hackett was pleased with himself.

"She got an envelope from the desk clerk. It might be something. What do you want me to do?" Stone asked.

"Stay where you are and keep an eye on her. Don't do anything. We don't know what's in the envelope. It could be nothing. If she leaves the hotel, follow her. Keep me informed." Hackett was in charge of this operation.

"Right." Stone hung up, putting the receiver back in its cradle. He turned and went back to his table and chair. This was the second lucky break today.

- - - - - - - - - - - - - - - -

About fifteen minutes later Monika hurried through the main lobby to meet Jack and get back to the hospital. Though she had not changed her clothes, she had had a chance to freshen-up and compose herself. She was glad she had taken Jack's advice but wanted to get back to James.

"That didn't take long," Jack greeted her as she opened the door and got in the car. He had parked about twenty feet from the lobby at the side of the hotel's driveway.

"I hope it wasn't too long for you. Thanks for waiting." Monika's energy level was vastly improved. She was almost back to her normal self despite the circumstances.

"No problem. Is everything all right?" Jack put the car in gear and pulled into the driveway headed for Wellington Street.

"Yes. Perfect. Thank you." She gave him a warm look as she faced him, conveying her gratitude for what he done.

Jack smiled in understanding. "No problem at all. I was glad to help out." He understood. He turned his attention back to driving.

- - - - - - - - - - - - - - - -

Seeing Monika leave through the lobby, Stone took some money out of his pocket and threw it on the table to cover his bill. Keeping a safe distance, he followed after her. He got to the lobby doors just as she got into Jack Callot's car and recognized the Ottawa police detective. He whistled to the parking attendant who had allowed him to leave his car parked at the side of the hotel's driveway after being given a twenty-dollar bill. The parking attendant acknowledged him and grabbed Stone's car keys from behind his stand. Stone hurried over to his car where the attendant gave him the keys.

"Thanks." Stone took the keys gave the attendant another twenty-dollar bill and, keeping an eye on Monika's car, got into his vehicle.

"Thank you sir," The attendant, who was impressed with the large tip, yelled as Stone sped away.

Callot's car was now fifty feet ahead of him at Wellington Street. He was not worried about losing her. He had a good idea where she was going.

- - - - - - - - - - - - - - -

Jack made the journey very quickly. By 6:15 pm he dropped Monika at the entrance to Ottawa Civic Hospital. They had been away exactly an hour.

"As promised. One hour." He put the car in park and waited for Monika to get out.

"Thank you. You've been so helpful. I don't know how to thank you." Monika sat for a moment. She felt better knowing she was back at the hospital.

"I'm just doing my job, but you're welcome. I'll

check back a little later and bring you some food," Jack offered.

"What about your own family? Aren't they expecting you?" Monika inquired.

"I'm divorced. No kids. So don't worry about it," Jack said almost apologetically.

"I'm not really that hungry." Monika didn't want to be rude, but ever since she had heard the news of James' accident, she had lost her appetite.

"I'll bring a coffee and doughnut anyway. If you don't want it, I'll have it. Deal?" He smiled at her.

"Deal. I'll see you later," she said her good-byes and got out. She waited a moment on the steps to the entrance and waved as Jack drove off. It was very cold outside. She ran up the steps into the warm hospital.

- - - - - - - - - - - - - - - -

Stone stopped fifty feet behind them at the hospital. He watched as Monika ran to the building alone. He took out his cellular phone and punched in some numbers. The phone rang twice.

"Hackett."

"She's back at the hospital," he informed his partner.

"Alone?"

"Yes. But she was driven by Jack Callot."

"Stay there. I'll get there as soon as I can." Hackett hung up.

Stone put the phone back into his jacket pocket. Putting the car in gear, he drove up to wait in the hospital's short-term parking.

Chapter 6

At 7:30 pm Hackett parked next to Stone in the short-term parking lot of Ottawa Civic Hospital. It was a crisp cool evening—typical for this time of year. The sky was clear and the stars shone brilliantly. Morgan Skinner was sitting in the front passenger seat with him. Both men got out and, before getting into Stone's car, made a scan of the surrounding area to be sure they had not been followed or were being watched. They were both cautious. It was a hazard of their job. Hackett then opened the front door to Stone's car and got in next to him. Skinner got in the back seat.

"Sir." Stone turned around and greeted his boss.

"Where's Ms. Queller?" Skinner got right to the

point.

"She hasn't come out this way. She's still inside." Stone was nervous. He did not want to say anything to upset his phlegmatic boss.

"She's probably upstairs in ICU with Anstey." Hackett confidently interjected. Both he and Stone looked a little like Tweedle-dumb and Tweedle-dee with their dark parkas and similar looks. Both men had brush cuts and taut facial features. They sat, half-turned, looking back at Skinner. Though Hackett was older than Stone, they were both in excellent physical condition and did all of C2's 'rougher' work.

"Good. What about Callot? Is there anyone with her?" Skinner knew it would be a lot easier to complete their mission if Monika were alone. He didn't want the added complication of the authorities.

"He left after he dropped her. She went in by herself," Stone informed.

"Good." It was time to act. Skinner knew this might be their only opportunity. This whole unfortunate situation with Jeneau, Anstey and now Monika Queller was getting out of hand. He couldn't afford another mistake. If anything went wrong he and his men would be scapegoats. He knew his political superiors would cover everything up and deny any knowledge of this covert operation. They would brand him a radical lunatic and he would be left out in the cold.

"Do you think she has the list?" Hackett asked.

"If she doesn't, I think she knows where it is. We have to find out. Now. It's time Ms. Queller and I had a face to face chat." Skinner had a plan. He could no longer afford to wait around. He had to take control and clean this up before his time limit ran out. There would be no second chances.

"What about the detective?" Stone wondered if Monika had shared the contents of the envelope with Callot on the journey from the Château Laurier to the hospital.

"We can't take any more chances. He's a casualty. I'll take care of him. I want you to go up there, get her and bring her to the office—and be careful about it. Let me worry about Callot. We don't want any more problems. Understand?" Skinner reached into his pocket and pulled out a small bottle and a piece of white gauze. It was chloroform. "This should do the trick." He sat forward and passed the items to Hackett.

"Don't worry. We'll have her there within the hour." He assured his boss as he took the items.

"Remember, this is a public place. I don't want any more screw ups." Skinner looked at both men threateningly through the darkness.

"Yes, sir." Hackett and Stone replied simultaneously.

Without saying another word, Skinner opened the back door and got out. Now that the door was open, the light in the center of the passenger compartment illuminated the interior of the vehicle and highlighted Hackett and Stone's worried faces. It was dark outside. The streetlight above them in the short-term parking lot was not working.

"Remember." Skinner had one last word of warning for them. "No more mistakes or you'll be shopping for boxes." He slammed the door shut, adding emphasis to his threat and stepped over to his car, got in and drove off.

Feeling relieved that Skinner had left, Stone faced Hackett and asked him, "How are we going to do this?"

"We'll go upstairs together. You wait in the stairwell and I'll get her. Once she's in the stairwell, we'll use this." Hackett lifted up the gauze and bottle. "Then we'll get her down to the car."

"But won't anybody notice?" Stone was concerned about abducting someone in such a public place during what were normally the busiest hours for visitors in a hospital. "There might be a lot of people in there."

"It doesn't look like the crowd has arrived yet. If we hurry we might be lucky and hit a down time. If anyone stops us, we'll just say she fainted and we're taking her outside for fresh air. It should work but we'd better hurry." Hackett pushed the knob of the car radio and the time was illuminated on the radio's LED dial. It displayed 6:35 pm. "People are still coming home from work and getting dinner. It'll probably get busy after seven."

"Okay. Sounds like a plan." It made sense to Stone. He trusted Hackett's planning abilities. They had never gone wrong in the past.

Hackett put the gauze and chloroform into his jacket pocket. Both men opened their doors and got out. They searched the short-term parking lot for interlopers but there was no one else around. They were still early enough to accomplish their mission.

Closing their doors, they turned and looked up to the lighted windows of the second floor ICU unit and made their way to the hospital entrance. If they were lucky and everything went as planned, they would be safely on their way with their package within fifteen minutes.

- - - - - - - - - - - - - - - -

Skinner did not usually get involved at this level of an operation. He had paid his dues many years ago and left such jobs now to Stone and Hackett. But there was no time to waste. Callot was a loose cannon and needed to be dealt with immediately. Over the last twenty hours there had been more loose ends to deal with than he liked. He wanted to get this situation resolved and get back to the normal clandestine operation of C2's activities. He looked at his car clock display. It was 6:40 pm. He took his cell phone out of his jacket pocket and punched in the number of the local division of the Ottawa Police.

"Ottawa Police. Staff Sgt. Cooche speaking," a woman answered.

"Detective Jack Callot, please," Skinner requested. He was not worried about using his phone. His number could not be traced or seen on the caller ID that the police used.

"I'll put you through to Homicide. Please hold." Though not rude, the sergeant's tone was curt.

Skinner waited for the connection.

"Homicide. Detective Ferisse." It was Jack's partner.

"Detective Callot, please," Skinner repeated.

"He's just left. Can I help?" Jean-Paul Ferisse was matter-of-fact. He was busy doing follow-up paperwork on the Jeneau case.

Skinner disconnected without saying a word. He punched in directory assistance.

"For what city?' the operator came online.

"Ottawa. Jack Callot." Skinner hoped the detective's number wasn't unlisted. He had neglected to get his home phone number at the office.

"Thank you." There was a short pause and an automated message gave him the number.

Skinner punched in Jack Callot's home phone number. He was glad he didn't have to find his number the harder way from the C2 office and waste precious time. The phone rang several times.

"Hello." Jack had just arrived home and was

opening the side door to his house, which led from the driveway to the kitchen when he heard the phone ring. He ran over to get the phone on the opposite wall before his service picked it up. He did not lock the kitchen door behind him.

"Stacey, please." Skinner made up a name. He did not want to make Callot suspicious.

"I'm afraid you have the wrong number," Jack's run to the phone made his words come out in short bursts.

"I'm sorry," Skinner said politely.

"That's okay." Jack cradled the phone. It was not often he received a wrong number but it did occasionally happen. He was not alarmed by it.

Happy to be home and have a chance to relax, Jack had finished his work at the station and was going to freshen-up before he returned to the hospital to keep Monika company. He planned to get there no later than 7:45 pm. He looked at his watch. Seven forty-five was an hour away and he wanted to have a quick shower. On his way to the hospital, which was no more than fifteen minutes away, he was going to pick up coffee and doughnuts. Not wanting to waste time, he crossed the kitchen and went down the hall that led to his bedroom and shower.

Skinner ended the call and put the phone back into his jacket pocket. He was pleased with himself. Detective Callot lived on Green Lane just off the 417, the main highway which traversed the center of Ottawa east to west. He was only minutes away. He remembered the address from Callot's file, which he'd checked at the office after Hackett had informed him of Stone's call from the Château Laurier. He knew this veteran of the Ottawa Homicide Department, though he had never made his acquaintance.

Having left Carlingview Avenue and the Ottawa Civic Hospital just a short time ago, he was now approaching the ramp to the westbound 417. He signaled and turned onto the westbound ramp. It was rush hour and the traffic was much slower than usual. He gradually made his way onto the highway and a short time later was on Green Lane, parked on the street opposite Jack's home.

Jack lived in the newer part of suburban Ottawa. Divorced from his wife five years, he had reestablished himself alone in this small modern ranch style bungalow with a carport instead of a garage attached at the south side. It was the only ranch style bungalow on this section of Green Lane. The rest of the homes were the more popular two-story design. The house stood on a large sixty by one-twenty foot lot. Ottawa was still under-populated enough that land was readily available.

Skinner shut off the car, leaned over and opened the glove compartment. He took out his revolver, checked it and sat back. Attached to his revolver was a silencer. He looked out his window to Jack's house. The snow was piled about five feet high along the street and driveway. Outside, the white porch light glistened off the soft white snow covered front lawn, illuminating a path that led from the driveway to the front door. Sitting in the carport, protected from the harsh winter elements, was Jack's sedan. The house was well-lit, indicating to Skinner that Detective Callot was home. There was not much activity on Green Lane and the other homes of the neighborhood, though well lit and occupied, were peaceful with their cars parked in their driveways. Skinner's car was the only one parked on the side of the street but it drew no notice, as everyone inside was busy settling in after a hard day's work.

Skinner checked the car clock again. It was 6:55 pm. If he waited much longer he would lose the advantage of surprise. He got out of the car and, closing the door quietly behind him, reconnoitered the area. Keeping his revolver tucked into his jacket, he walked across the street and up Jack's driveway to the side door that entered the house from the carport. There was no light on in the carport and he was concealed in the darkness. When he got to the side door he stopped and looked around. Very slowly, he opened the screen door and, without making a sound, pulled out his gun and listened for any sound coming from inside. Hearing nothing, he tried the doorknob. To his surprise it was not locked. He carefully twisted the handle and pushed open the door, stepping inside the kitchen of Jack's house. Skinner's pulse raced. Stealthily he closed the door and strained his ears for any sound of Jack. He heard nothing. Satisfied that his intrusion had not been heard, he made his way across the kitchen and down the short hallway. All the lights were on but there was no sign of Jack. As Skinner traveled down the hallway he heard the sound of the shower coming from behind a door at the end of the hall. Jack was in the shower.

Skinner smiled. This was going to be easier than he had expected. Like a hunter closing in on his prey, he went up to the door at the end of the hallway. Gingerly he placed his hand on the door handle and leaned forward to listen. All he could hear was the sound of the running water.

Slowly Skinner opened the door far enough to see into the room. He held his gun out in front of him. The room was full of steam and the sound of the shower was loud. It was a small but standard full bathroom. Directly opposite him were the opaque glass doors of the shower. As the steam escaped through the open door into the hallway, Skinner could make out the image of a man in the shower behind the shower door. He stepped into the center of the room and aimed his gun at the man.

Noticing the sudden draft, Jack opened the shower door to identify its source. Instantly he saw Skinner pointing his gun at him.

"Who are you? I'm a police officer. What do you want?" he called out over the sound of the shower, wiping water from his face. Though afraid he did not show it in his voice. The water from his wet hair dripped into his eyes and prevented him from clearly identifying the intruder. He knew from his police training that he must try and personalize himself to the intruder if he wanted a chance to survive this invasion. It was his only hope under the circumstances. He had nowhere to turn. If he could distract the intruder long enough he might be able to turn the situation around.

"Detective Callot?" Skinner inquired aiming his gun at Jack's upper torso.

"Yes," Callot answered, hoping to create a verbal bond between them.

Skinner fired off two rounds, hitting Jack in the chest. Jack was in shock. The impact of bullets pushed him against the wall. His blood stained the wall and mixed in with the water. He brought his hands up to his wounds in disbelief. He was unable to speak. His eyes were open wide in amazement. He opened his mouth in an attempt to speak but it was too late. Skinner fired one final round and Jack slipped dead to the floor of the shower.

Without flinching, Skinner put his gun into his jacket pocket and left the room, wiping the door handle with his handkerchief as he went. He felt no emotion. Shooting Callot at such close range in cold blood had no effect on him. He was a seasoned professional. It was only a job that had to be done. He made his way through the house and went out into the carport again, wiping the door handles as he left. The world outside was unchanged. He casually strolled down the driveway, crossed the street, got into his car, started it, and drove off. He was headed home. It had been a long day and he was tired. All he needed now was to get the list and then silence both Anstey and his fiancée. He expected that Stone and Hackett would easily complete their mission. By this time tomorrow C2's secrets would be secure. As he drove away, he became more relaxed. There was one less loose end to be thinking about.

- - - - - - - - - - - - - - - -

Stone and Hackett's timing was perfect. The main lobby of the hospital was empty. Even the candy-striper that Hackett had spoken with that morning was gone and her kiosk left vacant. They were in-between shift changes and the next volunteer had not yet arrived for her evening shift during visiting hours. They made their way across the lobby to the stairwell that led to the second floor. They leapt up the stairs. When they arrived at the second floor landing, they stopped.

"Wait here and be ready," Hackett commanded.

Stone backed into the corner. He understood what he had to do. He would stay out of sight until his partner returned. Hackett gave Stone the thumbs-up, opened the door and stepped into the second floor corridor. He hoped he was ahead of the rush and that the floor would not be busy with visitors. If that were the case, he would be back with Ms. Queller in the seclusion of the stairwell within a few short minutes.

Chapter 7

As Monika entered the Intensive Care Unit Geena greeted her from the nurses station. Tonight her shift ended at ten pm.

"Hi. You're back early?" From her tone, it sounded as if Geena thought something might be wrong.

"Yes. I just wanted to check into the hotel and freshen up. How is he?" Monika peered into the ward to James' curtained-off unit.

"There's been no change." Geena shrugged.

"Oh." Monika was disappointed and it showed. Somehow she had hoped James would be awake, sitting up and waiting for her but she knew that this was just a fantasy.

"Don't worry. That's a good sign." Geena

smiled trying to cheer her up. "Go in. He knows you're here. I'm sure of it." She wasn't sure but it made her and Monika feel better to believe it.

"Thank you." Monika hoped that Geena was correct and that James somehow knew she was nearby. She desperately wanted to believe he could sense her presence on some subconscious level.

She crossed through the ward to James' bed. Other than two other nurses who were tending their patients, she was the only visitor. This was not unusual for the ICU. These were patients who were seriously ill and needed solitude to recover. The unit understood this and did not encourage a lot of visitors. James' case was a rare exception to this otherwise strictly enforced policy. Usually families went along with it, not wanting to impede their loved one's recovery.

Monika took off her coat and placed it, with her small black patent-leather purse that matched her boots, on the chair that Geena had earlier put at the end of the bed against the curtain. She then gently sat down on the edge of the bed and gazed at James. She felt a little better since freshening up at the hotel and was now calmer about the manner in which she again found him. "At least," she thought to herself, "He isn't worse."

Monika was wearing a short black heavy cotton crew neck one-piece dress. It clung tightly to her petite body. Her hair was pinned up and she looked a lot younger—perhaps in her late teens and not her late twenties. As she sat there, she felt alone and wasn't sure what she would do if she lost James, who remained motionless. If it weren't for the beeping monitors surrounding him and the sound of his breathing, she would have thought he was dead. Raising her hands together to her chin, she closed her eyes and began to say a simple prayer.

"Please Lord. Let him live. I know it's selfish, but I need him. I love him. Please protect him and bring him from harm. Amen." She spoke quietly and when she had finished put her hands in her lap and opened her eyes. She hoped someone was listening and would answer her prayer. Though not a regular churchgoer, she was a very spiritual person. She leaned over and kissed James on the forehead after saying her prayer.

"Hi sweetie. I'm back." She caressed his cheek with her hand and sat up. Looking about the ward she felt sadness for the families of the other patients who were lying there. The smell of disinfectant permeated the unit. Several of the patients had small bouquets of flowers placed on their bedside tables. The colorful arrangements helped to break up the otherwise mechanical starkness of the typical, sterile white hospital ward.

Realizing it was going to be a long wait, Monika reached over for her handbag and gently put it on the bed in front of her. She opened her bag and found the envelope the clerk had given her at the hotel. She unfolded the envelope and noticed the 828 written in blue magic marker. She wondered what was inside.

Placing her finger under the flap of the envelope, she ripped it open and looked inside. To her amazement she found pieces of paper. She turned the envelope upside down and shook the pieces of paper onto the bed. There were about twenty pieces. She wondered why someone would send her ripped up pieces of paper. Carefully she examined each piece. Some were blank and others had handwriting in blue magic marker similar to the writing on the envelope. Anyone else would probably have thrown the envelope and its contents away after opening it, without taking the time to examine the pieces of paper, but Monika had plenty of time to spend puzzling over the pieces that lay before her. She began to slowly go through the pieces, looking for a pattern.

Monika enjoyed doing puzzles. She followed her usual pattern of lining up the corners and piecing the straight edges in between. The pieces had been torn by hand and she found it fairly easy to match them by their rip marks. She became very absorbed in the puzzle. Gradually, piece by piece, she managed to make progress. The paper was standard white eight and half by eleven. The blue magic marker on many of the pieces gradually began to form a legible pattern somewhat like ancient hieroglyphics. Bit by bit the symbols and the puzzle became clearer to her. When she finally pieced it all together correctly she discovered that the ancient hieroglyphics were really just somebody's handwritten message. Someone had written something in the center of the page and then torn it into little pieces. She could not understand the writing, as the letters did not resemble any script she was familiar with. The symbols weren't Egyptian or of any other culture she knew. They didn't appear to have any obvious pictographic origin.

After ten minutes of further contemplation, she sat back and stared at the completed puzzle before her. Someone had handwritten a combination of nine letters and symbols. It was definitely western English script, but she could not make any sense of it. She reached into her purse, found her pen, ripped the envelope in half and copied the letters and symbols onto it. She stared at the curious message before her, not understanding its meaning. She thought maybe it was a joke that someone had mistakenly sent to her. But she wondered why someone would take the time to send such a foolish thing. She reached over and placed the envelope on James' side table in front of a stainless steel water jug.

Picking up the pieces of the puzzle from the bed, she carefully put them with the pen into the change section of her purse. She did not want to throw them out until she deciphered their meaning. It was quite a mystery for her. She sat back and considered the puzzle. As she sat there thinking, she caught the distorted reflection of what she had copied onto the envelope in the stainless steel water jug. Suddenly she caught a recognizable glimpse of the letters and symbols of the message.

"Of course," she thought to herself. "It was a mirror image. Someone had written the message in a reflected image."

She reached for her purse and pulled out her pen. Standing up she tore off another piece of the envelope and manipulating the paper to an angle that allowed her to clearly see, held up her writing against the water jug. She twisted the envelope around a couple of times and then it became crystal clear to her. She smiled as she saw the perfectly legible image reflected in the water jug. How fortunate she had placed the envelope on the side table. She had been lucky to be able to decipher it to so quickly.

Pleased with herself Monika read, symbol by symbol, and wrote down what she translated as: 1720YQBCF. Though she did not see the meaning of the message at least now she could easily read what was written. There were four numbers and five letters. It was a coded message of some sort. She wondered who could have sent it to her.

Monika continued to stare at the message, trying to decode its meaning. Maybe this message really wasn't meant for her. Maybe it belonged to somebody else. Frustrated, she picked up the envelope and put it in the same section of her purse as the puzzle pieces. When she got back to the hotel she would talk with the desk clerk about it.

Monika liked a mystery and, no matter how she tried, she kept searching for some meaning to the decoded 1720YQBCF puzzle as she sat there. She went over the message again and again trying to make sense if it. It wasn't long before she wondered if the message had something to do with James' accident. Maybe the message had played a part in all that had happened to him and Craig. If that were the case, she knew she would have to be careful who she spoke to about the message. When Detective Callot arrived she would talk to him about it. She believed she could trust him. Maybe he could better understand its meaning. Until then she would not say anything to anyone.

Chapter 8

Hackett was relieved to discover that the Intensive Care Unit was as quiet as it had been earlier that day. He entered through the ICU doors and walked past the nurses station. Geena was no longer in the station. He paused and looked into the ward. There were no nurses to be seen. He assumed they were all busy tending to patients needs out of the ward. Scanning the right side of the ward he spied Monika. She was sitting at the end of James' bed in a chair. He hoped she was alone. He calmly made his way to her through the unit.

"Good evening, Ms. Queller." He put on his best act. "I'm Detective Philips."

"Oh. Hi." Monika was startled by the unexpected male voice behind her. She turned to face the man who had addressed her. "Couldn't Detective Callot make it?" Philips was a rough looking man and she couldn't help but notice his cold, penetrating cruel eyes. She didn't feel comfortable with him.

"No. He's been held up," Hackett fumbled at her mentioning of Callot and recovered. "He sent me instead. He'll be by later. I hope you don't mind?"

"No. Not at all. You have all been so kind and I appreciate it." She smiled, concealing her true feelings. There was something about Philips she didn't like but she overlooked it, since he was a colleague of Jack's.

"He wanted me to ask you some questions." Hackett did not blink as he looked at her.

"Go ahead." She readied herself. She wanted to do anything to help find the perpetrators of the crime against James and Craig.

"Would you mind if we went somewhere a little more private? It's kind of sensitive and there are ears..." Hackett indicated by a nod of his head the neighboring patients. He was concerned they might be able to overhear their conversation. That was something he wanted to avoid.

"No. I don't mind. That's fine. Where did you have in mind?" Monika stood up. Her five-foot two-inch height was much shorter than Detective Philips.

"I thought maybe I could buy you a cup of coffee downstairs and we could talk for a couple of minutes? It won't take long," he suggested. As he spoke his eyes wandered up and down her, tracing her curves.

"Sure. I wouldn't mind a hot cup of coffee." The detective's lecherous stare made Monika uneasy. He was not anything like the gentleman Jack was. She turned and, searching through her bag took out her wallet, which contained all her ID and money. She didn't want to carry a purse and felt it would be reasonably safe there in the ICU.

Hackett surveyed the room as Monika turned away from him to get her things. The rest of the ward was as quiet as when he had entered. No one else had come in and there was still no sign of the nursing staff.

"I'm ready." Monika started to walk towards the detective.

During her conversation with Hackett, Monika had not noticed what was happening with James. Distracted, she had not seen the sudden movement of the fingers of his right hand protruding from his cast. Just as she and Hackett began to walk away, James' one good eye began to twitch open. He was coming to. He was groggy and his vision blurred but he was awakening. He saw the blurred image of a petite blonde woman before him. He strained to better focus his eyes but he was unable to make any noticeable movement. He believed it was Monika. He tried to lift his right arm but there was something heavy preventing him from lifting it. His vision gradually cleared and he now saw Hackett walking away with Monika. Though he did not know him by name, James never forgot a face. It was all part of his training. It was an instinctual reaction. He knew that the man with Monika was responsible for shooting him. James realized from Monika's demeanor that she was not aware of this fact. He desperately tried to get her attention but she did not turn around. She kept walking farther away with the enemy. James knew she was in danger. He tried to call out but there was something down his throat preventing him from speaking. He tried to muster all his energy to make a sound to warn her but he was not strong enough. He was frustrated and didn't know what he could do. They soon left his limited line of sight.

"There's a coffee machine in the lobby downstairs. Why don't we go there?" 'Detective' Philips suggested as they arrived at the door to the second floor stairwell.

"That'll be fine. I don't mind machine coffee. At this point anything hot would be great." Monika felt the chill of the wintry weather and didn't want to leave the building. It would take a while for her to acclimatize.

"After you." Hackett pulled open the stairway

doors allowing her to go ahead.

"Thank you," she said and began to walk into the stairwell. She appreciated such chivalry and considered she might have been unfair in her estimation of the detective.

Hackett quickly looked over his shoulder and pulled the chloroform out of his jacket pocket. He soaked the gauze and followed Monika into the stairwell, closing the door behind him.

As Monika entered the stairwell she saw Stone, who was standing with his back to her blocking her way.

"Excuse me," she said trying to get the man's attention. The man had an offensive stale aroma that repulsed her.

Stone turned and grinned at her, alarming her. Her adrenaline surged and she felt danger. She was about to turn to call for Detective Philips' assistance when, from behind, she was grabbed and a strong smelling wet gauze was forced over her nose and mouth. She tried to twist and pull away from the foul smell. She wondered who was holding her and then saw it was Detective Philips who was manhandling her. She struggled harder and kicked at the detective, trying to break free, but he was too strong and overpowered her.

She could not prevent herself from breathing in whatever chemical saturated the gauze. The chemical had a bittersweet aroma. She was not able to scream for help. Philips held her head firmly against him, keeping the gauze over her nose and mouth. She put up a powerful fight, pushing and kicking. She tried to grab at Philips' coat and the bottle containing the chloroform fell from his pocket. There was a loud popping sound as the bottle shattered on the cement stairwell floor.

"Don't just stand there. Give me a hand," Hackett ordered Stone, who was watching and enjoying the sight of Monika squirming. Stone stepped over and helped subdue her.

"Feisty, isn't she," he chuckled. He was a perverse man and enjoyed being rough with women.

Monika's struggle seemed to last an eternity but in reality it only lasted a few short seconds. She was petrified. Her heart pounded in her chest and she found it difficult to breathe. She was forced to inhale large amounts of the fumes from the gauze. She thought they might be poisoning her but quickly realized by the sleepy feeling washing over her, that she was being drugged. These men wanted to abduct her. She did not know who they were or why they would do such a thing. Her mind turned to rape but this was more than that. Finally the chemical took effect. Monika felt an increasing light-headedness. She felt like she was getting drunk. Gradually her struggle slowed then ceased altogether as she succumbed to the chloroform.

"That was harder than I thought it would be."

Hackett caught his breath and held Monika's limp body. He picked up her wallet from the floor where it had fallen during their scuffle and put it in his pocket.

"She's a tough little thing. Let me get her arm." Stone lifted one of Monika's arms over his shoulder. Hackett lifted her other arm and they sandwiched her between them.

"Got her?" Hackett asked. She was not heavy but she was a dead weight.

"Yep." Stone was ready to move.

Monika was securely positioned between them with her head flopped down. Hackett and Stone carried her down the stairs into the lobby. In order to prevent her feet from dragging they lifted her up.

Several minutes later they entered the hospital lobby. There was no one there. They could not have planned it any better. They were just before the rush. They hurried across to the exit and went out into the cold night. In a matter of minutes they had Monika sprawled out on the rear seat of their car. Their mission successful, Stone started the car and they drove away from the Ottawa Civic.

- - - - - - - - - - - - - - -

James was still trying to call out but the tubing down his throat would not permit any sound to come forth. He tried to moan but found he could not make a loud enough sound to attract attention. He was too weak. The vision in his open eye was clear. He could see he was in an Intensive Care Unit in a hospital. He saw the cast on his leg and arm and his bandaged chest, but he did not feel any pain. He recalled what had happened to him the night before. At least he thought it was the night before though he wasn't certain how long he had been unconscious. He remembered hearing a chilling scream and then nothing. Everything was beginning to come back to him.

Nurse Geena had stepped away for a few moments on a break. When she came back to the ICU she did a quick routine walk-through. She had only been gone five minutes. The other two nurses on her shift were busy with housekeeping duties. Expecting to find Monika with James, she was surprised to find James trying to communicate. He appeared extremely agitated and she became concerned that he may do himself harm and open his wounds.

"Susan. Get a sedative," she called out to one of the other nurses who hurried to the nurses station and returned with a syringe. The doctor had written up an order just in case it was required.

James saw the syringe. He moaned and tried to shake his head to indicate 'no' but his protesting made him appear more hysterical.

"Relax Mr. Anstey. Don't upset yourself. Everything will be all right. We don't want you opening your wounds. Your fiancée is here. I know this is all a shock but you have to calm down. You'll be okay. I'll get the doctor." She injected the sedative into his IV and sat back comforting him until it took effect. Within seconds he was unconscious. The effect would not last long. She had only given him enough to calm him until she could get the on-call doctor. She was very happy he had awakened so soon after his injuries. It was an encouraging sign. She wondered where Monika had gone. Seeing her coat and purse on the chair made her think she had stepped out to the ladies room. She couldn't wait for her to get back so she could share the good news.

- - - - - - - - - - - - - - -

Within twenty minutes Hackett and Stone had parked their car and were carrying an unconscious Monika along Sparks Street Mall. It was almost 7:30 pm. While in the car, Hackett had blindfolded Monika and phoned Skinner informing him of the success of their mission. Skinner had told him to secure her in the C2 office. He said he would get there as soon as possible. Hackett was pleased with Skinner's reaction.

Moving quickly, they carried Monika sandwiched between them from the car to the office. A couple of the passers-by who saw them assumed Monika was drunk and were disgusted by such a public display. Hackett and Stone ignored their disapproving stares and soon found themselves at the entrance to the C2 office. Opening the door they turned sideways and lifted Monika inside, closing the door behind them. They breathed a sigh of relief feeling they were safe from the outside world. With difficulty they climbed the stairs with Monika and went into the office. Tired from their exertion, they welcomed the chance to put her down and rest while they waited for Skinner to arrive.

Chapter 9

"Here you go Jean-Paul. This just came up for you." A middle-aged uniformed officer dropped a file folder on Jean-Paul Ferisse's desk.

"Thanks George. I would've come down for that." Jean-Paul had been waiting for the print report. It had taken longer than usual. He looked at his watch. It was 7:30 pm. He had run the prints before ending his shift earlier that morning. He hated working the night shift. Though it was only once a month it upset his system.

"I needed the walk anyway. How's Jack?" The uniformed officer was a man in his sixties. No longer doing patrols or walking the beat, he was assigned to office work in the station. He was three weeks away from retirement. He knew Jean-Paul and Jack well.

"He's great. We're both a little busy this week. I'll tell him you said hi." Jean-Paul was anxious to see the print report. Usually he would have talked longer with George but he was curious and knew that Jack would want to hear from him right away. George was a man who had seen many years of service on the Ottawa Police force. Originally he had been a military policeman but he had given that up after his tour was over and moved into the Ottawa Police. He was originally from the west, from Calgary.

"Okay. I'll see you later." George understood the pressures on detectives in the early stages of investigating a homicide. He smiled and walked away through the department.

Jean-Paul opened the folder to find a thorough report on the prints. The prints belonged to Craig Jeneau, an RCMP officer currently assigned to Québec City. Jean-Paul was surprised. This was no ordinary homicide case after all. This meant there might be farther-reaching ramifications.

Picking up the phone, Jean-Paul dialed Jack's cell number. He knew Jack would want to get this information without delay. Before Jack had left for the evening he had told Jean-Paul his plans: first he was going home and then he was going to the hospital for an hour to visit with Ms. Queller. The phone rang about six times.

"Jack Callot," it was Jack's voice inserted into the automated message of the mobile phone company. "Is not available. Please leave a message after the tone." Jean-Paul did not leave a message. He put the receiver down.

Sitting back in his chair he wondered where Jack was. He felt certain he would not have gone to the hospital yet. He knew once Jack entered the hospital he would turn his cell phone off. It was the hospital's policy. Jean-Paul reached for the phone again and decided to try Jack at his home. He punched in the number and waited. The phone rang many times but neither Jack nor his service took the call.

"That's odd," Jean-Paul thought. Jack was usually very easy to get a hold of. He hung up the phone. His police instincts told him that something was wrong. Jack was too anxious about the print report not to answer his phone.

Picking up the folder, Jean-Paul stood up. Maybe his partner had gone to the hospital early. Jean-Paul decided to take the information to him there. With the folder under his arm, he walked through the homicide department and disappeared through the main doors.

- - - - - - - - - - - - - - -

Twenty minutes later Jean-Paul walked through the double doors on the second floor of the Ottawa Civic Hospital into the ICU unit.

"Good evening," Geena called out to him from

the nurses station.

"Good evening. I'm Detective Jean-Paul Ferisse with the Ottawa Police." Jean-Paul stepped towards the nurses station, pulled out his identification and showed it to Geena. "I'm looking for Detective Callot."

"He's not here. He left a couple of hours ago." Geena stood up from behind the nurses station to examine his ID.

"Really? Maybe you could show me to Ms. Queller?" Jean-Paul found it unusual that Jack was not there. He considered the possibility that he was just running late. But if that were the case, he wondered why Jack hadn't answered his phone.

"She's not here either. I think she stepped out for bit. She left her coat and purse."

"I see. How's Mr. Anstey?" Jean-Paul half expected Geena to say he wasn't there either.

"Much better. He woke up a little while ago." Geena smiled, her large eyes firmly focused on Jean-Paul.

"I'd like to see him." He had a few questions he wanted to ask James.

"He's in the last bed on the right but he's sedated."

"Sedated? Why?" It made no sense to Jean-Paul. He couldn't understand why a comatose patient would be sedated after having come out of his sleep.

"He's still very ill. He's still critical. He was very disoriented and upset when he awoke. He won't be out that long. I gave him a small dose of Valium. You can wait there if you like." Geena pointed to James' bed.

"Thank you. I think I will." Jean-Paul put his identification back into his pocket and walked through the unit to James and stopped.

Standing at the end of the bed, Jean-Paul carefully examined James' condition. He looked badly hurt and in a lot of discomfort. His right arm and left leg were in large white plaster casts. His upper torso was bandaged and his head wrapped. His right eye was badly bruised and swollen. Tubes were running into his nose and mouth. An IV drip line was attached to his left arm.

Jean-Paul noted Monika's coat on the chair next to the curtain. Her purse was sitting on it. He thought it odd that a woman would leave her purse unattended. He wondered where she had gone. He would have thought she would want to be constantly at her fiancé's side under the circumstances.

Scrutinizing the rest of the room, Jean-Paul saw a piece of an envelope lying on the bedside table in front of a stainless steel jug. He took three steps to the table and picked up the piece of envelope to examine it. He was in investigation mode. There was handwriting on the envelope: 1720YQBCF.

He wondered to whom the envelope belonged to and what the writing meant. He considered it might be some sort of secret code. But if that were the case, why would someone leave it out in the open so carelessly? He studied the writing. The only part that made sense to him were three letters: YQB. These were symbols for the Québec City International Airport. He had made many trips over the years to Québec City and these three letters immediately jumped out at him.

"Seventeen-twenty Québec City CF?" he said out loud to himself hoping that hearing the phrase would help. But it didn't.

He assumed that Monika had written these numbers and letters, as the writing appeared to be in a woman's hand. He stood puzzled for a moment and then returned the paper back to the table next to the stainless steel jug where he found it. He had learned a long time ago the importance, while investigating a case and finding clues, of leaving things as he had found them. Sometimes this was the best way to elicit their true significance. He wondered what this clue's significance was.

Jean-Paul remained standing while he contemplated the clue. He looked about the unit. Other than the nurses and the other patients, no one else was in the unit. He scanned the ward wondering why it was so quiet and where Ms. Queller had gotten to. He had expected there to be more visitors at this time in the evening. He also wondered why Jack had not yet arrived. These questions gnawed away at him. Something was wrong but he didn't know what.

He checked his watch and noted the time, it was almost eight o'clock. He decided to wait a while longer for Ms. Queller and Jack. Repositioning Monika's purse and coat on the chair, Jean-Paul sat down. He hoped he would not have to wait long. It had been a wearing, eventful day. He was bushed.

Chapter 10

When Monika came to she was groggy and afraid. She remembered the struggle in the stairwell of the hospital and the betrayal of Detective Philips. She had been kidnapped but she had no idea why. She was sitting in a hard chair with her arms and legs bound tightly to it. Her forearms hurt from the ropes. She was blindfolded and vulnerable.

"Good evening Ms. Queller, or may I call you Monika?" Skinner's voice shot out to her from across the room. "I'm sorry for the way we had to bring you here but I thought it was time we had a little chat." Skinner was sitting at his desk in front of her and going through her wallet. Hackett and Stone were quietly standing behind her in the two corners of the room.

"Where am I? Why have you brought me here?" Monika's belligerence came through as she realized her life was not in immediate danger. Her abductors wanted something and she knew that until they got it she would be safe. She faced and spoke to the direction she heard the voice coming from.

"Now Monika. Don't fret. No one's going to harm you. I just want to have a friendly little chat. I won't keep you long." Skinner was calm and confident. The clock on the wall over the door read 8:10 pm.

"Who are you? What do you want?" Monika tugged at her restraints, her tone fearful. From the sound of his voice the man sounded mature. She thought she detected a slight southern American accent.

"Right to the point. That's good. I like that quality. We won't be wasting each other's valuable time." Skinner smiled. He respected her bravado. "Who I am is not important. You have something I want."

"What? I don't even know you." Monika twisted her head as she spoke, not certain where the man now was. Her heart was pounding.

"And that's the way we're going to keep it. Your fiancé has been a bit of trouble for us," Skinner began.

"So you're responsible for what happened to

him. Did you also kill Craig?" she angrily interrupted.

"It was unfortunate. Things got out of hand. But let's not distract ourselves from our purpose. Craig gave your fiancé something that belongs to me and I want it back." Even though Monika would eventually be killed, Skinner was not going to give her any more information than he had to. Until he got the list he wasn't taking any chances. Too much had gone wrong already.

"What? I don't know what you're talking about." Monika's thoughts went immediately to the coded message on the envelope she got from the desk clerk at the Château Laurier. It was the only thing she could think of that might have a common connection to them all. So that's what this is all about, she thought. She wondered how such a simple thing could be so important.

"I hope for your sake you do, Ms. Queller and that right now you're just pretending you don't, to protect yourself. I'm not going to argue the point with you tonight. Let me just say this. I'll give you forty-eight hours—until Thursday morning—to return my property. If you and your fiancé want to live, I suggest you improve your memory and soon," Skinner's tone was threatening. "I hope you understand, Ms. Queller. This is not a game. There's a lot at stake."

"But I don't know what you want. I haven't got anything." She was not acting. She really did not understand what he wanted.

"That's too bad. You've only got a few hours. I suggest you find out." Skinner didn't believe her. She had to know something.

"Find out what?" she pleaded.

"Stop playing Ms. Queller. I know about the envelope." He used his trump card. Monika fell silent. He leaned back in his chair and smiled.

"Envelope?" Monika's timing gave her away.

"Come now. You see. I knew you were smart, but I'll play along. I want the envelope." He was enjoying their cat and mouse game.

"What envelope?" Monika played her expected role. The coded message in the envelope was certainly of importance. She conjured it up in her mind: 1720YQBCF.

"What do you take me for?" he sighed.

"But there was nothing in it." Monika lied. She was enraged by what this man had done to both Craig and James but needed to get out of there if she was going to have any chance at saving James and herself and getting retribution. She had to find out what the coded message meant before she handed it over to him. To accomplish that she needed to get away. She knew their lives only had value as long as he believed she had what he wanted.

"Of course. Have it your way." Skinner wrote something down on a small piece of paper and got up from behind his desk. He walked over and stopped in front of Monika. Monika felt his presence and tried to push away but was stopped by the chair.

"Don't worry Ms. Queller. I'm not going to hurt you. Not tonight anyway." Skinner reached forward and putting the piece of paper in Monika's wallet, put the wallet in her right hand.

"What are you doing?" She felt his rough large hands against her skin.

"When you're ready to deal call me at the number in your wallet. Don't lose it. If I don't hear from you by Thursday morning, then..." he let his unspoken thoughts linger on the air as he went back and sat behind his desk.

Monika felt relieved. She held tightly onto her wallet.

"Well, that wasn't that bad now was it? I think we're going to get along just fine." Skinner sat watching her reaction. He was pleased with their conversation. He sensed she knew what he was talking about and would comply with his wishes. He signaled to Hackett and Stone, who on cue came forward and began to undo her restraints.

"What are you doing?" Monika was startled and afraid. She tensed her body against the rough grip of the two sets of hands.

"Calm down, Ms. Queller. We're just untying you. But I'm afraid the blindfold will have to remain. Please don't make a scene. You will be dropped back at the hospital." Skinner used a softer voice to reassure her.

"I'm okay." Monika understood and gave up her struggle. She was safe for the moment. All she wanted now was to get out of this place. She settled herself down and cooperated.

"That's better. I knew you were a smart woman. I look forward to your call." That said, Hackett and Stone lifted her out of the chair. Monika could not see a thing. Before they walked out of the C2 office Skinner called out to her:

"One last thought, Ms. Queller. If you're thinking of telling anyone about our meeting, I wouldn't. We'll be keeping a close eye on you from now on. If anyone else gets involved it could be hazardous to your fiancé's continued recuperation."

- - - - - - - - - - - - - - -

Monika found it extremely cold outside without a winter jacket. By the time Hackett and Stone had gotten her to their car she was shaking. Though on several occasions she attempted to speak to them, neither of the two men said a word to her. She was not able to see where she was but she believed she was downtown judging from the traffic sounds around her. Once at the car, she was thrown into the back seat and Hackett sat beside her. The car started and she felt it pull forward, turn and speed up.

After several minutes she began to warm up. All she could hear was the sound of the car's heater fan on full. The car made many turns. She listened intently to any sound that might indicate her location but she did not know the area and was unable to identify anything that could help.

The journey did not last long. Just as she began to stop shaking and feel warm, the car stopped. Hackett opening the door, dragged her out into the cold night air. Monika stood still and listened. She heard the car door slam. The engine revved and she listened as the sound of the vehicle faded into the distance.

"Hello? Is anyone there?" She wasn't sure what she should do but she knew she could not stand out in the cold much longer.

She waited a few more seconds and then lifted the blindfold from her face. She was back at the entrance to the Ottawa Civic Hospital. There was no sign of her abductors. She wondered if they had really gone or if they were nearby watching her. She began to shiver. She opened her wallet and found a small piece of paper with a number scribbled in black. Ten numbers. It was a phone number. She put the piece of paper back in her wallet and ran over to the hospital entrance. She was shaking but was not sure if it was from exposure to the cold or from nerves. She felt happy to be free but upset by all that had happened. Her only thoughts now were to be with James.

Reaching the hospital entrance, she hurried inside. There were several people in the main lobby who gave her strange stares as she came in from the outside wearing nothing but a cotton dress. She paid no attention to them. She quickly went across the lobby to the stairs. When she got to the second floor she paused a minute and began to straighten her clothing and tidy her hair. She tried to compose herself. She did not what anyone in the ICU noticing any change in her, especially Detective Callot who she expected to be there waiting for her. She wondered how she was going to explain her long absence. She didn't want to answer his questions. She just wanted to be with James. She took in a breath, opened the door and stepped onto the floor and into the ward.

"Oh, Ms. Queller." Geena was relieved to see her. She came out from behind the nurses station. "There you are. I was getting worried about you. He woke up."

"What, he's awake?"

"Yes. We had to sedate him. You weren't here and he was upset."

"I'm sorry. I was walking around. How is he?" Monika's heart skipped a beat. James was all right. She was angry she was not there when he awoke. She would get even with Detective Philips or whatever his real name was.

"He's alright. Don't worry. It was only a mild sedative. There's a Detective Ferisse waiting for you." Geena felt the cold coming off her. "You want to be careful you'll catch your death. It's very cold outside."

"Thank you. I found out," Monika answered looking into the unit. She was excited to get to James but kept her guard up as she wondered who Detective Ferisse might be and what he might want. She would be careful this time.

Sitting in the chair by James' bed was a man she'd never seen before. She wondered if he really was a police detective or a fake like Detective Philips had been.

"I'll get you something hot to drink. I think you could use it. You go on." Realizing that Monika was very chilled, Geena went back into the nurses station to get a drink from the staff coffee pot.

"Thank you." As Geena left, Monika checked the time on the clock inside the nurses station. It was almost 9:45 pm. Other than Jack Callot, she was not interested in talking with another police detective, if he really was one.

Monika wondered why Jack was not there. He had told her he would return later. He did not strike her as the type of man who did not keep his word. She wanted time to think about her abductors' demands and did not want to waste time with this new detective. So much had happened since she arrived in Ottawa. She needed time to figure it all out. She was on her own, not knowing whom to trust. It was a difficult situation. She wasn't sure if forty-eight hours was enough time to solve this mystery but she had not been given a choice. She wondered what it was that had really caused

Craig's death and James' injuries. Suddenly she realized that James' trip to Ottawa to visit an old friend was really something more. Craig had stumbled onto something big and needed to confide in James. It was obvious that James was the only person he trusted. If she and James were to survive she knew she was going to have to be extremely cautious. She ran the coded message 1720YQBCF, through her mind again wondering what it meant. There had to be something more to it, but before she could work it out she had to get rid of this detective. He would only get in her way. She bolstered her resolve and walked through the Intensive Care Unit to James' bed.

"Ah hem. Detective Ferisse?" Jean-Paul Ferisse, slumped in the chair with his head flopped to one side, was taking a nap.

Chapter 11

"Ah hem." Monika tried to get his attention again. This time louder.

"Excuse me. I must have dozed off." Startled, Jean-Paul opened his eyes and stood up. He felt embarrassed to have fallen asleep. "Sorry." Sprawled out in the chair, he had wrinkled her coat. He picked it up, tried his best to undo the damage and folded it neatly over the back of the chair.

"That's okay." Monika didn't mind about the coat. She just wanted to be alone. She looked down at James to make sure he was all right.

"Your fiancé?" Jean-Paul turned his head to indicate James, noting her concern.

"Yes." She took an instant liking to the detective. His French Canadian accent especially in his pronunciation of fiancé was charming. She sat down on the bed.

"I'm Detective Jean-Paul Ferisse with the Ottawa Police. I'm Jack's Callot's partner." He pulled out his identification and showed it to her. "I was hoping to find Jack here. Have you seen him?"

Jean-Paul was polite. He had an endearing boyishly mischievous look about him. He smiled at her. He had lost his father in his early twenties and knew how difficult it must be for her to see a loved one so badly hurt. He did not wish to intrude on her, nor upset her further, but he needed to find Jack.

"He dropped me off after six but I haven't seen him since. He said he'd come by later. I guess he's not coming," she answered flatly, not wanting to encourage the detective to linger. She had James, Detective Philips and the coded message on her mind.

"So I understand you're from California? This must be quite a change for you," he changed the subject. There was no need to pester her about Jack. He would drop by Jack's house after he left the hospital. Monika was a lovely woman and he wanted to get to know her better. He now understood why Jack had gone out of his way to meet her at the airport that afternoon.

"Yes. The Los Angeles area. It never gets this cold there," she said politely making small talk, eventhough she didn't feel like it. She wondered why Jean-Paul wanted to see Jack so badly.

"What do you do?" It was not his standard question. Jean–Paul was investigating. He crossed over to the side table and leaned against it awaiting her reply.

"I teach." Again her answer was curt but he didn't seem to be bothered by it.

"I don't think I'd want to teach. I've heard too many horror stories. It seems a very corrupt 'profession'. Far more political and hazardous than police work." He smiled and moved away from the side table causing the ripped piece of envelope with the coded message that Monika had left next to the water jug to fall to the floor.

"It isn't that bad everywhere. Only in the inner cities." Monika, seeing the coded message fall, became friendlier in hopes of distracting him.

"How clumsy of me." He saw her eyes go to the piece of paper on the floor. Realizing he caused it to fall, he bent down and picked it up.

"Excuse me?" Monika pretended she didn't understand. She was not a good liar.

"This. Is it yours?" He showed the piece of envelope to her. He had gone through that whole routine in order to find out the truth about the coded message.

Monika took the piece of paper and, pretending

she had never seen it before, examined it.

"1720YQBCF. No. I've never seen this. What does it mean?" She continued her deception. She did not want to involve him. She did not want to be responsible for what might happen to him if she did. She handed the piece of paper back to him.

"1720YQBCF. The only thing that jumps out is Québec City. YQB is the airport symbol for Québec City. Someone must have left it here." He looked up at her, watching her reaction. He did not believe her. For some reason she was lying.

"Maybe it belongs to one of the nurses." She brightened. 1720 Québec City CF. She would never have been able to decipher the YQB without his help. She began to think about what the message might mean. Perhaps it was a flight number or the time of a meeting. Seventeen-twenty was five-twenty in the afternoon by the international clock.

"Have you ever been to Québec City?" Jean-Paul was curious. He had a very relaxed interrogation style.

"No." She was concentrating on the possible meaning of the message and considering who might have sent it.

"You should. Once your fiancé is better. Go. It's a quaint city. Be sure to stay at the Château Frontenac. It's right in the center of the Old City. It's a very beautiful place. You will ..." Jean-

Paul's French Canadian accent became more apparent as he described Québec City for her.

While Jean-Paul was speaking, Monika began to make sense of another part of the message. She tuned him out and ran the new possibilities through her mind. When Jean-Paul mentioned the Château Frontenac she instantly connected the Château Laurier and the 'CL' initials on its lobby doors with the Château Frontenac. She believed the CF in the message stood for the Château Frontenac. Something was happening at 5:20 pm in Québec City at the Château Frontenac. But which day? She wondered if it meant today, yesterday or sometime next week. Or maybe there was something wrong in her decoding of the message. She also wondered why the message had been in her hotel box. No one knew she was coming to Ottawa other than Jack Callot and the envelope was not from him.

"Of course," she said out loud, interrupting and stopping Jean-Paul in mid-sentence.

"Of course…What?" Jean-Paul waited a moment before asking for clarification. Her declaration was a non sequitur to him.

"Ah. Sorry. I was thinking about something else. I didn't realize I said anything. You were saying about Québec City?" Monika was embarrassed at being so rude. She wanted him to continue.

"I was just saying if you decide to go, let me

know. I can tell you some places you should visit." Jean-Paul realized he had overstayed his welcome. He looked at his watch. He had taken up enough of her time and he did not want to bother Jack too late at his home.

"Ooh. It is getting late. I had better go. Sometimes I talk too much," he confessed, his French Canadian accent showing through again.

"Thank you for the information. Québec. City sounds like a place I will go to soon." She was happy to have met him. She found his accent attractive. It gave him a debonair quality. She marveled at how men in uniforms or with accents could have such an effect on her. "It was nice meeting you."

"Well. Good night, mademoiselle. I will tell Jack hello for you. I hope your fiancé is better soon." Jean-Paul shook Monika's hand and walked off through the unit. He did not realize how much help the information he had given her would be.

Monika watched Jean-Paul leave. When he was gone she leaned over and kissed James on the forehead.

"Hi sweetie. I understand you've been awake. I'm back now. I won't leave again." She waited but James gave no indication that he had heard her. Disappointed, she sat up, her mind returning to the coded message. She had a revelation. Craig must have sent the message for James. Whatever

Craig had stumbled onto he must have been worried about who to trust. That's why he asked James to come up to Ottawa and meet him. She reasoned that she would have done the same thing under similar circumstances. Craig must have hidden something and sent a message to James as insurance against its being lost.

"Yes. That's it," she said out loud again. It was all beginning to make sense. Her abductors wanted whatever it was Craig had found. The envelope he sent to James only contained a clue as to its whereabouts. If everything had gone as planned, James would not have needed the clue. But obviously things had gone terribly wrong and now it was up to her to avenge Craig's death and finish his mission. She wondered what he had stumbled on that could cause this level of intrigue.

"1720, Québec City, Château Frontenac." She surmised that the message was not indicating a meeting but a location. Craig had hidden something in room 1720 of the Château Frontenac in Québec City. Monika tried to guess what it might be, knowing full well there was only one way to find out. In the morning she would have to fly to Québec City. It was the only way to put an end to this mystery and protect James and herself.

"Oh James. I wish this was all a bad dream," she sighed, leaned over, gently put her arms around him and closed her eyes. She wanted to feel him against her. She was afraid. Afraid for his recovery and afraid for whatever awaited her in the morning in Québec City. Exhausted, she fell asleep.

- - - - - - - - - - - - - - -

Jean-Paul started his car and took out the piece of paper he had discreetly taken from James' hospital table. Somehow he knew this was a valuable clue. When he got to Jack's he would show it to him. He pulled out of the lot. It was busier than it had been when he arrived.

Ten minutes later he pulled into Jack's driveway on Greenbank. Jack's car was in his carport and all the lights were on in the house. Jean-Paul glimpsed the time on his car radio. It was 10:15 pm. He picked up the file folder on the passenger seat next to him and got out of the car. Being careful not to slip on the ice of the driveway, he went to the side door. Opening the screen door, he knocked and waited. It was cold out but he was warm in his parka. When he didn't get an answer he knocked again, louder. He waited but Jack did not answer.

"Jack. Jack? It's Jean-Paul. It's getting cold out here," he called out, not wanting to disturb the neighborhood, but Jack did not answer. He tried peeking through the opaque glass window of the kitchen door but he could not clearly see into the kitchen. The kitchen light was on but he didn't see any movement. Jean-Paul had been around Jack long enough to know it was not like him to leave his lights on if he was not home. He tried the door handle. The door was locked.

Closing the screen door he walked to the rear of the carport. A small set of cupboards was fixed against the wall. He opened the door of the cupboard on his left and found Jack's spare key. He didn't like to enter the house unannounced but he was becoming concerned. So many strange things had been happening in the last twenty-four hours. His policeman's instincts were switched on and in high gear.

Going back to the side door Jean-Paul put the key into the lock and opened the kitchen door.

"Jack. Jack? Are you there? It's Jean-Paul. Jack?" he called out, stepping cautiously into the kitchen. There was no answer.

Feeling there was definitely something wrong, he put the file folder on the kitchen counter to his right and drew out his service revolver. He proceeded into the hallway leading from the kitchen into the main hall of the house. He listened and heard the sound of water coming from the shower. He relaxed. Jack was taking a shower. That was why he had not heard him at the door. He put his revolver away and walked down to the bathroom door.

"Jack. It's Jean-Paul," he shouted over the sound of the shower and knocked on the door. There was still no answer. He assumed Jack still hadn't heard him. He opened the door and went in.

"Come on Jack. You're going to drown in all that..." Jean-Paul abruptly stopped. His mouth dropped. Jack was propped up in the corner of the shower. His eyes were wide open and there was blood splattered everywhere. "Oh. Mon dieu!" In shock he reverted back to his native French.

Jean-Paul felt weak kneed at the sight of his partner. He sat down on the toilet to steady himself. Jack was definitely dead and it hadn't been for long. After several minutes Jean-Paul pulled out his cell phone from his jacket pocket and punched in the division number.

"Ottawa Police," a woman officer answered.

"Suzanne? It's Jean-Paul. I'm at Jack Callot's. He's been shot. You'd better send someone over here. He's dead." Jean-Paul switched into his homicide investigation mode. He disconnected the phone without waiting for Suzanne's response. Putting his face in his hands he wept. Jack Callot had been like a father to him.

- - - - - - - - - - - - - - - -

After they had dropped Monika, Hackett and Stone drove around the block and then returned to the short-term parking area of the hospital. They parked near the back of the lot within view of the entrance. Taking shifts they kept an around-the-clock surveillance on her. It was only a matter of time before she led them to what they wanted. Unbeknownst to them they also were being watched and followed. Every move they made was being electronically documented.

- - - - - - - - - - - - - - - -

Within half an hour of Jean-Paul's call, Jack's house was full of police detectives. Outside, six police cars, all with their lights flashing, were parked along the driveway and the road in front of the house. Pockets of neighbors were standing about gossiping and watching the activity. Jean-Paul was sitting in Jack's living room talking with another detective. He was in shock. Someone had given him a warm cup of coffee.

"There's no sign of a break-in. Jack didn't expect a thing. Whoever did this was a professional. This wasn't a botched burglary. They wanted Jack. Nothing's missing." Jean-Paul summed up the situation, trying to make sense of the killing.

"Why? Were you guys working on anything special?" Detective Ken Graham, a heavyset man in his early fifties, was sitting on the couch next to Jean-Paul. They were both very upset by their fellow officer's murder. Ken had known Jack well. Originally they had been partners.

"No. Just the thing in the Byward Market." Jean-Paul was trying to understand who would want to kill Jack.

"That's the CIA and RCMP thing, right? How's it going?" Ken brushed his graying mustache with his index finger as he spoke. He had heard the details surrounding the Byward case in the department.

"Yeah. Well, one's still critical. We haven't been able to interview him. The other was killed." Jean-Paul wondered who had told Ken about Craig Jeneau. Other than George and Jack, he thought he was the only one privy to the information.

"Maybe it's connected?" Not understanding why Jack had been murdered, Ken offered the suggestion.

"I don't know, but I'm going to find out." He hoped he would be able to talk to James after the sedative wore off. With Jack murdered he had a lot more questions that needed answers. Jean-Paul drew in a deep breath. He was emotionally spent.

"Why don't you go? I can finish up here." Ken saw how tired Jean-Paul was. He felt sorry for him. It was hard to lose your partner. It was like losing a wife. He put his hand on Jean-Paul's shoulder to comfort him and looked him in the eye.

"Thanks. I think I will. If you need me, I'll be at home." Jean-Paul stood up. There was nothing more he could do. Ken had everything under control.

"I don't think I will but if I turn up anything I'll let you know right away. Get a good sleep. I'll talk to you tomorrow." Ken stood up, patted Jean-Paul on the shoulder and said goodbye.

Jean-Paul made his way through the living room and out the front door, oblivious to the other officers. Stopping a moment on the path that led to the driveway, he observed the scene. Jack's house was an anthill of police activity. The property had been cordoned off with yellow police tape. There were plainclothes and uniformed officers everywhere. The lights from the police cars lit up the neighborhood like a dance club. He did not feel the biting cold. He was numb. He put his right hand in his jacket pocket and felt the piece of envelope from the hospital. He pulled it out and read allowed: "1720YQBCF." Somehow he knew this clue was connected to Jack's death. In the morning he would return to the hospital and get some answers. Monika had lied to him about the piece of paper and he was going to find out why. He did not like being lied to, especially when it had possibly caused the death of his partner. He felt a wave of anger rise up within him. He was frustrated at the impotent way he felt.

Putting the paper back into his pocket, he headed to his car. The first thing he would do when he got home was pour himself a stiff drink. He missed Jack terribly already.

- - - - - - - - - - - - - - -

Nurse Geena brought Monika a hot coffee. Seeing she was asleep, she did not say anything. She did not want to disturb her. Putting the coffee on the side table, she went back to the nurses station and found a spare blanket and returned to her. The romantic scene of Monika and James moved her. Gently she placed the blanket over them. Though it was against all regulations for visitors to remain in the ICU, she was willing to make an exception in this case. She felt empathy for Monika. By the look on Monika's face, it was obvious they were very much a part of one another. She hoped James' awakening was a good sign and that he would make a complete recovery but it was still too early to tell. He was very seriously injured and had a long way to go before being removed from the critical list.

Geena stood admiring them. She checked her watch. Her shift ended in an hour-and-a-half. She had her reports to finish. As she walked away, she wondered if she would ever find someone to love the way Monika appeared to love James.

- - - - - - - - - - - - - - -

Monika began to dream as soon as she fell asleep. Her emotionally exhausted subconscious mind needed to be mollified. In her dream, she was taken on a journey to the last time she and James were intimate. It had been only a few days ago. James had been working late and she prepared a surprise for him when he got home. It was a warm night. She put a small note on the fridge door. All she wrote was 'Open for a surprise." She knew the first place James would go was the kitchen when he got home.

Inside the fridge was a bottle of Moët & Chandon, her favorite French champagne. Attached to the bottle by a delicate red ribbon was another small note. It said, "Upstairs." Two glasses were chilling beside the champagne.

When James got home at ten, he called out for Monika but, getting no answer, went directly to the kitchen before going upstairs to bed. He wondered where Monika had gone. When he got to the kitchen and saw the note, he opened the fridge and smiled. He took out the champagne and glasses and opened the bottle with a loud pop. The champagne overflowed from the bottle to the kitchen floor. He filled one of the glasses and took a large gulp.

Going back through the kitchen he went to the stairs that led up to the second floor. On the stairs was a trail of Monika's discarded lacy lingerie. He picked up each piece as he climbed the stairs to the second floor landing and smelled her soft perfume. The second floor was dimly lit by two night lights. At the top of the stairs the trail continued with small red rose petals leading him to the bathroom door. The door was closed. He stopped and grinned. Monika was full of unpredictable surprises. It was one of the things he loved most about her. He slowly pushed open the bathroom door and looked in.

The bathroom was lit by many candles scattered throughout, each giving off its own delicate aroma. Monika was waiting for him in the bathtub semi-concealed beneath her bubble bath. He stopped to admire the scene. She was asleep and looked like an innocent angel in the soft glow of the candlelight.

He put down the champagne and glasses and slowly undressed and then went over to the tub. He leaned down and kissed her on the lips and pulled back to watch her awaken from whatever heavenly place she was in. Her skin was soft to touch and sweet to taste. She was beautiful.

"What took you so long?" Monika opened her sparkling blue eyes, put her arms around him and pulled him into the bath with her. She had been faking sleep.

"Hey. You," he complained, but she knew he was really turned on by her seduction scene.

They began to kiss each other with a longing desire. The water in the tub was warm and overflowed onto the floor but they did not care.

She felt his firm hard body against hers and she went soft inside. He had a power over her that she reveled in. She breathed in his bittersweet aroma mixed in with the candles and the blue lavender scented bubble bath and became more intoxicated by his presence. She felt an uncontrollable need to taste every part of him in every way. Her passion was building and overwhelming her senses. She felt his hand on her shoulders and heard him saying her name.

Chapter 12

"Good morning, Ms. Queller." It was 7:00 am. A doctor in his early fifties with thinning brown hair was trying to wake her. He was wearing his white medical coat. Dr. Will Keene was embroidered in blue script over the left breast pocket.

"Ms. Queller?" Dr. Keene stepped over to her and gently shook her shoulder.

"Oh. Yes?" Monika awoke, startled by his touch. She expected to open her eyes and see James but realized quickly she had been dreaming. She sat up and tried to get her bearings.

"Hi. I'm Dr. Keene." Will Keene was a soft spoken man who exuded a subdued but self-assured personality. He was of Scottish descent and had a rugged debonair charm that even at his age was appealing.

"Hello Dr. Keene. I'm James' fiancée, Monika Queller." Monika got up from the bed, straightened out her dress and presented her hand to him. "I hope it was all right that I stayed." She did not really care what he thought. She would have stayed regardless.

"Yes. It was probably best. Nice to meet you." Dr. Keene shook her hand. He had a very delicate grip for a man. "I operated on your fiancé."

"Oh. I see. Thank you for everything you've done. I just arrived last night. How is he?" Monika realized Dr. Keene's reason for stopping at James' bed. This was the doctor who had saved his life. She was grateful and felt indebted to the man whose skill had repaired James' broken body.

"He was pretty bad." Dr. Keene referred to a chart he was carrying as he spoke. "Broken leg. Broken arm. Two broken ribs. A cracked skull. Concussion. Cuts, bruises and a bullet wound that fragmented after entry. Part of the bullet pierced his left lung and nicked his heart. .He had lots of internal bleeding."

He put the chart down and looked directly at Monika. "The serious wound is the one to his lung. I managed to stop the internal bleeding and resection the lung. He was very lucky. He might need more surgery. If he had gotten here any later

I don't think we could have saved him."

"Is he going to be all right?" A chill ran through Monika as she listened to the doctor's clinical enumeration of James' injuries but she managed to keep her composure as she took in the seriousness of his condition.

"I hope so. As long as we keep him still and the internal bleeding doesn't start up again. The next forty-eight hours are crucial." Dr. Keene was not trying to frighten her. He was merely informing her of his medical opinion. He realized by looking at her, and hearing her speak, that she was an intelligent woman.

"He woke up last night but was sedated. I don't understand why they would do that?" James was still unconscious. She had hoped the effects of the sedative given last night would have worn off by now. She desperately wanted to speak to him about everything and anything. Speaking to him would reassure her he was better.

"Yes. I know it does seem a little odd but it really was for his own good. He woke up traumatized and disoriented. It's not unusual in these cases. Sometimes it's better to keep the patient sedated and allow them to remain still until they're further along in their recovery. We really didn't expect him to wake up so soon." James had been so agitated that it was likely he would have opened his internal injuries and started to hemorrhage again. That was not something Dr. Keene wanted. It was wiser to sedate him.

"But why is he still unconscious? I thought he'd be awake this morning." Monika and Dr. Keene were looking at James as they conversed.

"Every case is different. The fact that he woke up so soon is an excellent sign. Most of these cases remain unconscious for days. He's certainly a fighter. Don't worry. We're going to keep a close eye on him and monitor him carefully. In fact we're going to remove the tubing in his mouth during rounds this morning. I just came by early to check on his progress." His manner was reassuring and his gray eyes conveyed his caring nature.

"I have to go to Québec City this morning. Will he be okay?" Monika realized that, under the circumstances, her leaving must seem callous but she had no choice. She had to comply with her abductors' demands by Thursday and the clock was ticking.

Dr. Keene remained silent for a moment, considering his answer. He did not judge Monika for having to leave. He had been a doctor for twenty-two years and it had taught him there were usually valid reasons for people's actions. He did not become Chief of Surgery by being unfairly judgmental and intolerant. If it were him, he would stay. James' condition was critical and could change without a moment's warning. But he was not her. He decided to be straightforward.

"There are no guarantees. I really can't promise he won't get worse. The only unusual thing about this case is that he woke up so soon after surgery. Based on that I'm inclined to think he will make a good recovery. If you have to go, try and keep in touch with the unit. If there is a dramatic turn for the worse you could hurry back. Québec City is only an hour by plane. How long will you be gone?"

"Just the day. I should be back this evening." She hoped the excursion would only last one day. She wasn't sure how to find the list but believed she could do it within that time frame. She read between the doctor's words. He was not judging her for leaving but he was trying to let her know, without causing her to lose hope, that James was not yet out of the woods.

"I think he'll be okay. As long as you understand I can't promise. These things are hard to predict in the best of times," Dr. Keene gavc his final opinion.

"I understand. I'll keep in touch. I'll give the nurse my cell phone number just in case." She appreciated his candor.

"That would be a good idea. Well. I've still got a few more patients to see upstairs before rounds. It was nice to meet you. I'll see you when you get back." Dr. Keene put out his hand.

"Thank you again, doctor." Monika took his hand and gently shook it. Their eyes met. She knew he would continue to do his best. James was in good hands.

"It's what I do. Take care." He saw the depth of her gratitude. He held her hand a little longer than usual and then, letting go, walked off through the unit.

Monika sat back down on the bed. It was time to go. The sooner she got away the sooner she would get back. She stared lovingly at James.

"I have to go. I want you to be strong and get better. I'll be back tonight," she said to him as if he was conscious. It made her feel better. She hated her abductors for making her leave like this. She leaned over and kissed James on the lips. He did not kiss her back.

"God bless, sweetie. I love you." She sat up and pulled herself away. Picking up her purse, she stood up and grabbed her coat. As she walked away she took one last look. She silently prayed he would be there when she returned.

"I have to go out but I'd like to leave you a number where I can be reached," Monika, standing at the nurses station, called out to the nurse who was sitting inside doing paperwork.

"You are?" The nurse got up and came over to the counter.

"Monika Queller. Mr. Anstey?" She wrote down her cellular phone number on a piece of paper and handed it to the nurse as she introduced herself.

"Ah yes. I'm sorry." This nurse was not as nice as Geena. She took the phone number but neglected to tell Monika her name. "I'll put this with his chart." She was efficient but cold. She was in her early twenties and obviously the new generation of nurse.

"How do I get a taxi?" Monika was preoccupied with her mission and didn't bother to ask for the nurse's name. By the time she returned it would be Geena's shift.

"Right outside the front. There's usually several taxis at this time of the morning." The nurse returned to her paperwork without saying goodbye.

"Thank you." Monika checked the time on the clock in the nurses station. It was 7:30 am. She assumed there would be frequent flights from Ottawa to Québec City. She would go directly to the airport and take the first available flight. There was no need to go to the hotel and get her suitcase. She had everything she needed for her short trip.

Monika walked away from the nurses station, through the ICU doors, down the stairs and through the main hospital entrance. The weather outside was noticeably colder than last night.

She hurried down the steps and crossed the sidewalk to a white taxi that was waiting at the curb. As she walked over the fresh dusting of snow that had have fallen in the early hours of the morning, she could hear the crunch of her boots on it. There was a bite in the air she inhaled and the billowing clouds of her exhaled breath lingered about her. She opened the door to the taxi and got in.

"The airport, please," she directed the driver. There was a stale vinyl smell inside the cab.

"Yes ma'am." The driver acknowledged her request. He turned on the meter and pulled into the street.

- - - - - - - - - - - - - - - -

"There she is." Hackett sighted Monika coming out of the hospital and getting into the taxicab. "Stone. She's going somewhere." He was relieved to finally have something to do other than wait.

"What?" Stone roused from his sleep. He was stretched out in the front next to Hackett.

"There. See. She got into that cab." Hackett put the car in reverse and backed out of his parking space. It had been a long and uncomfortable night. They had taken three-hour shifts and had not expected her to be leaving the hospital so soon.

"It seems Ms. Queller knows more than she let on last night." Stone sat up and buckled his seat belt. His back was sore from sitting so long on the uncomfortable car seat.

"Yeah. I wonder where she's going so early?" Hackett pulled out after the taxi.

The taxi drove along Carlingview Avenue away

from the hospital. Hackett increased his speed. He did not want to lose sight of the cab. Behind Hackett and Stone a late model, dark green Ford Explorer with dark tinted windows pulled out after them. It was not possible to see the occupants of the SUV. The three vehicles kept a safe distance from each other, the first two unaware they were being tailed.

- - - - - - - - - - - - - - - -

"Thank you. How much is it?" Monika opened her purse when the taxi pulled up to the departures section of the Ottawa International airport. The airport was small but busy. It was crowded with middle-aged businessmen wearing similar business attire.

"Twenty five dollars," the driver said as he turned to face her. It was the most he had said during the trip. Monika was used to the constant chattering of the cabbies in California and found it a nice change.

"Here you are. Keep the change." She handed him thirty dollars and got out.

"Thank you. Have a safe trip." He took the money and, after she closed the door, drove away.

- - - - - - - - - - - - - - - -

"Get out and follow her. She's going somewhere in a hurry," Hackett ordered Stone. He pulled up and stopped a couple of cars behind Monika's taxi.

"What do you want me to do?" It was clear to

Stone that Monika was going to catch a flight.

"Stay with her. I don't care where she's going. Just don't lose her," Hackett said emphatically. He knew what would happen to them if she got away.

"Okay." Stone opened the door and got out. There was a crowd of businessmen on the sidewalk. He tried to stay concealed among them. Monika was entering the terminal. He went after her.

- - - - - - - - - - - - - - - -

Monika walked through the terminal to the Air Canada ticket counter. There was just a short line-up. Most of the passengers were pre-booked and using the self-serve check-in kiosks instead of using the ticket counter.

"Good morning. When's the next flight to Québec City?" she asked a young uniformed man sitting behind the counter.

"Good morning. There's one at 8:45. It just started boarding. If you're fast, you can make it." He was very clean-cut and looked more like an enthusiastic employee of Disneyland than a major airline. He was fresh, young and friendly. When he smiled his teeth glistened. He had the whitest teeth she had ever seen.

"Thank you. One please. Return." She was pleased with her timing. Not wanting to miss the flight, she put her purse on the counter, took her credit card from her wallet and handed it to him.

She did not ask the price of the ticket but assumed it would be expensive.

"Thank you, ma'am. Would you like to reserve your return now?" He smiled politely and started to input her information into his terminal.

"No. Leave it open." Something inside her told her not to book it now.

"That's not a problem." He continued to enter her particulars.

"Is the flight very full?" She didn't want to be cooped up with a lot of people and hoped the flight would not be overly crowded.

"Let me check." He typed on his keyboard and examined the reservations for both the flight out and back. "No. It's very light going out. There's plenty of room. There won't be a problem. Will that be business or economy?" he asked.

"Economy's fine." Monika relaxed. She continued to answer the agent's questions and he quickly completed the ticketing process.

"Are you checking any luggage?" he asked. There was not much time before the plane left.

"No. Just carry on." Monika felt awkward about traveling without luggage, but it didn't phase the agent. He was used to people traveling to Québec City on business without luggage. "Normally you would have to check-in at the next counter, but since the flight's already boarding I will check you in."

"Thank you. I don't want to miss the flight."

Monika appreciated his help.

You're on flight 8242 departing gate 'C', arriving in Québec City at 9:50." He handed her her credit card, ticket and boarding pass.

"You should go to the gate right away. It's over there. You'll have to go through security first. The last flight tonight is Air Canada 8250 at 6:00p.m. The next after that is Thursday morning. I've noted it on the ticket. Thank you for choosing Air Canada." He pointed her in the direction of the passenger security check.

"Thank you." She took the ticket and, putting her wallet back into her purse, hurried over to the security check. She had a lot to do by 6:00 pm.

- - - - - - - - - - - - - - -

"Good morning." Stone came up to the same ticket agent that Monika had just spoken with and flashed his fake police badge. "I'm Detective Moodie with the Ottawa Police. Can you tell me where that woman is going?" he got right to the point.

"Certainly detective." The agent was nervous. "Québec City, 8:45 flight." He did not question the detective's authority.

"Book me a seat," Stone was not asking.

"The plane has boarded and I don't know if you'll make it." The agent was checking the flight information on his terminal while he spoke.

"Do it. Let the gate know I'm coming. It's official business." Stone took out the credit card that matched his identity. He was not going to miss the flight.

"Yes sir. Economy or Business?" The agent didn't argue. If the detective wanted to make the flight he needed to process him right away.

"Economy. One way." Stone kept his eye on the security entrance that Monika had gone through.

The ticket agent complied. He wondered what the woman had done to warrant a police detective chasing after her. She had seemed so innocent—not at all the criminal type—but he was too timid to ask. He started typing the detective's information into his terminal, and as it was processing, picked up his phone and dialed the gate.

"Hi. Yvette. I have one last passenger for flight 8242. He's coming now. Hold for him."

Stone pulled out his cellular phone from his jacket pocket and while the agent was preparing the ticket dialed his partner in the car outside the terminal.

"Hackett," Stone's partner answered his cell phone.

"She's booked on the 8:45. Air Canada flight to Québec City. I'm getting a ticket," Stone informed him.

"Québec City? That's a little coincidental isn't it? The Summit of the Americas is being held there next week and Skinner is going there this afternoon."

"Yeah it is," Stone agreed. Like Hackett he

wondered if Monika had some clandestine purpose for going to Québec City a week before the Summit.

"Stay with her and don't lose her. Keep me updated. I'll inform Skinner." Hackett disconnected.

"Excuse me. Detective Moodie. Your ticket. I've checked you through." The agent handed Stone his credit card, boarding pass and ticket.

"Thank you. Gate 'C' is over there. You should hurry. They won't wait long. Thank you for choosing Air Canada." Again the agent pointed out the security entrance.

"Thanks for everything." Stone took his card and boarding pass. He hoped Monika was well ahead of him and had already boarded the plane. He did not want her to see him if he could avoid it. Though he did not believe she would remember him from the stairwell, he didn't like to take the chance.

He crossed over to the security check-in. He wasn't worried about his gun. His police ID would permit him to carry an unloaded handgun on board. He would remove the ammunition at security when they checked his ID.

- - - - - - - - - - - - - - -

The Ford Explorer stopped at the Departures section of the Ottawa airport a few cars behind Hackett. After Stone walked into the terminal a short man in his twenties wearing dark sunglasses and a black goatee, got out. He was dressed in casual business attire and a black fur trimmed parka. He was careful not to be seen by Hackett or Stone. After he closed the door, the Explorer drove off. Normally he worked with a partner but for this mission he was on his own.

He followed Stone into the terminal and watched as he bought a ticket from the Air Canada counter. When Stone disappeared into security he went over to the counter. It had been a long day and night of surveillance. He welcomed the chance to get some rest on the plane.

Chapter 13

The plane was new but small. Monika thought it might be a Dash 8. A center aisle ran its length with two rows of seats on both sides. The business class section held twenty passengers and was separated from the economy class, which could hold eighty. For the short fight to Québec City the plane was large enough. Other than the government and business traveller, there was not much demand for Québec City in January. Most of the traffic was during the Winter Carnival in February and during the warm summer months.

Monika found her seat, 10A, and was making herself comfortable by the window. No one else was sitting in her row and she was relieved. She was not in the mood to make inane conversation with a stranger. She was glad to have the privacy for the hour-long flight. She fastened her seat belt, pulled out the airline magazine from the seat pouch in front of her and began to flip through it but her mind was elsewhere. Slipping the magazine back in the pouch, she sat back and closed her eyes.

She could not believe she had gotten herself entangled in another mystery. She wondered what it was that Craig had hidden in room 1720 at the Château Frontenac. She wondered if she would find it or if someone else already had. She wondered what she would do if she couldn't find it and had as a result nothing to give to her abductors. She was full of questions to which she didn't have answers. She was at a loss and wasn't sure what was going to happen next, so she resolved not to think too far into the future. She had until tomorrow to find the list and she knew from experience that a lot could happen between now and then. All she could do was take it one step at a time. She knew no matter what happened her abductors were not going to allow any witnesses to survive. Whatever it was Craig had stumbled into, it was big.

Monika wished there was someone she could turn to for help under these circumstances, but there wasn't. She didn't know who her abductors were or what far-reaching influence they might have. The fact that they wanted the return of a list led her to believe they were trying to protect people who might secretly be working for them. Since Craig had called on James for assistance and not the police or his own RCMP, it made her more cautious about who to trust. The only people she felt certain about were James, Craig and Jean Atero her police detective friend in Los Angeles. But James was comatose, Craig was dead, and Jean Atero was too far away to be able to help even if she asked him. She wasn't sure about trusting Jack Callot or Jean-Paul Ferisse with this type of information, so that left her back where she started—alone. She realized it was up to her to remain calm, find what Craig had hidden and find a way out of the danger.

She ran the coded message through her mind, double-checking it. 1720 Québec City Château Frontenac. That was definitely its meaning. She wondered why Craig had gone to such extremes. Why hadn't he hidden the list in Ottawa along with the coded message? Why had he gone to the trouble of hiding it in Québec City? She knew there had to be some reason. There had to be something important about Québec City that was somehow connected to the case. She hoped she could figure it out before it was too late.

After several minutes of contemplation, Monika opened her eyes. She checked her watch. It was eight-forty. In five minutes the plane would be on its way. She wondered if she should get off and go back to the hospital to be with James but she knew it was wishful thinking. There was no turning back. She was trapped. She stretched her neck and looked around the plane. There were only eight other passengers scattered throughout the economy section. A curtain was drawn between business and economy class, preventing her from seeing who was there.

The sudden movement of the curtain opening drew her attention. She caught a glimpse of a man in a midnight blue parka with a brush cut walking into the economy section. There was something about the man that was familiar but she was not able to place him. As the man entered the compartment, his eyes momentarily caught hers but he quickly averted them and turned his back to her as he continued at a quicker pace along the aisle in search of his seat. He seemed nervous, which only made Monika more curious about him. She scoured her mind in an attempt to identify this man. She trusted her instincts and she didn't doubt that she somehow knew him.

Gradually the man made his way down the aisle and passed her row. He did not look her way and was trying to keep his back to her. As he passed by her, she caught a whiff of his body odor. As soon as his stale aroma reached her, she instantly identified him as one of her abductors. She panicked and recoiled into her seat, turning her head toward the window in an attempt to hide. She was not sure if he had recognized her. She knew he was the other man in the stairwell at the hospital, who had stood in her way before Philips had forced her to inhale what she believed was chloroform. She sat petrified for a few moments and then gradually twisted her head 'round to see where the man had gone.

Stone hurried past her. He was sure she had recognized him. For a moment he was angry with himself but then realized it might be beneficial. It would remind her to quickly complete her task and not attempt to get outside help. He considered she probably expected to be followed and now she knew for sure. He made his way out of her sight and found his seat, which was near the back of the plane. He sat down and buckled up. Whether she recognized him or not, he would keep a safe distance from her.

Monika could not see where Stone went. She assumed he was somewhere in the back of the plane. She turned her head to the window and peered out at the Ottawa airport. The plane was taxiing away from the terminal. Snow was piled along the runway, giving the place a fairyland appearance. She felt as if she were in a winter scene inside a sealed glass container before it was shaken up. She stared out the window and wondered who might be behind all this. Whoever it was, he was not an amateur. Now that she knew she was being followed, she realized she would have to be very careful when she found whatever Craig had hidden. If she didn't play her cards correctly, she and James would be dead. Once she found the list she would have to act decisively in order to guarantee their future.

"Good morning Ladies and Gentlemen. This is Captain Alexander. We're just about to leave Ottawa. Please put your seats in the upright position and fasten your seatbelts. Our flight this morning will take just under an hour. The weather in Québec City is overcast and minus fourteen degrees Celsius. We'll be serving coffee and doughnuts after takeoff. I hope you have a pleasant flight. Attendants to your stations." The pilot went through the customary remarks before commencing the flight.

Monika reached into her purse and found her cellular phone. She'd forgotten it was still on. She turned the phone off and put it back into her purse. Placing the purse under the seat in front of her, she sat back and stared straight ahead. She prayed that everything would turn out all right.

Chapter 14

Jean-Paul had not been able to sleep. He had paced away the night around his apartment trying to make sense of what had happened. He was terribly disturbed by the gruesome scene of Jack's brutal murder, which still lingered in his mind. Every time he tried to close his eyes the scene was there vividly in front of him. He wondered who might be responsible for such a cold-blooded act. He also wondered if Jack's death had any link to Monika, James, Craig and the coded message. Knowing he would not be able to rest until he got some answers to his questions, he decided to go to the hospital, check on James' condition and hopefully get a chance to talk with Monika. He believed she was somehow connected to events of the past twenty-four hours.

Jean-Paul arrived in the ICU at 9:15 am. The unit was very busy. There was no one at the nurses station as he entered the unit. There seemed to be some sort of emergency. He walked farther into the unit and discovered what was going on. All the nursing staff was scurrying around James' bed, along with a man dressed in a white lab coat that he assumed to be a doctor. A sense of dread struck Jean-Paul as he realized what the emergency might be and how it would impact his case.

He rushed over to James' curtained space. Standing in the background he watched as the doctor tried to determine what was wrong with his patient. One of the monitors attached to James' chest was sounding an alarm and he was convulsing.

"Let the OR know we're coming up. I think he's bleeding internally. I was afraid of this. Maybe he tore something. We're going to have to open again," Dr. Keene's tone of voice was guarded as he directed the nurses. This was not an expected turn of events. The look on his face conveyed his uncertainty concerning James' prognosis.

"Yes, Doctor." One of the three nurses complied with his orders and hurried past Jean-Paul without acknowledging his presence. It was clear to Jean-Paul that James was in a life or death crisis.

"And you'd better call his fiancée. This doesn't look good," the doctor called out to the nurse as she neared her station.

Jean-Paul suddenly realized Monika wasn't there. He found it odd. Though he had not known her long, he assumed her to be the type of person who would have remained at her fiancé's side until he was out of danger. His instincts, which were seldom off the mark, told him there was something wrong about her not being there. He wondered where she might be and what was so important that she felt she had to leave her critically ill fiancé.

"Who are you?" Dr. Keene seeing the detective for the first time, demanded. He did not like unknown outsiders around under such circumstances.

"Detective Ferisse. Ottawa Police. I'm investigating this case," Jean-Paul replied. He did not appreciate the doctor's tone. He noted his name embroidered on his jacket.

"Well, you'll have to keep out of the way." Dr. Keene said reluctantly allowing Jean-Paul to stay. He returned his attention to James while the remaining two nurses prepared the bed for transportation.

"Is he going to survive?" Jean-Paul got right to the point. He needed to know right away. He did not want to wait for bad news. James was his only witness and he needed him alive.

"It's touch and go. I'll know better after we get into the OR. Don't worry detective. I'll do my best to keep your witness alive, but I can't make any promises." Dr. Keene understood the detective's professional concern.

"Thank you, Doc. He's my only lead." Jean-Paul had no personal feelings about James; to him James was just a case that required solving and it was a lot easier to solve a case that had breathing witnesses. Jean-Paul couldn't allow his emotions to get in the way. If he did, he would not be an effective investigator. It was his job to do what most people would not. A job that, like Dr. Keene, he took a great deal of pride in doing to the best of his ability. His emotional separation was a requirement to keep his mind clear and focused on the facts. He had learned this from Jack many years ago.

"I'm sorry his fiancée isn't here. I thought he was more stable. I hope Québec City is worth it." The doctor was concerned that Monika would not be able to get back in time once she was notified of James' change of condition. He felt sorry for her. It would be a difficult blow for her to bear.

"Québec City? When did she go?" Jean-Paul's interest perked.

"This morning. I spoke with her earlier. Why?" Dr. Keene was waiting for the nurses to finish their preparations.

"No reason. Just curiosity." Jean-Paul immediately connected the coded message to Monika's rush trip to Québec City.

"Doctor. We're ready."

"Let's get into surgery." Helping them maneuver, Dr. Keene pushed the bed with the nurses through the intensive care unit. It rolled easily. As they went, one of the nurses held James' IV above him allowing it to continue to drip while the other helped the doctor push the bed. Dr. Keene was a very hands-on medical practitioner.

"Detective, I'll let you know as soon as I'm done," he called out before leaving the unit.

Jean-Paul watched as James was rolled out through the ICU doors. He hoped for his as well as Monika's sake, that Dr. Keene could do something to save James. He would wait in the hospital until he found out.

Believing it would be a while before there was any news on James' condition, Jean-Paul crossed through the unit. He decided to go down to the lobby and get a coffee. When he came to the nurses station he paused.

The other nurse following Dr. Keene's instructions had called the OR and was now dialing Monika's cellular phone number. The clock on the wall displayed 9:25 am. Monika would still be on the plane and unable to answer the call. The line rang several times and then was forwarded to an automated message. The nurse hung up the phone. She would try again later when she had some news of James' condition.

"Couldn't get through?" Jean-Paul asked the

nurse as she hung up the phone.

"No." She sat down at her desk. It was the same young, unfriendly nurse that Monika had spoken with earlier that morning.

"I'm getting a coffee but I'll be back." Jean-Paul did not wait for her to reply. He pushed open the ICU doors and made his way to the stairwell. He wondered where Monika was. He felt there was something strange about her absence. This case was presenting many interesting twists and curves.

- - - - - - - - - - - - - - -

Hackett arrived back at the hospital at 9:00 am. He was sitting on the second floor about fifteen feet away from the ICU adjacent to the elevators in a small waiting area. He had a clear view of the corridor and the ICU doors. He had witnessed all the commotion and the arrival of a man who he sensed was a plainclothes police detective. He did not know Detective Ferisse but his arrival on the floor put Hackett on guard. He carefully watched as a patient was shortly thereafter wheeled from the ICU to the elevator next to the waiting area. He tried to stay concealed as the doctor and nurses waited at the elevator with their patient. He stretched up a little from his seat and was able to identify that their patient was James. There was clearly something wrong. He watched as the elevator doors opened and James' bed was rolled in. As the doctor and nurses entered the elevator he overheard snippets of their conversation. James had relapsed and they were taking him upstairs for surgery. The prognosis was not good.

Shortly after James had been taken upstairs, Hackett saw the plainclothes detective leave the unit and go downstairs. He knew the detective would remain in the hospital until James' condition stabilized.

Though it was against hospital regulations, Hackett pulled out his cellular phone. No one else was in the waiting area and he would keep his phone call brief. He dialed Skinner's private number. The phone rang several times but went unanswered. He disconnected and tried the C2 office.

"Canadian International Institute," Marylyn answered.

"Marylyn. Is Mr. Skinner in?" Hackett did not like to call her but he knew Skinner would want the update on James' condition.

"No. He's catching the 10:15 flight to Québec City. Do you want to leave a message?" For some reason she was friendlier toward him today.

"Yes. Tell him Ms. Queller has gone to Québec City and Stone is with her." He disconnected and changed his phone ringer to vibration mode, putting it back in his jacket pocket. He didn't realize Skinner was leaving for Québec City that morning. He decided to try him again later on his cell phone when he knew more about James' condition. He knew Marylyn would give Skinner the message by the time he arrived in Québec City.

Hackett picked up a magazine from the small table in front of him and sat back to relax, accepting that it might be a few hours before any information on James' status was forthcoming. He didn't mind. He was used to waiting.

- - - - - - - - - - - - - - - - -

"Ladies and gentleman. The captain has put on the 'fasten seatbelts' sign. We'll be landing in a few minutes. Please place your seats in the upright position and fasten your seatbelts. For those passengers requiring assistance please wait until all the other passengers have disembarked and we will assist you. Thank you for choosing Air Canada," the flight attendant announced in French and then English.

Monika's heart began to race. This was it. Once the plane landed she would get up quickly and try to get away from the man who was following her. Though she did not know the airport, she expected it would be small. She knew that Québec City, unlike Canada's two largest cities, Toronto and Montreal, was smaller than Ottawa. If she could get to a taxi, she might be able to lose him at the airport. She did not want him to know where she was going. She wanted the security of secrecy.

The plane began its descent. Monika looked out her window but it was too overcast to see beyond the wings of the airplane. Out of the blue her awareness focused on James. She felt a strange pang in her heart. She did not like the feeling. She hoped it was being caused by the stress of her current situation and not a premonition. She wanted to accomplish her mission in Québec City and get back to him. She felt as if he were calling to her. Taking a deep breath, she centered her thoughts. She needed to remain focused. Being distracted would not help her with whatever lay ahead. She prayed everything would go smoothly, but from her experience she knew deep inside there was a good chance it might not.

Chapter 15

The moment the plane came to a stop, Monika undid her seatbelt, picked up her purse and coat that she had put on the empty seat next to her, and started down the aisle to the exit. She did not look behind to see if her pursuer had followed her lead and gotten up before the other passengers blocked his progress. There was only one person in front of her as she nervously stood waiting until the flight attendant opened the main hatch to the gangplank.

"Have a nice stay in Québec City. Good-bye," the flight attendant said from her place in front of the cockpit door.

Stone also had the idea of getting ahead of the other passengers but didn't want to be seen by

Monika. As a result, he hesitated a moment longer than he should have and by the time he got up he saw her making her way down the aisle. The other passengers in front of him had already bottlenecked the aisle, preventing him from following her. He was pinned behind a man who was having difficulty getting his things down from the overhead compartment. There was no way to get around the man. Stone tried to keep track of Monika while he waited. He was frustrated. She was getting away.

Monika stole a quick look behind before leaving the plane. Seeing the bottleneck in the aisle she took advantage of the opportunity and hurried onto the gangplank. She did not pay attention to the flight attendant as she said goodbye to her. She was too focused on losing her pursuer by getting to a taxi before he could reach her.

It was cold in the walkway. She put on her coat as she walked but left it unbuttoned. She pulled her hat out of her coat pocket and put it on hoping it might help to disguise her. The walk from the plane to the building was very short and within seconds she entered the Québec City International Airport terminal building.

The airport was designed in the mid-seventies and decorated with modular furnishings in earth tones. A small building by most airport standards it consisted of one large rectangular space. She found herself walking through a futuristic tubular walkway at ground level that ran the length of the terminal, connecting and separating the arrival and departure gates from the main building. It carried every passenger to and from the nerve center of the terminal. The walkway walls were made of clear Plexiglas and its supports were thin metal strips painted in a burnt orange. She was able to clearly see every area of the terminal as she made her way through the walkway. There was a bar / restaurant immediately beside her arrival gate and opposite the bar was a small convenience store and a cafeteria-style fast-food restaurant. She made her way along the walkway and exited into the terminal. A large array of empty seats filled the main area of the building between the bar and the fast-food restaurant. Under other circumstances she would have been happy that the airport was not busy, but today she wished there were more people, so she could mingle among them and hide. The handful of people she did see appeared to be employees of the airport and not passengers.

Directly ahead of the exit from the walkway, about twenty yards away, were the main sliding doors of the terminal to the street outside. Without looking back she increased her pace and made her way to the exit. She hoped she was far enough ahead of her pursuer that she would be able to find an available taxi and make her getaway.

Stone became very impatient once the hatch

door to the aircraft was opened. He helplessly watched as Monika left the plane ahead of him. The man blocking him was still having difficulty with the overhead compartment and not allowing anyone to pass. Stone had not come this far to lose her now.

"Excuse me. I need to get by," Stone angrily informed the man.

"I've just got to get my things. What's the hurry?" the man arrogantly replied. He was not going to let Stone pass. He was determined to make him wait.

"Excuse me." Stone was not in the mood for such an obstinate ass. He did not waste time arguing with the man. Monika was getting too much of a head start. Catching the man off-guard he pushed him down into the seat and hurried down the aisle, ignoring his complaints.

He ran down the gangplank into the tubular walkway of the terminal. Monika was nowhere to be seen. He began to panic. There were a dozen passengers ahead of him who were chatting and slowly pulling their luggage, finding their way along the walkway. Stone searched through them but did not see Monika. Then he looked through the Plexiglas of the tubular walkway and spotted her hurrying through the main area of the airport to the terminal exit. Realizing he was about to lose her, he started to run through the walkway. He pushed a couple of slower passengers out of his way in his efforts to stay with her.

Monika went through the terminal's sliding doors onto the sidewalk. She was noticeably struck by a wave of sub zero air. It was a good ten degrees colder than Ottawa. She held her coat together to prevent herself from losing too much body heat. The sky was overcast and the snow was piled deeply along the freshly plowed streets. The glare from the pristine snow caused her to squint. It felt like it was going to snow again soon. She never thought she would need sunglasses this far north in the winter.

Three taxicabs lined the outdoor walkway waiting for customers. The taxis appeared to be independently owned and doubled as personal family cars in their off-duty hours. Their typical rooftop signs were temporarily secured in place by bungee cords clipped to the upper door frames. It was so cold, no one was standing outside. The drivers of the taxis were waiting inside their warm, running cars. Monika walked up to the first gray sedan taxi, opened the rear passenger door and got in.

"Bon sure. J'allay aux l'hotel Château Frontenac, sil-voo-play." Her French was not good, but she had read somewhere if you tried to speak in French first in Québec, then the Québécois would be nicer and more willing to switch to English, if need be. She nervously peered through the window, checking for her pursuer.

"Certainment, madam," the driver, a pudgy man in his late forties agreed. He was wearing a gray winter jacket over a mustard-colored plaid vest, white shirt and tie. He wore a gray Tyrolean style hat with a small blue panache on its left side and had a half smoked cigarette hanging out of his mouth burning closely to his debonair dark mustache. Though eccentric, the driver was stylishly dressed.

"Mercy." Monika smelled the smoky staleness of the cab's upholstery but did not comment. Distracted by the sight of her pursuer exiting the terminal en route to her taxi, she ducked out of sight. "Ploo veet, sil-voo-play," she called out to the driver to get going before she was spotted.

"Mais oui." The driver watched Monika's odd behavior through his rear view mirror but complied with her wishes, she was either hiding or trying to getaway from someone. He put the taxi into gear and pulled away from the terminal. It was obvious from her poor attempt to speak French she was Anglo. He thought he detected an American accent and would treat her like a tourist and not as an English Canadian. He was rather enjoying this unusual twist to the first run of his day.

Causing upset as he forced his way through the terminal, Stone finally made his way into the center of the sidewalk outside the arrivals area.

Monika was not there. He had fully expected to find her waiting on the sidewalk. A gray taxi was pulling out into the airport roadway but there was no one other than the driver inside. He angrily threw down his hands and cursed. He wondered where she could have gone. A small white commuter bus, with the picture logo of La Québécoise bus company painted on its side, was parked next to the sidewalk waiting for passengers who wanted to be taken from the airport to the downtown and surrounding areas.

Stone ran over to the bus and looking through the windows, thoroughly examined the passengers who were seated with their luggage, waiting to go. Monika was not inside the bus. Stone turned and reexamined the sidewalk along the road outside the terminal. Other than the few passengers who were standing waiting for their rides, taxi or bus, Monika was nowhere to be seen. He knew it was impossible for her to disappear. Other than the one taxi that had pulled out just as he exited the terminal, no other vehicles had gone by. He suddenly realized what had happened. Monika must have been hiding in the gray taxi.

He ran over to the next waiting taxi. A man in his mid-thirties, wearing a dark brown overcoat, was about to get in but Stone forced his way ahead of him and got in.

"Hey. That's mine!" Stone was so threatening in his size and manner that the man did not protest too loudly for fear he might be physically harmed. He stepped back and allowed Stone to take the cab. It was not worth a confrontation. There would always be another taxi.

"Follow that car," Stone blurted out to the fat woman driver as he slammed the door behind him. He was anxiously keeping his eye on the gray taxi, which was a fair distance ahead but still within sight.

"Pardon monsieur?" The woman was being smart. She thought she would have some fun with this Anglo.

"That car. Up there. Don't let it get away," Stone was frantic. He understood what the woman was doing. He had no time for political statements.

"Comment?" she played dumb, pretending she could not understand, but Stone knew better. He put his hand into his parka and pulled out his revolver. Sitting forward he shoved the gun into the woman's neck.

"I said follow that car. Now. Comprenez-vous?" Stone meant business and spoke perfect French.

"Oui monsieur." Startled, the woman stopped the game. Believing a crazy man had gotten into her taxi, she put the car in drive and pulled out after the gray sedan.

"Don't lose it." Stone added pressure with the gun against her neck. He was giving her some good advice. "And stay off the radio."

"Oui monsieur." She sped up in fear of what might happen if she lost the gray taxi. She wanted to get this man out of her taxi as soon as possible. She looked into the rear view mirror to better identify him. Stone sat back in his seat and put his gun into its holster inside his parka.

"What are you looking at?" he sneered at her. "Keep your eyes on that taxi."

"Oui monsieur." She focused on her assigned task, afraid of what her passenger might do next.

- - - - - - - - - - - - - - - -

"There is no one following us. You can come out," Monika's driver called out as he checked for her in his rear view mirror. He spoke English well with a heavy French Canadian accent.

Monika slowly sat up in her seat and looked back through the rear window. "Thank you. Sorry about all that."

The Qućbec City International Airport was in the rural outskirts of Québec City, about fifteen minutes from the old town. Monika marveled at how quickly one could get into the farmland in Canada from a major city. The land here was undulating and snow-covered. She had never seen so much snow in one place. A blanket of white covered not only the ground but also the rooftops of any farmhouse or building they passed. Scattered amongst the farmhouses was the encroaching growth of newly built homes and stores that were sprawling outward from the city core. The homes were much smaller than the ones she was used to. Everything seemed to be on a smaller scale. There was a charming provincial quality to the place.

"Not at all. Is something wrong?" the driver began his conversation, keeping one eye on the road and the other on his passenger through the rear view mirror. He was captivated by her fresh 'peaches and cream' complexion, which added softness to her sparkling blue eyes.

"No. I met some guy on the plane and…" she made up a story that she thought he might accept.

"Mais oui. Je comprend," the driver chuckled. He understood how a man would approach such a beautiful woman. Though it was not right, there was no harm done in his mind by such an attentive man. It was only natural under such conditions. He believed it was the price a woman such as his passenger paid for being so attractive.

"No. I don't mean he was bothering me. I just didn't want to share the ride with him. I don't think my fiancé would approve," she blurted, trying to correct the impression she had made. She did not want the driver to think she was being threatened.

"Don't worry. I understand. C'est la vie." The driver continued to smile. He liked this woman and could understand how any other man would feel the same way.

"How far away are we from Québec City?" she

changed the subject. They were entering a residential area, which she guessed marked the city limits. She found it interesting how people had constructed temporary enclosures, large tent frames covered with heavy plastic, over their cars in their driveways. Even the entrances to their homes and small businesses had awnings to keep not the sun but the heavy snow problem away.

"This is Sainte-Foy. It is a suburb of Québec City. We are very close now. Maybe five more minutes. Is this your first time to Québec?"

"Yes. There is so much snow here but it's beautiful. I live in California." She checked the rear window again to reassure herself she was not being followed.

"It is much warmer there than Québec at this time of year, non? I have never been. But I am sure it is nice." He glanced in his rear view mirror and caught Monika checking the traffic behind them. "Don't worry. There is no one there. No one can catch Pierre Laroc." He smiled and looked away.

Realizing he had caught her in her paranoia, Monika turned around and faced forward. "Then I am lucky to have such a skilled driver." She found her English starting to reflect the same intonation as the driver.

"Merci, mademoiselle," he thanked her and, changing the way he addressed her, concentrated upon driving through the heavier traffic of Sainte-

Foy.

Feeling more relaxed and secure, Monika sat back and silently took in the sights. She hoped Pierre Laroc was as good as he claimed to be and that her pursuer was lost at the airport, but she realized it was unlikely. In a small place like Québec City it would be easy for a professional to find her. She would have to be careful and keep an eye out for him.

Several minutes later Pierre Laroc turned off the major roadway and onto the smaller streets that were typical of Québec City. The buildings became more charming and the streets narrower. The landscape was hillier, reminding Monika of downtown San Francisco. Tiny houses of all shapes and designs were sardined together and standing precariously on the steep streets. Beyond these sights, she noticed a predominance of churches. Québec City seemed to have a church every couple of blocks. She counted fifteen or twenty churches or religious institutions on the drive into the City before giving up. It was obvious that religion played a big part in the lives of these people. The city had a European feel that pleasantly surprised her. Québec City steadily became more quaint, more charming, and more old worldly European the closer they got to the heart of the city. She found herself wishing she was there with James.

"This is Porte Saint-Louis. It is one of the city

gates. We are entering Vieux-Québec." The driver pointed out the entry to old Québec City.

Québec City from its earliest beginnings in the sixteenth and seventeenth centuries, was a fortified garrison that overlooked the St. Lawrence River. The walls that had been constructed around this hilltop city protected it from invasion. To this day these walls were maintained and still impressively surrounded the city though there was no longer any threat of invasion. Inside the city walls not much had changed over the years. Most of the old city's cobblestoned streets were intact and so narrow they only permitted traffic to move in one direction.

Forgetting her troubles for the moment, Monika admired the sights from her taxi window. A recent heavy snowfall had left the streets covered, causing traffic to slow. The plows of the works department had not yet managed to clear it away. Still, this mess did not stop the pedestrians from making their journeys. There were many more people outside than Monika had expected to see at this time of year in such cold, snowy conditions.

Along both sides of the rue Saint-Louis, the street they were driving along, people were coming in and out of a multitude of two-storied stone buildings that had been renovated and contained a variety of restaurants, gift shops, and other tourist attractions. It was apparent that Québec City, though it was the political seat of Québec and home of the National Assembly, depended primarily on tourism to survive.

Those walking on the streets were dressed warmly and wore hats that covered their ears. Their exhaled breaths lingered behind them as they scurried to wherever they were going. Under different circumstances it would have be nice to explore this city.

"The best time here is in the summer when it is warm. The flowers are in bloom and the trees have their green leaves." Pierre continued.

"I like it like this. It reminds me of 'A Tale of Two Cities' or 'A Christmas Carol'. It's very romantic." She admired the way the Old City had been maintained according to its original seventeenth century French origins. The architecture was far more interesting and ornate than the more spartan utilitarian cities of English-speaking Canada.

"We are almost at the Château Frontenac. It is on the right," Pierre added, directing her attention to the road ahead.

The rue Saint-Louis opened into the Place d'Armes, originally the parade grounds but now a large rectangular parkette to the immediate north of the Château Frontenac. The Place d'Armes along with the Château Frontenac was the focal point of the city.

Surrounding the park and running many blocks to the north and west was a maze of tiny cobblestoned streets and side streets that were lined with tiny renovated medieval buildings full of restaurants stores and shops. In the summer people would meet in the parkette and enjoy warm summer evenings overlooking the St. Lawrence River, but at this time in the bleak mid-winter, its trees stood like petrified skeletons, its lawn deeply tucked beneath a heavy blanket of snow. Only the parkette's sidewalks were cleared to allow pedestrians to cross from the Château Frontenac to the Québec tourist office and other stores that were housed in the museum-like buildings surrounding the Place d'Armes on rue Sainte-Anne or rue du Trésor.

Upon reaching the Place d'Armes, Pierre Laroc signaled and turned his taxi through an arched brick opening that was built into the side of the Château Frontenac, allowing entry into the hotel driveway. All thc hotel needed was a moat in place of the rue Saint-Louis and a drawbridge to resemble a medieval castle's fortified entrance. He drove up the narrow driveway and stopped in front of the flight of steps that led up to the lobby doors. Seeing the taxi arrive, a doorman leapt down the steps and opened the passenger door to allow Monika to get out.

"Thank you. How much is it?" She sat forward taking her wallet out from her purse.

"Twenty-five dollars, mademoiselle." He turned off the meter and faced her.

“Thank you for all your help.” She handed him thirty dollars.

“Thank you. I hope everything will be all right. Here’s my card. When you need to return to the airport, give me a call.” Pierre took the money and gave her his card. It was the custom in a tourist town like Québec City for a taxi driver to try and set up return trips.

“Thanks. I will. Or-rev-voir,” she used the French for ‘see you later’ put the wallet back into her purse and stepped out into the Château Frontenac courtyard.

“Bonjour madam,” the doorman, a young man in his twenties wearing the stylish uniform of the hotel, greeted her. He had on a charcoal gray greatcoat and was wearing a beaver pelt hat that made his head look larger than it actually was. The hat reminded Monika of a turn-of-the-century guard in the Russian Czar’s palace in St. Petersburg.

The courtyard was completely surrounded by the hotel. The driveway was made of cobblestone and the snow had been plowed away. Opposite the arched entryway, about seventy feet on the other side, was a similarly designed arched exit. She waited and watched as her taxi went up the drive and, turning right, disappeared through the exit.

She was alone. She stood on the stairs to the lobby and admired the architecture of the Old

Château. On the side opposite the lobby several cars were parked in front of what she assumed were offices for the hotel. She looked up through the open courtyard to the sky about twenty stories above. She could easily see the green tarnished copper turreted roof and the dark overcast sky beyond. She felt a little claustrophobic in the face of the towering solid gray brick walls of the Château Frontenac surrounding her.

"Bon sure," she replied to the doorman who was waiting to guide her into the hotel lobby. She was scared. She was not sure what she was going to do next. "Is the hotel very busy?" she asked before going up the steps.

"No, Madam. We'll be busier with the Summit. This is our slowest time of year," the doorman replied as he started up the steps to the lobby doors ahead of her.

"The Summit?" Monika didn't understand. She followed him up the stairs, stopping in front of the lobby doors while he reached over to open them.

"The Summit of the Americas. It's being held in the Citadel next week. It will be very crowded then. This week is the calm before the storm," he informed her as he pulled open the door.

"Thank you. I see." She went in. She was impressed that Québec City would be chosen as the location for such an important meeting. The Summit of the Americas was an opportunity for the leaders of North and South America to get together and discuss issues and policies that affected them. Holding the meeting here would put Québec City on the international map.

The lobby of the Château Frontenac had a very old-world feel. All of its walls were paneled in dark wood. To the left of the lobby was a magnificent set of stairs that lead up to the mezzanine. The stairs were covered in a dark patterned carpet that blended in with the lobby's maroon carpet. A large chandelier hanging from the ceiling above illuminated the lobby stairs and mezzanine. Straight ahead of her opposite the lobby entrance was a long corridor that contained several little shops. A small sign on the wall at the side of the corridor indicated that the bar and restaurant were down the corridor.

Two sets of green leather couches were placed at both ends of the large lobby—one in front of the front desk and the other by the stairs to the mezzanine. A woman was sitting on the couch in front of the stairway to the mezzanine reading a newspaper. Diagonally across from the lobby doors on Monika's right was the front desk. Other than herself and the hotel employees behind the front desk, the lobby was vacant.

Monika was not sure what she should do next. She looked at her watch. It was 10:20 am. She stood in the center of the lobby considering her options. The easiest thing to do would be to check into room 1720 in the hotel. She hoped there really was a room 1720 and that she had not been mistaken in deciphering the coded message. If she was lucky she would quickly find whatever Craig had hidden. She wasn't sure what she would do after she found it but she decided to worry about that afterwards. She drew in a breath and, setting her plan in motion, crossed over to the front desk.

"Good morning. I'd like a room. Is 1720 available?" She took off her hat and placed it with her purse on the countertop while she spoke to the young female clerk standing at her station behind the front desk. The young woman was in her early thirties. She had long dark hair without much makeup and wore French rectangular designer glasses.

"Good morning. I'll check." The woman focused on her computer screen as she typed an inquiry. "You are lucky. It's not reserved but it won't be available until eleven thirty or so." The hotel was not fully booked. The woman looked up at Monika.

"That's okay. Should I come back later?" Monika was relieved there was a room 1720 and that it was available. It would make things go a lot easier. She had expected the hotel to be so busy that room 1720 would be occupied.

"No, you can register now but the key won't work until after eleven or so."

"Is there someone in it?" Monika was curious.

"No. There was. They checked out early this

morning. Housekeeping hasn't gotten to it yet. I do have other rooms that are ready now." She was very accommodating.

"No, thank you. 1720's fine." She could wait a little longer. It would give her a chance to get something to eat and relax. The short down time would not cause any inconvenience to her, "Is there some place I can get a coffee?" Monika pulled her wallet out of her purse. She expected a hotel like the Château Frontenac was going to be expensive and hoped her credit card wasn't maxed out.

"Yes. If you go down the corridor to the bar, they serve coffee and donuts until eleven. The restaurant doesn't open until 11:30 am. Will that be on your credit-card?"

"Yes. Just one night." Monika handed the clerk her card. This trip was getting expensive.

"Ms. Queller. Do you mind if I ask why you want that particular room?" The clerk asked out of curiousity as she typed Monika's information into the computer.

Monika thought quickly. She needed a story that was believable.

"That's where my father asked my mother to marry him. I wasn't sure it would still be here."

"Ah. How nice. Yes we have been here many years. We have not changed much since then. Of course it was before my time." She smiled.

"And mine too." Monika watched as the young

woman processed her credit card without incident. She breathed a silent sigh of relief.

"Here you go, Ms. Queller. Room 1720. I'm sure anytime after eleven the room will be ready. I've put a rush on it. You can use the elevators there. You can leave your bags with the concierge if you like." She handed Monika her room key and credit card.

"Thank you." Monika did not want to admit she was traveling without any luggage. She turned away from the front desk, and headed for the bar at the end of corridor. She was thrilled that everything had been so easy. She hoped it would be just as easy to find whatever Craig had hidden in room 1720 before meeting James in Ottawa. If it was the list her abductors wanted, she wasn't certain what she would do with it once she found it. She again wished she knew someone in Canada that she could trust. It would be helpful in deciding what to do next. She also wished she knew where her pursuer had gotten to. Her escape from him was only temporary. She knew he would not give up until he found her. She hoped she could stay concealed from him until she could decide what to do to better protect James' and herself.

"Oh no." She suddenly realized she had not turned her cellular phone on after disembarking from the plane at the airport. Maybe the hospital had tried to call. She quickened her pace down the corridor. When she arrived at the bar and ordered her coffee, she would call the hospital.

- - - - - - - - - - - - - - - -

Stone's driver was nervous. She had managed to catch up with Monika's gray sedan taxi very soon after it had left the airport only to lose it after it left the main roadway on the rue Saint-Louis. She had lost it before the gate to the old City. There were many places where the taxi could have gone. There were a variety of small bed and breakfast hotels as well as larger major hotels along the route, assuming whoever the man was looking for was planning on staying over.

"I have lost them," the driver reluctantly informed Stone. "I am sorry. They could have gone anywhere." She waited, expecting the worst.

"What? Damn." He knew it was not the driver's fault. Québec City was riddled with a maze of streets, hotels, restaurants and shops, any one of a thousand places Monika could go. He did not believe she would stay overnight but would return to Ottawa after she found the list, which was obviously hidden somewhere nearby. He wondered if the list was hidden in a locker at the train station, but he didn't want to run around chasing hunches. The list was too important to make an incorrect guess. He considered his best options.

"Drive around the city. If we don't spot them then go back to the airport." He realized even if he could not find her, he might be able to find her taxi. He could then find out where the driver had taken her.

"Yes, sir." The driver didn't like the idea of keeping her passenger in her car. She wanted to get rid of him as fast as possible. "But I think I know the driver of her taxi. His name is Pierre Laroc. He only drives to and from the airport. I am sure he will return to the airport after dropping his fare.

"Really." Stone was pleased that the city was so small that most of the airport taxi drivers knew each other.

"Yes." The driver relaxed a little, realizing she had helped her passenger.

"Then turn around and let's get back to the airport. I don't want to miss him." Stone felt less panicked. It was now only a matter of time before he could discover Monika's whereabouts. He sat back in his seat searching for the gray taxi or Monika along the street.

The driver continued along rue Saint-Louis, following the same route that Monika's taxi had taken only ten minutes before. They passed the same picturesque scenes that Monika had admired but Stone did not take the time to look as closely. He had been to Québec City many times and was neither interested nor impressed. His only concern was to find Monika. It was important to find her and make sure the list did not fall into any other hands.

Coming to the Place d'Armes his driver went

around the parkette and turned onto the rue Sainte-Anne, headed back to the main roadway and the airport. She drove faster on this return trip. She knew her best chance of finding Pierre Laroc was at the airport and she wanted to get back there as quickly as possible. She hoped Pierre had not picked up another fare but would be there waiting. She did not want to keep this man in her company until Pierre showed up after dropping another passenger. She knew there was another flight from Ottawa arriving at 11:15 am with passengers looking for rides into the City.

As they rejoined the main roadway to the airport, Stone took out his cellular phone and punched in Hackett's number. Though he didn't want to report he had lost Monika, he knew under the circumstances it was wiser to do so.

- - - - - - - - - - - - - - - -

Monika entered the bar at the end of the corridor. It was a circular room that overlooked the Dufferin Terrasse in front of the Château Frontenac and then, far below, the St. Lawrence River. It was a magnificent view. The bar resembled a conservatory from a nineteenth century English country Estate. There were two fireplaces opposite each other along the circumference of the room. Tables and chairs ran around the room with a large circular bar in the center. Around the bar were several stools. A man in his late twenties was sitting at the bar drinking a coffee with his back to Monika as she entered. The bartender was leaning over the counter chatting with him.

Monika walked into the room and sat at a table next to the small fireplace on the right hand side. Seeing her settle in, the bartender immediately stood up and came over to her table. He was a large man in his late twenties. He looked like a big kid with his crew cut hair, baby fat, and clean-shaven face. He wore a maroon vest over a white shirt and black tie with black dress pants. Though he was probably the most gentle of people, his size gave him a threatening demeanor.

"Good morning. Can I get you anything?" for a man of his size, he spoke in a higher tenor voice than expected.

"Just coffee, please," Monika smiled. She was beginning to warm up. She took off her coat and draped it over the chair opposite her small round mahogany table.

"Would you like a donut or muffin? I have some freshly made," the bartender gave a convincing nod and raised his eyelids.

"Yes, thank you, a muffin would would be nice." Monika was hungry. The sound of freshly made muffins was appealing.

The bartender went back to the bar to fill her order. Monika sat back and looked out the window just beyond her table at the panoramic view before her. White snow was everywhere. Even the St. Lawrence River was full of large pieces of flowing ice. In the distance, crushing its way through the ice flow on the river, was a ferryboat heading for the side opposite Québec City. Her attention focused for a moment on the river, she did not notice the man drinking coffee at the bar pay his bill and leave. She then took her phone out of her purse and turned it on. The signal was strong. She pressed zero and put the phone to her ear.

"Bonjour…" the phone rang quite a few times and was answered by a French Canadian operator at the cellular phone company. The only part Monika understood of what the woman said was the first word. The woman spoke quickly and with a heavy local accent.

"Bon sure. I'd like the number for the Ottawa Civic Hospital in Ottawa, sil-voo-play." Monika hoped the operator spoke English.

"I'll connect you to the Ottawa operator. Please wait," the operator replied in perfect English.

"What city, please," after several moments another operator answered in English.

"Ottawa."

"Go ahead," the operator was matter-of-fact and had a nasal tone in her voice.

"The Ottawa Civic Hospital please."

"Would you like me to connect you? There's a fifty cent charge."

"Yes please. Thank you," Monika accepted and waited while the operator connected her. The phone rang three times.

"Ottawa Civic Hospital," the hospital switchboard operator answered.

"The Intensive Care Unit, please."

The hospital switchboard operator did not answer. She immediately directed the call to the ICU nurses station. The phone rang. Monika stared into the red ambers of the slow burning fire beside her table feeling the warmth from its flame. She drifted off wondering if James was better. The phone kept ringing and was routed back to the main switchboard.

"I'm sorry. No one's answering. Please try again later," the hospital operator came back on line.

"Thank you." Monika disconnected. She was disappointed and wondered why no one had answered. She checked her watch. It was 10:30 am. Perhaps the nursing staff was too busy to answer the phone. After her coffee she would try again. She put the phone back into her purse and tried to relax, but she couldn't. She was worried about James.

- - - - - - - - - - - - - - -

Stone held his phone to his ear and took a deep breath while the phone rang.

"Hackett."

"I've lost her in Québec City. She got ahead of me." Stone tried to conceal his embarrassment from him. He knew how unprofessional Hackett would think he was for losing Monika.

"Jesus," Hackett swore, his voice low. He was still in the waiting area on the second floor of the hospital. James had not yet returned to the ICU. He was not prepared for Stone's bad news. He didn't want to face Skinner's wrath when he reported the loss.

"But I think I can find out where she went." Stone tried to redeem himself.

"How?" Hackett welcomed any good news.

"I can find her taxi driver and get him to tell me. It'll take about an hour." Stone didn't know how long it would take, but he gave the time to add credibility to his ability to quickly resolve the problem.

"All right. I'll let Skinner know. He's on his way there now. FIND HER! Let me know as soon as you do." Hackett disconnected. He hoped by the time Skinner arrived in Québec City, Stone would have better news. He decided to wait forty-five minutes or so before calling Skinner. He did not want to leave a displeasing message on his service.

"Damn. Are you sure you know the driver?" Stone was upset. As soon as Hackett hung up he had become incensed. He needed to find the driver as fast as possible.

"Yes. He will be there," the woman answered confidently. She silently prayed she was correct.

"Then get there as fast as you can," he ordered. He only had an hour.

"Oui monsieur." That suited the woman fine. She stepped on the gas and the taxi sped up.

Stone stared out the window lost in thought. When he found Monika's driver, he would not waste any time getting the answers he needed. He put his hand over the gun inside his jacket. It was cool and smooth to touch; its texture comforting to him. He was prepared to do anything to redeem himself.

- - - - - - - - - - - - - - - -

"Here you are, ma'am." The waiter placed a white cup and saucer on the table in front of Monika and filled it with coffee from a small carafe. "A gentleman asked me to give you this." He handed her a small folded piece of paper. "Would you like cream and sugar?"

Monika took the piece of paper and looked around the room but did not see the man who had sent the note. She was confused. "What gentleman?"

The waiter turned around to identify the man who had given him the note but he was no longer in the bar.

"He was just here. I'll get you your cream and sugar." Unperturbed, he went back to the bar.

Unsettled, Monika brought the paper closer and unfolded it. A note was scribbled in black ink.

"If you and your fiancé want to live, go to the confessional in the Basilique Notre Dame right away. DON'T WAIT."

The last two words of the message were written strongly in capitals. She turned the paper over to see if she had missed something but there was nothing else on the paper. She wondered who had left the message. She nervously scanned the room again but did not see anyone other than the bartender. She sat and considered what she should do. She wondered if her pursuer had found her but if he had, why would he leave her such a note. She did not have any answers to her questions. Standing up, she picked up her coat and put it on. There was only one thing to do.

Seeing his customer get up to leave, the bartender hurried over. He carried with him Monika's cream, sugar and a small bran muffin.

"I'm sorry it took so long. Is something wrong?" He put the items on the table and waited for an answer. He was worried he might have done or said something to cause her to leave.

"No. Thank you. I forgot. I have to meet someone right away. Can you put these on my room?" Monika picked up her purse and placed it over her shoulder.

"Don't worry about it." He was relieved he wasn't the reason for her leaving.

"Is the Basilique Notre-Dame near by?" she asked him for directions since she had no idea where to go.

"Yes. It's ten minutes away. When you leave the hotel lobby go back to the Place d'Armes, the parkette on the rue Saint-Louis in front of the hotel. Take the rue du Trésor, it runs north on the west side of the Place d'Armes, to Rue Baude. It will be the first street you come to. Then turn left. You can't miss it," he instructed, giving the directions as simply as possible.

"Thank you. I think I've got it." She ran the directions over in her mind.

"You're welcome. I'll keep the coffee pot hot." It was his way of saying good-bye.

As she left the bar and went down the corridor, Monika considered what lay ahead of her. She worried about who might be there waiting at the basilica and if she was going into a trap. A confessional was an odd place to have a meeting, especially with an unknown stranger. She wondered who might know she was there in Québec City other than the man on the flight. She felt a chill as she realized she might be being watched even now. She was afraid to go but had no choice. The past twenty-four hours had all been absurdly surreal to her. Very much like a scene out of a cloak and dagger mystery. If it weren't for the fact that James was lying critically ill in a hospital bed with a gunshot wound, she would have thought this meeting nothing more than a foolish prank. But James was shot, Craig was dead and she was alone in Québec City searching for a secret list.

Chapter 16

"There. He's here." Stone's driver was overjoyed at the sight of Pierre Laroc's taxi. She pulled up along the arrivals section of the terminal and parked three cars behind him. Pierre's taxi was idling second in line waiting for passengers. This meant she would be rid of her crazy passenger right away.

"Now I don't want you getting any ideas about telling anybody about our little ride." Stone took his revolver out of his jacket and, leaning over the front seat, pushed its muzzle against the driver's neck. "Do you understand?"

"Yes monsieur. I would not think of such a thing." The woman was very nervous. As long as she got out of this in one piece she was not going to add insult to injury by reporting him to the police. It was clear to her the man would leave her alone as long as she kept silent.

"I'm glad. I wouldn't want to have to come back and find you. Just consider this a lesson in life." Stone leaned back, holstered his revolver in his jacket and pulled out two twenty-dollar bills from his pants pocket. "Here. This will cover your trouble." He threw the money on the seat next to her.

"Oui. That's fine." She saw the two bills fall beside her. Normally she would have charged fifty dollars for the round trip but forty was close enough under the circumstances. She was happy to be in one piece and rid of him. She did not move to pick up the money. She was waiting for him to get out.

He slid over to the passenger door next to the sidewalk and got out. He trusted the woman would not say a thing to anyone. But if she did, he wasn't concerned about the local authorities. C2 knew some very highly placed people in the police department. People whose names were on the list.

The terminal was not busy. He checked his watch. It was 10:50 am. He had lost Monika almost an hour ago. He needed to find her whereabouts quickly. He picked up his pace and walked up to Pierre Laroc's taxi. Looking through the car's windows he saw a large man wearing a Tyrolean style hat, sitting behind the wheel reading a newspaper and taking an occasional sip from a steaming cup of coffee. He opened the rear passenger door and got in.

"Pardon monsieur. Ce n'ai pas le taxi premiere dans le queue. Vous…" Pierre put down his paper and turned to face the passenger in the rear seat. The man looked like he was in the military. Pierre was intimidated by his mean appearance.

"Just drive," Stone interrupted, not allowing Pierre to finish his sentence.

"But sir. I am not the first taxi. The other drivers will report me. It is not permitted. You must take the first taxi. It is the law." Hearing Stone's southern American accent, Pierre was polite and switched to English.

"I said drive," Stone grated out. He was not asking. There was an implied 'or else' in his voice.

"If you insist." Pierre gestured with his hands and capitulated. It was obvious to him; his passenger was not in any mood to discuss it further. He had tried his best to enforce the rules but was not about to physically remove this individual from his taxi. If the other drivers complained he would explain to them why he had accepted the fare. Putting the car in gear, he turned out into the roadway.

"Where are we going?" Pierre tried to break the tension in his taxi by asking for a destination. He carefully juggled his coffee as he turned the steering wheel.

"Québec City," Stone answered monosyllabically. He looked through the taxi windows and checked to be sure nothing was amiss. He did not want any uninvited company on this trip.

"Any particular place in Québec City? It is a big place." Pierre's tone was sarcastic. His passenger was not making it easy for him. He wondered why he was being so vague. Usually passengers knew exactly where they wanted to go and had a name of a hotel or an address where they were going, ready.

"About an hour ago you drove a young woman—a blonde, pretty, into the city. I want to go where you dropped her." Stone leaned forward and stared into the rearview mirror.

Pierre was taken aback. So this was the man his lady passenger was afraid of. It was instantly apparent to him why she had been so afraid. Even he was not comfortable with this man.

"A woman? I think you are mistaken sir. I only just come on duty." He looked into his rear view mirror pretending not to understand, trying to protect Monika, but his eyes twitched when he caught the penetrating stare of his passenger glaring knowingly at him through the mirror. The terminal was getting farther behind and he was driving through the more desolate section of the airport roadway. There was no one nearby who could help if he stopped. He was on his own until he got closer to Saint Foy.

"Oh. That's too bad." Stone pulled out his revolver and, similar to the previous taxi ride, pushed its cold rigid muzzle into Pierre's neck.

"Hey. What're you doing? Don't shoot. Mon dieu." Pierre had not expected this type of behavior. He was not paid enough to risk his life over a fare. He started to come undone.

"Where did you take her? I won't ask again." Stone cocked the hammer of the gun.

"Okay. Okay. There's no need to get upset. I dropped her at the Château Frontenac. She's staying there. I just came back from there. I will take you. Free. But monsieur...please put the gun away. It is difficult to drive that way, you know?" Pierre was unnerved and babbling, his accent becoming stronger as he pleaded for his life. He didn't care about the money. All he wanted was to get out of this situation unharmed. Whatever this man wanted, he would do.

"That's better. No more tricks." He uncocked the revolver. The clicking sound made Pierre flinch. His reaction amused Stone. Putting the gun back in his jacket, he sat back in the passenger seat. "Remember. No tricks," he looked into Pierre's eyes through the rearview mirror, scolding him with his index finger. He was entertained by Pierre's fear of him.

"No sir. No tricks." Pierre was placated and would offer no further trouble.

Pierre was nervous. He concentrated on his driving and did not say a word. He kept an occasional eye on his passenger through the rearview mirror as he drove. He continued along the roadway and eventually came to the exit for Saint Foy, taking the same route he had driven with Monika.

They passed the same picturesque sights that she had admired, but Stone had been to Québec City many times and was not interested. His only concern was to find Monika. It was important he find her and make sure the list didn't fall into any other hands before he tracked her down.

Arriving at the Place d'Armes the taxi pulled into the arched courtyard entrance to the Château Frontenac and stopped in front of the lobby steps. Again the doorman, who a short while before had helped Monika from her taxi, came down and opened the passenger door for Stone. Stone knew how much to give the driver without asking. He paid him and got out of the taxi. Pierre was relieved and quickly drove off, wanting nothing more to do with the crazy man. He would report this incident to the authorities, after he had had a drink and calmed down. He would be sure to remember his passenger not only because of the gun but because he had given him exactly twenty-five dollars with no tip.

"Bonjour. Good morning sir," the doorman, in his usual pleasant way, greeted Stone. The Château Frontenac had high standards of conduct.

Stone ignored him and leapt up the stairs. He

was anxious to see if Monika had checked into the hotel. If she had, he knew she would not be far ahead of him. He would be able to reestablish his surveillance. Opening the door he hurried into the lobby and crossed over to the front desk. He knew the Château Frontenac well. The American Consulate was only half a block south along the Dufferin Terrace. He had been to the Château Frontenac many times for drinks at the bar.

"Good morning," he said to the same female clerk who had checked Monika in. "Can you tell me if a Monika Queller has checked in?" Though he knew many of the staff of the Château Frontenac, he did not know this young woman. She was new.

"Yes. She arrived a little while ago. She's in room 1720 but I think she's gone to the bar. You might catch-up with her there." The clerk was very friendly and accommodating. She assumed the man was Monika's boyfriend or husband.

"Thank you." He did not need directions. He went away from the front desk believing his luck had changed.

- - - - - - - - - - - - - - - -

Skinner's flight arrived five minutes ahead of schedule. By 11:05 am he was walking out of the tubular walkway into the main passenger area of the Québec City Airport terminal en route to the exit. He was dressed in business attire with a dark trench coat. He could have been mistaken for an important diplomat or government deputy minister. He walked confidently through the terminal. He was familiar with the airport from his weekly trips to the city. All he carried was his matte finished black leather attaché case.

He went right across the passenger area and headed through the sliding glass doors of the terminal to the cold Québec mid-morning. He was displeased by the bone chilling, dull day. He hoped it wouldn't snow before he finished his business there but there was the feel of it in the air. He didn't want to be stuck in Québec City any longer than necessary.

A few of his fellow passengers who disembarked ahead of him were getting into the taxis lined up at the sidewalk. Skinner walked out to the curb as a large black Ford Crown Victoria with tinted windows drove up and stopped beside him. A chauffeur dressed in traditional uniform and cap drove the Crown Vic. Skinner reached out, opened the rear passenger door and got into the vehicle. This was the Président's personal car.

The inside of the limo was plushly laid out in black leather. The passenger compartment was separated from the driver's by tinted glass. Skinner had no need to speak with the chauffeur. The chauffeur knew the procedure. Immediately after he got in and shut his door, the chauffeur pulled out into the roadway.

Skinner made himself comfortable. He put his

attaché case on his lap, released the two locks on either side of the leather grip and opened its lid. Inside on top of some folders was his cellular phone. Turning on the phone, he pressed the button to connect him with his voice mail service. He discovered he had two messages. One was from his secretary Marylyn and the other from Hackett. He smiled as he played back their messages. Apparently Ms. Queller had come to Québec City on the flight before him and Stone was hot on her trail. He felt it would be only a matter of time until he had possession of the list. Once C2 was protected he would dispose of James and Monika, who he believed were the only remaining people who might expose C2's activities. Whether they actually figured out what they had stumbled onto or not didn't matter. They were a threatening shadow that he didn't want hanging over him or C2. He disconnected from his mailbox then punched in another number and waited for the call to be answered.

"Hackett." Hackett was still in the hospital second floor waiting room.

"I just arrived in Québec City and got your message. How's Anstey doing?" Skinner, all business got right to the point. He wanted to confirm the good news, move ahead and settle the account with Mr. Anstey and Ms. Queller.

"I'm not sure, sir. They haven't brought him back from the operating room. He didn't look good going up," Hackett informed him quietly, not wanting to be overheard by any of the staff on the floor.

"Maybe they'll do the job for us. We don't need him alive anymore. If they bring him back, make sure he never wakes up," Skinner ordered.

"No problem sir. They won't suspect a thing. So, did Stone find Ms. Queller again?" Hackett was also relieved. He wasn't worried about killing James. It was up to Stone to take care of the girl and his to make sure James didn't survive. He had a special syringe in his pocket. Once he injected its contents into James' IV the lethal drug would do its work in a matter of seconds. He was more afraid of Skinner's reaction if Stone had lost Monika. Now that he had the go ahead, he assumed all was going as planned. Soon they would retrieve the list and all potential threats would be eliminated.

"What do you mean?" Skinner's confident tone changed.

"He lost her at the airport about an hour ago. I haven't heard from him yet. I assumed he called you." Hackett's voice betrayed his nervousness. He had spoken too soon.

"I haven't heard from him. Only you. What the hell's going on? Can't you guys get even simple things right?" Skinner raised his voice, disappointed by this turn of events. Every time he came close to finalizing things, one of these two screwed up.

"He said he had a lead. I'm sure he's found her by now," Hackett explained, trying to soften the blow. He was angry with Stone for putting him yet again in an awkward predicament with Skinner.

"Hold off on Anstey until we know about Ms. Queller. I'll see what I can do from this end." Skinner abruptly disconnected. Hackett was happy it was over even if it was for the moment. Though he had delivered the bad news it was his partner who had messed up. He would not want to be Stone right now.

Skinner punched in Stone's cellular phone number. As it rang he cursed his two field agents for being so inept. After this was over he would reassign them, permanently. He angrily waited for Stone to answer, not paying any attention to the progress of his ride into the city.

"Stone." The number being displayed on his screen revealed it was Skinner calling. He guessed why his boss was calling and put off answering as long as he could.

"Have you found her?" Skinner didn't have to say anything more to convey his anger. His four words cut into Stone.

"Not quite, sir. I'm at the Château Frontenac. She checked in an hour ago but she's not in her room." He prepared himself for what he knew would follow.

Skinner paused and considered his plan of action. There was no point in berating Stone. It would be counterproductive. He could reprimand him later after everything was resolved. At least he knew where Ms. Queller would end up. Now that he was in Québec City it would be easier to control the situation. He could get the help of the local police easily. Once found, Ms. Queller would not leave Québec alive, list or no list. He was growing tired of this game.

"Stay there. Let me know the second you spot her. And don't lose her again. She's probably got the list on her. When she comes back, find out. We've wasted enough time being nice. Let's get down to business. I'll see what I can do."

"Yes sir." Stone heard the click as Skinner disconnected. It did not go as badly as he had expected. He would remain in the lobby of the hotel and keep an eye out for Ms. Queller. He sat back into the comfortable leather couch at the end of the lobby next to the mezzanine stairs. He hoped it would not be a long wait. He was tired and hungry.

Skinner put his phone back into his attaché case and closed its lid. He needed to act rapidly. There was not much time left to secure the list and keep C2's secrets before his own deadline expired. He knew if he did not retrieve the list soon his career would be over. He had worked too hard and long to allow that to happen. He also wanted to find out who had betrayed C2 and caused all their upset. Whoever it was, once he found them they would suffer a long and excruciatingly painful death.

Within five minutes of hanging up from Stone, Skinner's car turned left off Grande Allée to rue des Parlementaires on the north end of the Parliament buildings, a stone's throw west of the Porte Saint-Louis and the old city of Québec.

The Parliament buildings were imposing with their light gray blocks and Second Empire style. The building consisted of four wings, each approximately one hundred meters long and four stories high. The Québec flag dominated the sky-line on the central tower with its oxidized green copper, turreted roof and crown designed wrought iron cupola. The tower rose four stories above the main building.

The back of the Parliament was not as elegantly decorated as the front facade, which contained twenty-two weathered, bronze statues of historically important Québec figures displayed in arched niches along its exterior. The building reminded one, in its small way, of the Palace at Versailles. The car turned into the 'Members Only' drive and passed a security guard who, recognizing the Président's car, waved them on through the members' entrance.

After the car stopped the chauffeur got out and hurried around to the other side of the car to open the passenger door.

"Thank you," Skinner said as he got out into the cold wintry air and crossed to the building's entrance. The chauffeur nodded, and without a word, got back into the car and drove off. It was not often that Skinner made the trip to the Président's office in the National Assembly. He did not like to be seen too often with the Président. He was concerned about the suspicions it might raise.

Skinner entered the north wing of the parliament buildings and walked down the ornately decorated corridor to the office of the Président of the National Assembly. Along the hallway were life-size portraits of past and present Québec parliamentarians. These classically rendered oil paintings made the building feel more like a museum or an art gallery than the seat of Québec provincial politics. Everything about its design exuded French culture including the intricate mosaic floor tiling, which was representative of an artisanship of a by-gone era.

Skinner came to a door at the end of the hall. He opened the door and stepped into the reception area of the Président of the National Assembly. It was much less ornately decorated than the hall.

"Bonjour," the receptionist, a dark haired woman in her thirties wearing a smart, stylishly cut gray suit, looked up and greeted Skinner.

"Bonjour. Morgan Skinner to see the

Président." Skinner crossed over to the woman's desk, which was cluttered with papers, keyboard and a large computer monitor. Her modern desk and computer were in stark contrast to the rest of the late Baroque-styled room.

"Oh yes Mr. Skinner. He's expecting you. Please go right in," she spoke beautiful English without a trace of an accent. She did not get up to show him the way or buzz the Président. The chauffeur had informed her of Skinner's arrival and before he had come into the building, she had notified the Président.

The Président, Claude Bonneau, was a man in his early fifties. He had been in politics most of his adult life representing Jonquière, a zealous separatist riding. Though he was an elected official, his position as Président was attained via political patronage, coming from the recommendation of the Premier of the province. He and the Premier were good friends. They had both helped to promote and expand the separatist movement until it resulted in its majority government today. It had been a tremendous achievement for Québec and, more importantly, C2.

Monsieur Bonneau was charged with the duty to oversee the daily running of the Parliament in and out of session assuring members' strict adherence to the Standing Orders. He was also responsible for the operation of the physical plant.

Also called the Speaker of the House, Bonneau

was an extremely powerful and influential person, commanding respect from all levels of government. Nothing could be done within the Parliament buildings without his knowledge or consent.

"Thank you." Skinner indicated to the secretary that he knew where to go, and walked the five feet beyond the receptionist's desk and opened the door that led into the Président's inner sanctum.

"Morgan. How are you? Come in. Take off your coat." Bonneau's face beamed, a welcoming look that was a practiced, polished, public persona. One that served him well in the public arena. His curly, light hair was heavily receding but he kept it long and over his ears, giving him the look of a younger, more vital man. He wore a neatly trimmed, graying moustache that he kept cut to the size of his upper lip. "Close the door and have a seat."

Bonneau half stood up from his chair behind his large Louis XIV wood desk. He directed Morgan with a small hand gesture to a matching high-back chair in front of the desk. The office was large and tastefully wallpapered in a rose color. Its floor was tiled the same as the corridor and its two large windows overlooked the members' drive that Skinner had just taken. A picture of the English Queen, which Skinner always found out of place taking into account Québec's turbulent history, hung on one wall to the Président's right and a smaller framed picture of the Premier hung on the left. On the wall behind the desk was a beautifully painted landscape of the Parliament buildings. It was all very impressive but the most striking feature of the room was the fifteen foot high ceiling, which gave the space a regal feel.

"Thank you Claude." Skinner took off his overcoat and threw it over the back of the chair and sat down facing Bonneau. He was wearing the same conservatively cut suit and white shirt as the day before. The only different part of his outfit was his blue striped tie.

"So what's going on?" Bonneau asked as he sat down. While he waited for an answer, he stretched over to the right side of his desk, picked up the phone and pushed a red button below the keypad. He waited for his secretary in reception to pick up.

"Michelle. No interruptions," he instructed then quickly hung up. "We won't be bothered," he assured Skinner. His secretary always followed his orders.

"I wish I knew. Someone made contact with Jeneau and gave him the list. So far there's only three parties involved that we know of. One's been taken care of but there could be more." Skinner brought Bonneau up to date. Though he was in charge of C2 and Bonneau fell under his control, he deferred to the Président for appearance's sake.

"The list is just names. Is it not? No one could possibly make a connection. Maybe we shouldn't be so worried about it? So they have a list of names—big deal." Bonneau didn't see the greater significance of the list.

"There shouldn't be anybody knowing or looking for such a list. We've been top secret since the beginning. Half of the current government is probably on that list. You know how suspicious Canadians are of the separatists. We don't want to start any unwarranted investigations. This is just another step along the way to expose us and we've worked too hard for too many years to finally get into political position and blow it now. It's been good for us.

Thirty years ago the Canadian dollar was worth seven cents more than the US's. Now it's only sixty-five cents. When you consider that seventy percent of trade is done between Canada and the US, it's easy to see how we continue to benefit. Our economy is booming. US interests control or have bought up businesses, products and land over the years at bargain prices without political issues of direct annexation, and we've managed to work in the background and slowly infiltrate Québec politics. No one has ever considered the possibility of what really was behind the separatist movement. Even during the FLQ crisis no one suspected other motives. They thought it was France or the Arabs interfering. No one would have believed it possible that a separatist government would come to power, a government controlled by us, but here we are.

We've managed to maintain political uncertainty for over thirty years. The instability caused by the constant bickering between English and French Canada has done nothing but benefit the US. This is the first indication in thirty years that someone might suspect foreign involvement in Québec politics beyond France. Who knows where it might lead. If they have a list it will be easier for them to zero in—then it's only a matter time before they begin to really understand what's been going on in Canada. Head office won't let that happen. Think of the political ramifications. We can't let that happen.

This is a very delicate situation, especially now before the Summit. Nobody wants this to blow up in our faces and you can be sure if it does we'll find ourselves branded as rogue independent radicals. We'll be thrown out into the cold and it won't be survivable. If we don't get the list, we're all in serious shit," Skinner explained.

"The Front Libération du Québec," Bonneau smiled. Skinner's reference to the FLQ made him nostalgic. He had been a young man in his early twenties and just starting his infiltration into the separatist movement. It had not been hard to incite some of the more radical Québécois of the time to action in the FLQ. "We really had people worried." He chuckled at the memories.

"Yes and that's the way we want to keep it. We don't want to go back to the days of the Canadian dollar being worth seven cents more than U.S.'s That will bust our economy and send Canada into a downward spiral that will ripple throughout the States. With the Premier stepping down we've managed to set up even more instability in Québec politics. We don't want people finding out that his best friend, his 'American' best friend, his confidante and advisor, is one of our moles and her name, like yours, is on the list. If this ever gets connected with the US government the impact would be felt for a century. It would undermine every relationship we have with every country on the planet. Our international position would be undermined. All because of a stupid list in a country that is so stupid to allow itself to be so vulnerable because of the French. They don't understand the half of it. With the list they might finally start putting it together. This goes far beyond Canadian-American friendship. It's in our national interest to keep C2 secret and operational. Just think of the other places in the world that the US is running similar operations. Forget about us. They'll all come under scrutiny." Skinner surmised correctly.

"So what do we do?" Bonneau accepted the severity of the situation.

"Jeneau did not have the list on him. He tried to

contact a CIA agent in Ottawa."

"The CIA?" Bonneau was alarmed and interrupted.

"Yes but he didn't get the list."

"But the CIA. If they're involved..." Bonneau did not finish.

"Its okay. Jeneau is dead and the CIA agent will be taken care of. But there's a woman, her name is Monika Queller, she's the agent's fiancée. I think she knows where the list is and she is a threat." Skinner stared at Bonneau.

"I don't understand. How can you not be worried about the RCMP or the CIA, but be worried about his fiancée?"

"Because she has come to Québec City and we lost her and there are only a few days before the Summit and we haven't retrieved the list. We don't know if she has turned to anyone for help. We don't know where she is. All we know is she checked into the Château Frontenac about an hour ago and then went out. We have to find Ms. Queller, find out where she has been, who she's talked to and get the list before it's too late." Skinner's agitation was growing. He did not like the uncertainty that Monika presented to C2.

"If she's in Québec City, we will find her." Knowing this woman was in his city, Bonneau felt more confident.

"I thought you might think that." Skinner reached for his attaché case, put it on Bonneau's desk and opened it. He took out the top green file folder and threw it over for Bonneau to peruse. “Here’s her file. Her picture’s inside.” Skinner sat back and watched Bonneau’s reaction.

Bonneau picked up the file folder and took out Monika’s eight by ten photo. “She is pretty. It’s too bad she got involved.”

“Don’t let her looks fool you. She’s smart and she’s had experience. It’s all in her file.” Skinner directed his attention to Monika’s dossier.

Bonneau quickly scanned through Monika’s background. “I see what you mean. She is an amateur detective with quite a track record. But I think she is no match for us.” He stretched over and picked up his phone, pressing the intercom button. “Michelle. Could you come and get something?”

As soon as Bonneau put his phone down there was a knock at his office door and his secretary Michelle meekly stepped in.

“Yes, sir?” she asked her boss, not liking to interrupt. Skinner sat silently in his chair and did not look at her. He kept his eyes forward and fixed on Bonneau.

“Get this to Paul Charbonne right away.” He held out Monika’s photograph. Michelle hurried across the room, stole a glance at Skinner and took the picture.

“I’ll do it right away, sir.” She turned and taking the picture with her, went out of the office, closing the door behind her.

"Paul Charbonne?" Skinner did not know him and was curious.

"He is the new Chief of Police. He's reliable and he owes me one." Bonneau picked up his phone and dialed Charbonne's private office number. He motioned for Skinner to remain quiet while he spoke to the Police Chief.

"Paul. It's Claude Bonneau." Bonneau, speaking in French, put on his gregarious public persona. Skinner listened to Bonneau's half of the conversation, filling the gaps with what he imagined was being said by the Police Chief.

"Yes. They're all fine, doing very well. How 'bout everyone in your house?" Bonneau listened to the Chief's answer.

"I'm sending you a photograph of a woman. She is in Québec City. Arrived today. Staying at the Château Frontenac. I need you to do me a favor." He fell silent again as he listened.

"No. No. It's a personal matter. It's a little embarrassing. She's disappeared. I need you to find her but I want to keep it quiet." He listened again as Charbonne asked a few questions.

"I'd rather not go into it over the phone, if you understand. Just keep it unofficial and take her to the cells in the Citadel when you find her." He listened again.

"Well. I appreciate your help. I'll wait for your call. Thanks Paul." Bonneau hung up.

"It's all taken care of. If Ms. Queller is in Québec then he will find her. He will send a man over to the Château Frontenac and get her picture out to every car. She won't be able to go anywhere without being seen." He had switched back to flawless English.

"Can he be trusted?" Skinner was a little uneasy getting such extensive police involvement.

"Yes. We are all one family here. This will be kept unofficial. No one will know. I have used him before and it has always worked out."

Bonneau did not doubt Charbonne's ability to help out while at the same time keep everything quiet and unofficial. Québec City was really a very small town where people scratched each other's backs no matter what the circumstances or legalities. It was all a matter of personal gain. The French Canadian had learned to live that way in order to survive under the regime of the Church and the officials of New France. They were used to dealing with each other in this manner. It was a way of life for them. It was not necessarily doing a wrong that was so bad, it was the getting caught doing it that was bad.

"What if she doesn't have the list?" Bonneau asked the unthinkable question.

"I'm sure she does or at least knows where to find it. She knows if she gives it to anyone else she, or more importantly, her fiancé's dead. She won't betray us. The only thing keeping them alive right now is her. She has something we want and knows it very well. That's why we can't waste anymore time. We have to find out if she has the list and where it is." Skinner did not accept the possibility that Monika did not have the list. Why else would she have come to Québec City so soon after her 'meeting' with him in the C2 office in Ottawa?

"She must realize all this. She won't just give up the list without assurances." Bonneau was right. Monika was probably afraid but not stupid. She would not just hand over the list without first guaranteeing she and her fiancé's safety: a safety that they all knew was impossible to guarantee.

"I know. It's the only wild card. That's why we have to get to her. If we give her too long to plan she will find a way out and someone to trust that may not be acceptable to us. If we can retrieve the list before she realizes its importance, then she and her fiancé's fate will be sealed."

"But what if she has already made contact with someone and figured it out?"

"Who?"

"I don't know. The RCMP, the CIA?" Bonneau guessed.

"She doesn't know anybody here. The only contact with the RCMP is dead and her fiancé is in a coma. She was smart enough to know that Jeneau did not know whom he could trust. She will be very cautious about whom to approach. Besides, she hasn't had long enough to react and she probably hasn't realized the ramifications of what she's involved with. No. I don't believe Ms. Queller has spoken to anyone yet. If she had we would have heard about it by now through one of our people. Over thirty years we've managed to place moles in every official department of the province. Ms. Queller has good instincts and would also know this. But if we give her enough time she will find someone and our advantage will change." Skinner, as usual, was correct in his analysis.

"So it comes down to time." Bonneau sat back in contemplation. If Skinner was correct, then both their futures hung precariously in a delicate balance controlled willingly or not by this woman.

"Yes. We have to find her before she finds them and it has to be done right away. I have my orders." Without telling him specifically who had given the orders, Skinner wanted Bonneau to understand they had come from above.

"Don't worry we'll find her. There isn't anywhere she can go. Charbonne will do the job quickly."

Knowing Skinner would not have allowed Ms. Queller to get out of his sight so easily, Bonneau wondered why he wanted his help. She would have been under constant surveillance and even now Skinner's men would be scouring the streets in search of her. The fact that he was here and asking for his help could only mean that he was having difficulties and was desperate. He had never known Skinner to ask for help in the past. It was a very risky endeavor. For Skinner to take the risk he must have reached a critical point of no return. Bonneau felt a chill of fear ripple through his body. He momentarily thought about spending the next twenty-five years in prison for treason and was horrified by the thought. Like Skinner, he would not allow anything, under any circumstances, to expose them.

"I see you understand." Skinner could tell what Bonneau was thinking. "It isn't a pretty picture, is it?"

"No. It isn't. Who do you think is responsible?" Bonneau asked again, now fully appreciating the necessity to discover and seal the leak. Just retrieving the list would not be enough. As long as there was a leak in C2 there would be others like Ms. Queller and Craig Jeneau.

"That's the problem. It could be anyone. It could be you," Skinner tested, staring across at Bonneau.

"Do you really believe that?" Bonneau was angered by Skinner's aspersion.

"No. But it is someone that we trust—that we know."

"But why now? After all these years." Bonneau was at a loss. The timing made no sense to him.

Surely there had been better opportunities in the past.

"I don't know. But it has to be someone close—someone who had access to the most sensitive information. That's why I'm handling this personally. I'll find out who it is and when I do..." Skinner didn't need to finish his sentence. Both men understood the severity of Skinner's justice.

They sat speechless for several moments considering their next moves. There was nothing else available for them to do. They could only wait until Ms. Queller was apprehended. Bonneau checked his watch. It was ten to twelve.

"It's almost twelve. Why don't we go to the members' restaurant and have some lunch. Michelle can notify me the minute she hears from Charbonne. Unless you have other plans?" Bonneau suggested. He needed a break from the stress of their meeting. He did not like the feeling of dread their conversation had stirred up within him. Lunch would be a welcomed distraction. He had no other commitments for the day. His priority was to help Skinner and extricate them from this difficult situation.

"That's a good idea. Maybe we'll have better news after lunch," Skinner agreed. He hoped Stone or the police would find Monika by then. Time was running out and, though he didn't show it, he was nervous.

"Good. Follow me." Bonneau got up from his

desk and crossed to his office door. Skinner got up and followed him.

Before opening the door Bonneau saw that Skinner was carrying his attaché case. "You can leave that here it if you like. It will be safe. No one will come in."

"Thank you. I think I will. I'll just get my phone." There was no need to lug the attaché case about. There was nothing in it of particular value and he would prefer not to carry his case with him through the building. Resting the case on the arm of his chair, he opened it and took out his phone. He placed the phone in his jacket pocket, locked the case, put it on the floor beside the chair and draped his overcoat over it.

Bonneau opened his office door and ushered Skinner out. The two men walked through the reception area.

"Michelle. I'll be in Le Parlementaire. You can reach me there when Charbonne calls," Bonneau informed his secretary in French. She was busy at her keyboard.

"Oui monsieur," She confirmed without taking her eyes off her screen.

Bonneau opened the outer office door and they stepped into the hallway. Le Parlementaire was in the central part of the building—a three-minute walk away.

Chapter 17

Monika hurried through the lobby of the Château Frontenac, fiddling with her coat to make sure it was done up as she walked to the hotel's inner courtyard driveway. She stopped in front of the lobby's revolving doors and, finding her hat, placed it snugly over her head and ears before going out. She was not used to such biting cold. It amazed her how quickly the low temperatures affected her. She had thought she would be able to spend a longer time exposed to the elements but she was mistaken and was happy she had brought her hat. A ten-minute walk outside under these conditions without the proper clothing could easily lead to frostbite.

Feeling better protected, she went down the stairs and turned right, headed down the driveway through the arched entrance to the rue Saint-Louis. She stood on the sidewalk next to the street and observed her surroundings. The Place d'Armes opened out in front of her. There were no other pedestrians walking about. She felt alone and her nervousness about what she might find at the basilica increased. She hoped there would be someone there who could help her if things went terribly wrong.

Distracted by this thought, she crossed rue Saint-Louis and started along the west sidewalk of the Place d'Armes along the rue du Trésor. A large four-storied sandstone building took up most of this side of the street rising majestically beside her. It looked like it had been built like all the other buildings around the Place d'Armes, at least a hundred years ago. Though it had been renovated and modernized, it still had an Old World charm. The building had an official austere design and, from a small plaque mounted on the wall, Monika noted it was indeed a government office building.

She picked up her pace to keep warm. Along the right side of the sidewalk opposite this government building was a circular kiosk displaying advertising and announcements. It had a tiny conical roof with a black and white checkered band running around its fascia board. The kiosk had a festive, carnival look. Four newly planted Maple trees ran along the edge of the sidewalk next to the rue du Trésor.

On the other side of the street was the Place d'Armes. Several turn-of-the-century styled gas lampposts lined the edge of the street. Monika recalled reading somewhere that Québec City put on a tremendous winter festival. She thought it would be nice to experience it one day with James, after he recovered. The thought of James brought her back to reality. She became emotional at the thought of losing him.She determinedly pulled herself together. She had to extricate herself from her present situation first, before she could make any plans for their future.

Continuing to the end of rue du Trésor she came to the second building that dominated the block. It was a rectangular light gray brick building with a high-pitched green copper 'A' roof. She thought it might be a church, but she could not find a sign to indicate what the building was. Monika gazed down rue Saint-Anne. It was a quaint European-style street lined with buildings on both sides, none of which were higher than three stories. Most of them had snow-covered, high-pitched roofs. Not much traffic passed along the road or the sidewalk so Monika crossed over to the continuation of rue du Trésor as it became a pedestrian walkway no wider than fifteen feet.

The short walkway was lined with half a dozen

artists standing out in the cold, under makeshift clear plastic canopies, displaying their paintings. But she did not allow it to distract her. She realized she must get to the Basilique Notre-Dame before it was too late. She wanted to get back to the hotel early and check out room 1720.

At the end of the walkway she came to rue Baude just as the bartender at the hotel had directed. Again this street, which ran east-west, was lined with quaint, picturesque, renovated turn-of–the-century buildings on the south side all closely jammed together. These buildings housed restaurants and shops of all sorts competing for the same tourist trade. Colorful awnings and signs hung from many of the buildings.

On the north side of the street, directly in front of her, was a large gray stone building. The structure was different from the tiny stores of the south side and contained many arched windows and a massive green copper roof. This building rose high above the stores and restaurants on the south side and had the look of a church. Monika assumed it was the back of the basilica. Her heart began to beat rapidly realizing she was almost at her destination. She took in a few short breaths of cold air to sober herself, resolved to meet whatever fate awaited her.

She turned left and went along the south side of rue Baude, deciding to find the front of the basilica and get a better look at the structure before going in. Within a couple of minutes she came to rue Sainte-Famille, which fronted the basilica and opened onto a parkette which was surrounded by four streets lined with tiny stores and restaurants. On the farthest side of the parkette, along the rue des Jardins, was what appeared to be another government building.

Monika surveyed the area. It was busier here than at the Place d'Armes. The parkette contained a large monument but she could not make it out. She stopped on the sidewalk and regarded the front of the Basilique Notre-Dame. Though the building was massive, taking up the whole block and towering above every other structure along the street and parkette, it was not as impressive a cathedral as she expected it to be. Its exterior was not at all ornate. In fact, the building was stark. On its right hand corner rising up four stories was a circular bell tower. It had a badly oxidized copper arched cupola that was open to the elements and a metaphor for the declining power of the Catholic Church in Québec. On its left corner rising up three stories was a rectangular tower, with arched windows in each of its three stories. In between these two towers the center of the basilica offered two large arched doors as its main entrance. Above the entry, running the complete height of the second and third story, was an arched stained glass window with a Romanesque brick facade above it.

Monika crossed the street and headed to the main doors. When she opened the door and stepped into the building she came into a small anti-room. She turned right and went through another set of doors that led into the church. In contrast to its stark, plain exterior, the basilica's interior was striking in its late baroque design. She stood amazed, absorbing the marvelous spectacle.

Directly opposite the entry was a small chapel and forty or fifty burning candles in small opaque red containers were arranged on a table. Though she was not Catholic, she understood that the candles were lit in memory of departed loved ones.

To her left was the center aisle of the basilica. There must have been at least fifty rows of boxed–in wood pews running the length of the church leading to an ornately decorated dais and altar. Gold leaf adorned the altar and its arched pillars, reflecting the lights in the ceiling and giving the area a yellow glow.

Several feet to the left of the dais and altar the pulpit rose five feet above the pews. It had an intricate and imposing design and was also laden in gold leaf. The basilica impressed anyone entering its doors with its wealth and the power of the Catholic Church in New France.

Along the east wall of the church was a narrow aisle adjacent to the row of pews to the left of the center aisle pews. Adorning the wall of the east aisle was a set of stained glass windows, each was a priceless work of art, rich in color and religious motif. A marble baptismal sat along this side of the basilica.

Monika's eyes were drawn upward to the main arched ceiling of the basilica. She had never seen anything like it in North America. It was brightly and ornately decorated, instilling in her a humble but uplifting feeling. The arches of the ceiling led visually to the right side of the church and the west aisle, and another set of the stained glass windows.

At the far end of the aisle to the right of the altar Monika saw a confessional constructed of dark wood. She had found her destination.

She looked around the church and saw no one else around. She was completely alone, though she felt as if she were being watched. She stepped past the entrance, careful not to make too much noise on the hard floor with her boots, and took the aisle on the right hand side. She did not remove her hat. Somehow she felt she should leave it on inside such a traditional, sacred place.

Walking at a normal pace she carefully checked out the basilica for any sign of tourist or priest as she went up the aisle. About ten feet in front of the confessional she came to a crypt. A lifelike bronze statue of one of the early bishops of the basilica was stretched out along the marble sarcophagus. The statue was beautifully carved and realistically detailed. He was sleeping with his hands held in prayer. It certainly was a work of art but Monika found it creepy. It gave the church the feel of a mausoleum. She hurried past the crypt and came to the confessional.

The confessional had two doors. She slowly opened the door on the right, fearing that she might find someone inside. To her relief, the tiny cubicle was vacant and she stepped inside. She couldn't help but think that when this confessional was originally built the people must have been small. The space was very cramped. She sat down on an uncomfortable old wood chair and looked at a small-screened eye level opening to the cubicle on the other side, where she imagined a priest would discreetly listen to parishioner's confessions. She quietly closed the door. A dim twenty-watt bulb mounted in the ceiling of the cubicle, provided an eerie illumination. She felt claustrophobic and unsettled.

She sat there for several minutes wondering what she was meant to do. Sitting there alone in the silence, surrounded by the smell of wood mingled with incense, she began to relax thinking perhaps the note she had received in the bar really had been nothing more than a silly prank. Someone had obviously been playing a game with her.

Just as she was about to give up her vigil and go back to the hotel, she heard the door on the other side of the confessional open and close. Someone sat down on a chair in the other cubicle. She tensed, confronted with the reality of her situation. This was not a prank. Someone really was on the other side of the confessional. She thought it might be a priest who, seeing her come into the basilica, had come to hear her confession. She sat and waited nervously, not wanting to be the first to speak.

"Ms. Queller?" It was a man's voice. He sounded young and soft spoken.

"Yes?" She remained seated but tried to squint through the screen to see who was on the other side. However, the screen mesh was too dark and prevented her from seeing more than the man's shadow. She knew she did not know him or she would have recognized his voice.

"Sorry to meet you this way. I thought it would be safest for both of us." The man was well spoken and seemed to have a slight French accent.

"Who are you?" she asked cautiously. She did not want to say too much until she had a better understanding of who he was and what he wanted. She was surprised to find she was no longer afraid.

"My name is François Jolliet." He was also cautious. He was trying to feel her out.

"What do you want?" she asked outright in an attempt to get this over with and get back to the reason for her being in Québec City—finding whatever Craig had hidden.

"I'm with the Canadian Security Intelligence Service. I'm investigating a conspiracy involving the Québec government and I think you're involved," he answered matter-of-factly and to the point.

"Who?" Monika did not understand.

"CSIS. It's like your FBI and CIA. We're the investigative arm of the RCMP," he explained.

"I don't know anything about a conspiracy." She strained to get a look at him through the screen but was not successful. She could smell his musky aftershave lotion. She wondered if there really was an organization in Canada called CSIS or if this was just another red herring. Maybe this was just another part of the game being played by the people who had abducted her in Ottawa in order to get what they wanted.

"Maybe not. But I believe Craig Jeneau and your fiancé did," François continued. He wasn't sure if Monika was telling the truth but he gave her the benefit of the doubt. All the research he had on her indicated she was nothing more than a friend of Craig Jeneau's and the fiancé of his contact James Anstey.

"You know them?" Monika was surprised. She began to believe that perhaps François was who he claimed to be. If that was the case, he might be of some use to her.

"Not personally. We've been running an operation over the last few months and came across Craig Jeneau. We've been keeping an eye on him."

"But Craig's dead. If you've been watching, why didn't you stop it?" Monika was perturbed. She wondered why Craig was allowed to die and James be so badly injured. She questioned why CSIS had not intervened earlier.

"Things went wrong. We didn't expect it. By the time it happened it was too late. I'm sorry." He understood why she was upset. He knew that her fiancé was in the Ottawa Civic ICU on the critical list. But his job was to observe and do nothing until he could get evidence to build their case. He did not want to frighten those involved into hiding.

"So why should I help?" Since he had not been able to do anything for Craig or James she didn't see thc point in making herself more vulnerable.

"We suspect the Canadian International Institute in Ottawa is involved," he expanded for her benefit.

"I don't understand?"

"They are the people who abducted you. I saw them take you to their office on Sparks Street Mall."

"What?" She did not know what to say. She had not known the name of her abductors or whom they represented. She fell silent and began to piece it together. François knew more than she expected.

"Yes. We have their office under surveillance. They call themselves C2. We're not quite sure who they are but we think they have a connection to the US, maybe the CIA. From what we can tell you have something they want and we'd like it before they get it." He understood her silence. He appreciated it must be a tremendous shock for her to realize what she was in the middle of.

"I didn't know. Is that why they killed Craig and tried to kill James?" She was appalled that her own government might be involved in such a despicable plot.

The events of the last few days were beginning to make sense to her. The information on the list had to be very incriminating. She now grasped the desperateness of her predicament. There would be no way C2 would allow her or James to survive after they had retrieved the list.

"Yes. Whatever Craig stumbled on, it's big. Do you know the whereabouts of their list?" He let her know he was aware of the list. He knew of the list by the bugs he placed in the C2 office and the pay phone outside the coffee shop.

"No. I'm not sure. I think I might know where Craig hid it. That's why I'm here in Québec City. But I'm being followed and I haven't found it yet." She wasn't sure how much more CSIS or François really knew or how much he was bluffing. She decided to remain vague and not tell him everything yet. She wasn't sure if she could really trust anyone. After all, Craig had turned to James and not CSIS. There had to be a reason why he hadn't gone to them. Prior to making any decision she wanted to find whatever Craig had hidden in the Château Frontenac before she informed anyone of its whereabouts or contents.

"Yes I know. The men following you work for C2. One of them is here and the other is at the Ottawa Civic keeping an eye on your fiancé. We've been keeping tabs on them for a couple of days." François was trying to gain her confidence. It was imperative that she trust him and give him whatever Craig had hidden as soon as she found it. He didn't want to press her and ask where she thought the list was hidden. It would make her distrust him. Eventually she would have faith in him.

"James. Is he safe?" Her concern for James remained her overriding concern. She felt trapped. If her abductors discovered she was talking with the authorities, James' life would be worthless. Until she found a way out of this mess she had to be certain not to allow herself to be seen talking to anyone who might cause her abductors to panic. "If they know I'm talking to you, they'll kill him."

"I suspected as much. That's why I asked you to meet me here. No one will see us here and I don't think you were followed," François reassured her.

"No. I think I lost him. But I'm sure it won't be for long. So what do we do now?" Monika wanted to see what François had in mind. She was still trying to decide if she could trust him. Even if she decided she could, she was not going to risk James' life or her own until she had an escape planned. She knew how government agencies tended to take care of themselves first before worrying about others.

"I want to keep in touch. When I leave, I'm going to put the number where you can reach me on a piece of paper on the chair. Give me a minute to go and then come get it. As soon as you find the list, call. I can help. C2 won't leave any potential witnesses alive." He wanted to underscore the seriousness of what she was involved in.

"As soon as I find it, I'll call." Monika wasn't sure she would call, but she knew this would placate him until she could decide.

Monika heard François open his confessional door and leave. Their meeting was over as abruptly as it had begun. She found herself wondering what François looked like. She wondered, when she finally met him, if he would resemble what she imagined him to be like from his voice, aftershave and footsteps.

The sound of François's leather shoes on the floor of the basilica echoed and grew fainter until there was no longer any trace of him. Monika hoped no one had followed her to the basilica or seen her with François. She got up, opened her confessional door and stepped out into the openness of the church. She quickly looked around to see if anyone was there but saw no one. The church was quiet. She wondered if she had just imagined the conversation she had had inside the confessional with François.

"Maybe," she thought in denial, "It was a dream." She didn't want to accept how deeply entangled in a dangerous web of conspiracy she had become.

She opened the door to the other side of the confessional, which was a mirror image of hers, and looked in. On the wooden seat of the chair was a piece of paper. She reached in and picked up the paper. Written in the same black ink as the note she had been given in the bar of the Château Frontenac were eleven numbers. She did not recognize the area code. The conversation with François had been real.

Putting the paper in her right hand jacket pocket, she closed the door and crossed to the center aisle and turned to face the altar. She paused and then knelt down on one of the two rows of carpeted steps that led up to and ran the length of the dais. She crudely made the sign of the cross in the manner she believed it should be done with her right hand in front of her. She bowed her head and began a silent prayer. She was not Catholic, nor much of a churchgoer but she did not think God would mind.

- - - - - - - - - - - - - - -

At the time Monika was saying her prayer in the Basilique Notre-Dame, James was in the operating room with a team of three surgeons, an anesthetist and nurses frantically working to save him.

"How's his pressure?" Dr. Keene, the chief surgeon, fully outfitted in his operating scrubs and using a pair of bloody rib expanders, looked over his patient to the anesthesiologist, and asked. There was a tinge of nervousness in his voice. He was afraid James was slipping beyond his ability.

A large bloodstained sheet was draped over James, hiding him from view. Dr. Keene had cracked open his chest in a desperate effort to find and stop the cause of the internal bleeding threatening James' life. The rectangular opening in the sheet revealed the bloody mess in James' chest cavity. They had been operating for an hour and half and had still not stabilized him.

The other assisting doctors were similarly stressed. The operating room was brightly lit by a large powerful lamp over the operating table. The room was jammed full of monitors and equipment. Several nurses were checking the equipment and assisting in the background.

"He's barely holding on. I don't think he

can take much more of this," the anesthesiologist evaluated James' condition. Though he was completely concealed behind his operating gown and mask, his tenseness was apparent as he glanced at the chief surgeon.

"Just a few minutes more and I'll have it. Suction," Dr. Keene ordered the nurse who was assisting him.

The sound of suctioning filled the room. Everyone fell silent in an effort to better concentrate on the work of saving their patient, not one of them certain if he was strong enough to withstand the surgical trauma. James had been through too much over the last twenty-four hours. They were doing their best but their combined surgical skill, talent and technology was stretched to its limits and their effectiveness was uncertain. They felt frustrated by their human shortcomings. They worked feverishly in a perfect choreography, but James was in need of a far greater level of performance than any of them were able to achieve.

Chapter 18

Monika checked her watch. It was 11:25 am. The lobby of the Château Frontenac was luxurious with its paneled mahogany walls. She noted what she thought was a man reading a newspaper sitting on the couch at the north end of the lobby by the staircase leading to the mezzanine, but was not able to identify him as he was concealed behind the newspaper. She hoped her room was ready and her key would allow her entry. She wanted to thoroughly search the room, find whatever Craig had hidden, call the hospital to check on James' condition and then get everything over with. She was not clear how she was going to proceed once she found the list; she just wanted to get back to

Ottawa and be by James' side. She needed to be close to him. She resented her abductors for forcing her on this journey.

Crossing through the lobby to the elevators Monika pressed the black plastic call button mounted on the wall on a brass plate in between the elevator doors and waited. She was distracted by her thoughts.

She ran her meeting with François Jolliet in the basilica over in her mind. It had been so unusual. So cloak and dagger. She felt as if she had stepped into an 'Agatha Christie' or 'Murder She Wrote' mystery novel. She wondered why Craig, an inspector in the RCMP, had not trusted CSIS, why he had called upon James to help him and not someone else in Canada? CSIS was the investigative arm of the RCMP. It would be natural for Craig to confer with them. She also found it hard to believe that the US government would be so actively involved in Québec politics. If what François said was true and C2 was somehow connected to the US, then she understood why her abductors wanted to retrieve their list and protect not only themselves but also their political masters. Over the years she had begun to realize the clandestine manner in which certain government departments operated. It was not impossible for such an operation to be run in Canada, but she would never have imagined that her government would involve itself in subverting Canadian political stability as they commonly did in developing nations throughout the world. Unlike those developing countries, Canada was not a threat to the United States in any way whatsoever. In fact, on the surface at least, Canada was essentially American. Even Québec had adopted many aspects of American culture. The cars, the style of dress, were all of American influence. Monika did not feel she was in a foreign country but rather another State. A State that was perhaps unique but still American. It was disgusting how her own country would be so imperialistic to such a good neighbor and friend.

The elevator doors opened. The elevator was empty. Monika stepped in and pressed the button for the seventeenth floor. The interior of the elevator was laid out in mahogany panels with brass trim. Everything was restored and in impeccable condition. The highly polished brass doors reflected her image perfectly. As the elevator effortlessly floated up, a large Art Deco dial, situated above the doors, displayed the floor numbers. For some reason riding up in this elevator reminded her of a hotel in Rochester New York where she had gone as a young girl to visit family friends with her parents. The hotel there had been of the same era as the Château Frontenac and equally as well maintained. The memory restored a warm, safe feeling within her. She hoped it was a sign of good things to come.

Arriving at the seventeenth floor, the elevator slowly stopped. The trip had taken less than a minute. The elevator doors opened and Monika stepped out into the corridor. It was the same corridor that Craig, disguised as a hotel employee, had pushed the housekeeping cart along several days ago. From the artistically swirled plaster ceiling along its wood-paneled walls, to the deep maroon carpet, Monika was impressed by the corridor's Old World charm. On the wall opposite the elevator was a brass plaque displaying directions to the rooms on the floor. 1720 was to her left.

While the elevator doors closed, Monika walked down the hall looking for room 1720. The floor was very quiet. She had expected to run into more people. The winter months before the carnival was not the prime tourist season in Québec City.

Coming to the end of the hall Monika stopped at the last room. The number on the solid mahogany door was 1720. Surprisingly she was not nervous or concerned about being followed. She was happy to be close to discovering Craig's hiding place of the list. She took the key the hotel clerk had given her from her purse and placed it into the narrow slot at the top of the door handle. She hoped the room was ready and the key would work. She did not want to spend any more time waiting. The sooner she found the list the sooner she could get back to James. A small light in the door handle changed from red to green unlocking the mechanism. She pushed down the handle and opened the door. She was relieved. It was nice to see that the hotel housekeeping was efficient. She went into the room, closing the door behind her.

The interior of the room was tastefully laid out. To her immediate left was a modern bathroom. Its door was open and Monika could see it was pleasantly decorated in off-white. A large mirror filled the wall it shared with the hallway outside. Immediately adjacent to the bathroom door was a small open concept closet. She walked the five feet from the room door past the closet into the room.

The room was not large but it was cozy. A set of off-white patterned cotton drapes framed the large picture window. A small desk with a high back wood chair neatly tucked under it, was kitty cornered to the right of the window. On the wall adjacent to the desk was a mahogany colored wood armoire in which she saw the television set. Next to the armoire was an ornate gold-framed mirror. A large king-sized bed with a dark patterned bedspread that she did not particularly like, was up against the wall opposite the mirror and took up much of the room's available space. She walked over to the bed, took off her jacket, along with her purse and threw them on the bed. Placing her hands on her hips, she examined the room, wondering where Craig could have hidden the list.

There did not seem to be any obvious hiding place.

Not wanting to squander her time, Monika began to search. She carefully scrutinized every aspect of the room. Not really knowing what she was looking for, she didn't know where to start. She decided her best approach was to methodically start at one corner and go through every item in the room. She went over to the left side of the window and pulled back the drapes. Checking the wall and floor behind it, she found nothing. She looked up to the valance to see if anything might be hidden there. Other than the curtain rod there was nothing.

She continued along the wall. Under the large picture window, which looked out over the snow-covered property of the Château Frontenac fronting Dufferin Terrace, the Old City and the St. Lawrence River, Monika examined the room's heating unit. She got down on her hands and knees and carefully searched underneath and around the unit but there was nothing other than the freshly vacuumed carpet. There was no way anyone could have hidden anything inside the metal box that housed the unit against the wall under the window.

She kept moving along the carpeted floor on her hands and knees to the curtain on the other side of the window and desk. She carefully searched the underside of the chair and desk in case something was taped to them. Standing up, she opened each of the drawers but only found the hotel guest stationery and a bible. She placed her hand deep into each drawer, feeling the insides, but again found nothing. She rifled through the hotel information binder sitting on the desktop but other than information on the hotel there was nothing of interest.

Similar to her search of the desk, she thoroughly went through the armoire. Inside the armoire a twenty-inch television sat on the top shelf above three drawers. She pulled out each of the drawers and meticulously inspected them as well as the space inside the armoire behind them but again there was nothing. She was beginning to panic.

"Maybe someone has already found Craig's hiding place and the list," she thought. "Maybe housekeeping stumbled upon it while cleaning the room." If that were the case, what would she do next? How would she find the list? She wondered.

She tried to calm down, telling herself not to let her imagination runaway with itself, nor to give up on the search so easily. Finishing with the armoire, she walked over to the closet and checked the shelf above coat rack. She was again disappointed.

Turning on the lights next to the closet, she went into the bathroom. Pausing a moment before entering, she visually scanned the vanity to her left, the toilet several feet in front of her and the bathtub / shower unit to her right. The only obvious place to hide something in there was the toilet. Not liking the idea of searching the area around the commode, she crossed over to the toilet and lifted its heavy ceramic tank lid, thinking something might be hidden within it. The lid clanged loudly, hitting the tank as she lifted it. She looked inside and, finding nothing out of the ordinary, placed the lid back carefully. She leaned over trying to see behind the tank where the toilet attached to the wall but was not able to see much from her standing position. She got down on her knees next to the toilet hoping housekeeping did their job and had thoroughly cleaned the area. The white ceramic floor tile was cold. Without touching the toilet, she peered under and examined the space behind the toilet. Again she found nothing.

Staying on her hands and knees she crawled over to the vanity that ran under the mirror and checked under it. The underside of the vanity was filthy. It was not a part of the room that most guests would see or a place that housekeeping would consider cleaning. It ruined the hotel's grandeur for her.

Standing up, she checked herself in the mirror. Her hands were dirty and her black tights were soiled around her knees with fluff from the bathroom floor. She turned on the gold taps and, picking up a bar of soap beside the sink, unwrapped it and watched her hands. The dirt came off quickly. She turned off the taps and dried her hands taking a small white cloth that was folded in the shape of a swan placed next to the sink and then used it to brush away the dirt from her knees. She checked her face and hair and, satisfied, walked out of the bathroom.

The only place she had not checked was the bed. She went over to the bed and took her hat, coat and purse from it and threw them over the back of the chair, which she had pulled away from the desk during her search. She lifted up the bedspread and ran her hands over the sheets to see if she could feel anything. The bed was freshly made and the sheets were crisp. It was not likely that Craig would have hidden anything under the sheets.

Moving back she got down on her knees and lifted the mattress from the box spring. The mattress was awkward and heavy for her. Holding it up with one hand she managed with difficulty to check underneath. She skirted around the bed to be sure none of it was left unchecked. Finding nothing she put the mattress back down and lifted the pillows. Again there was no result. She stretched across the bed and looked behind the mahogany headboard and looked up. Seeing a small-framed landscape picture of the Québec area on the wall above the bed she became excited. She stood up on the soft bed and lifted the painting slightly from the wall and peeked behind it. Her hopes were dashed.

Getting off the bed, she got down on the carpeted floor and proceeded to look under the bed. Though an unlikely place to hide something, it was worth checking. To her amazement halfway under the bed was a piece of crumpled paper. She again became excited, thinking it was the list.

Realizing the paper was beyond her reach, she lay down on the floor and stretched her arm under the bed. Gradually she managed to reach the paper and pulled it into the light of the room. She sat up and leaned against the bed holding the paper in her hands. She straightened it out only to find it was garbage. It was information from a tour company about trips to the Ice Hotel fifteen minutes northeast of Québec City.

She got up off the floor and sat down on the bed holding the piece of paper in her right hand by her side. She was very disappointed. There were not many places in a hotel room to hide something. The thought that someone had already found Craig's hiding place was becoming a stronger possibility in her mind but something inside was telling her not to give up; that if she continued searching she would stumble upon it but where? She couldn't for the life of her figure out where it might be hidden. She had searched everywhere and there was not much time left before her abductor's deadline. She worried if she did not find the list then her abductors might do something to James. James. In all the turmoil she had forgotten to call the hospital back.

She got up from the bed and went over to her purse on the chair in front of the desk. She rifled through her purse until she found her cell phone. The phone was on and the signal strength strong. Staring out the window to the river, she pushed zero and waited for the operator. She was not worried about the language difference, knowing now that Québeckers would speak both French and English.

"Bonjour…" the phone rang twice and was answered by a French Canadian operator at the cellular phone company.

"Bon sure. I'd like the number for the Ottawa Civic Hospital, sil-voo-play." Monika tried to improve her French without much success.

"I'll connect you to the Ottawa operator. Please wait," the operator answered in English.

"What city, please," after several moments another operator answered in English.

"Ottawa," Monika answered.

"Go ahead," the operator said matter-of-factly.

"The Ottawa Civic Hospital, please."

"Would you like me to connect you? There's a fifty cent charge."

"Yes please. Thank you," Monika agreed and waited while the operator connected her.

"Ottawa Civic Hospital," a switchboard operator at Ottawa Civic answered.

"The Intensive Care Unit, please."

The switchboard operator immediately directed the call to the ICU nurses station.

"ICU." Nurse Geena, early for her shift, was sitting in the nurses station by herself. She was on a rotating shift this week. One day starting early, one day starting late, in twelve-hour shifts. It was hard on her system but she got several days off in a row because of the schedule and she liked the trade-off.

"Hi Geena. It's Monika Queller. I'm calling about James. How's he doing?" Monika recognized Geena's voice and was pleased that she had answered the phone. She did not like the nurse from the morning shift. Geena was more compassionate and friendly.

"Oh Ms. Queller. Didn't anybody call? He was taken up to surgery this morning." Geena was kind and apologetic.

"What? But he was all right this morning. What happened? Is he okay?" Monika held her breath expecting to be told terrible news. A sudden wave of emotion overpowered her. A tear fell from her eye to her cheek. She wiped it away.

"He came out of surgery all right. He's in recovery now. I'm just coming on my shift and I don't have all the details, but it looks like he had a relapse this morning and they had to operate. He should be back in ICU later this afternoon." Geena was embarrassed that no one had called her earlier. It was unforgivable under the circumstances. After their conversation she would find out who was responsible and have strong words with them.

"Thank God. I'll be there soon as possible. Would you call me if there's any change?" Monika was relieved. She didn't want to tell Geena she was in Québec City. Though she didn't have to, she felt awkward and didn't want to explain. She felt guilty for having left James but there had been no choice. She wanted to get back to him right away but before she could do that, she knew she had to find the list.

"Yes. I'm on until midnight. Is there a number, in case I need to reach you?" Geena wanted to make sure she had her phone number.

"Yes." Monika gave Geena her cell phone number. "Thank you. Please call me if there is even the slightest change."

"I will. Don't worry," Geena reassured her.

"Thank you." Monika disconnected. She began to weep. The stress and strain had gotten to her. Crossing over to the bed she lay down and rested her head upon the fluffy pillow. She wished she could talk to someone but there wasn't anyone there to talk to. She felt an urgency to leave Québec City. The only thing stopping her was the list. She had to find the list. It was the only way she could get back to James.

After several minutes, Monika calmed down. She would be of no help to herself or James if she did not take control of her emotions. She put her feelings to one side and turned her attention back to the search for the list.

"It has to be in the room somewhere. It has to be here. I must have overlooked something," she told herself as her eye caught a reflection from the mirror opposite her. She was then drawn by the mirror's ornate gold leaf frame. It was the only piece in the room that did not completely fit in with the decor. It was of a different period and far more decadent than the rest of the furnishings. She wondered if all the rooms here had such a mirror or if this was the only one. She lay there thinking when it dawned upon her that the only thing she had not checked in the room was the mirror.

Jumping up from the bed she went over to the mirror. She was excited. For some reason she believed she would find whatever Craig had hidden there. Very carefully she scrutinized the mirror and ran her fingers around the surface of the frame. As she ran her fingertips along the surface she noted the consistency of its touch. She ran her fingers along both sides and then along the top of the frame. About halfway along the top on the right hand side near the back of the frame was a small imperfection. Not being able to see the imperfection, she focused her touch on it. It was a small smooth circular surface and had a different texture than the gold leaf paint of the frame. She needed to have a look.

She got the chair from the desk, leaving her coat and hat draped over its high back, and placed it in front of the mirror. She then climbed on the chair and looked down at the top of the mirror. On the right hand side of the mirror pushed in close to the wall was a brass colored thumbtack. It looked like it had recently been put there. She examined the tack. A thin piece of clear fishing line was wrapped around the tack and ran behind the frame. She instantly knew this was it—this was Craig's hiding place! She believed it was the only reason to find a piece of fishing line attached to a mirror in a hotel room.

Balancing herself on the chair, she pulled the frame away from the wall and pulled up the fishing line. There was definitely something attached to it. She carefully lifted the line and discovered a Kraft nine-by-twelve inch envelope.

Grabbing hold of the envelope she ripped it from the line and got down from the chair. She was proud of herself for finding Craig's hiding place. She opened the envelope and looked inside. Inside was a single piece of paper. She pulled the paper out and examined it. At the top of the paper was the blue logo of the Québec National Assembly and the Office of the Président. Typed on one side of the paper was a list of names. Monika read through the names. Next to each name was listed what she assumed were the departments or positions each person held in the government. One or two of the names had no department or position listed next to them. She did not recognize any of the names, but from her conversation with François Jolliet, she understood what this list was. She now knew why her abductors at C2 were worried. In their position she would also be concerned. It was a list of all the operatives within the Québec government. Whoever controlled this list could inflict a lot of damage and cause tremendous embarrassment to the United States government.

Monika was pleased she had found the list but was saddened by the cost exacted upon Craig, James and herself for becoming aware of its existence. She marveled at how such a simple piece of paper could have had such a devastating impact on people's lives. She was not sure how she herself would use the list but she knew she had to do something. She now understood how Craig must have felt when he realized the importance of the list. She was now also faced with the same dilemma.

Sitting down in the chair, she checked the time on her watch. She had been searching for thirty-five minutes. It was 12:15 pm. She stared at the list considering her options. She knew she had to call her abductors and let them know she had the list in order to prevent any harm befalling James, but she also knew she could not just give it to them. Once they had the list she and James would be eliminated. She wondered if she could trust François Jolliet and CSIS. She had her doubts. The only thing she was certain about was she had to decide quickly. The choices she would make in the next few minutes would have a critical impact on her future.

Chapter 19

Stone was sitting in the lobby. He had seen Monika enter the hotel through the revolving lobby doors and quickly picked up a newspaper to hide behind so she would not see him. Fortunately she did not recognize him. He watched being careful not to alert her to his presence as she crossed over to the elevators and entered into a waiting car. Once the doors closed he put down his paper and observed the floor numbers on the dial over the doors. The numbers steadily rose until finally stopping on the seventeenth floor. Monika was going to her room.

Stone remained seated, considering what he should do. He was in no hurry to confront Monika. He did not know where she had gone after losing him or for what purpose, nor did he know if she had the list. The list was very important. He decided to wait and see what happened. His orders from Skinner were very clear. He was to find Ms. Queller and keep her under surveillance.

Skinner wanted the list returned. There was no point in phoning him to let him know he had found her until he had a better idea as to whether or not it was in her possession. As long as Monika was in her hotel room there was nothing for he or Skinner to worry about. There was no way for her to exit the hotel without him spotting her. As long as she didn't suspect she was being followed again, she would have no reason to be suspicious or evasive. If she did leave the hotel Stone believed she would exit the way she had come in via the lobby. He would wait a half an hour and then make his move. He wanted to give her as much time as possible to find the list. Without the list the whole purpose of his being here was wasted. He hoped she had the list.

About forty minutes after Stone had first sighted Monika, a police officer dressed in the dark uniform of the Québec City police entered the lobby from the street and walked over to the front desk. The police officer was young and Stone thought he might be a rookie in his early twenties. He had a brush cut and a very muscular physique. His appearance reminded Stone of a German storm trooper from World War II. Stone immediately perked up. This was not an everyday occurrence in a hotel. The police officer had an official air and appeared to be in the hotel on business. All Stone's senses told him something was up.

The officer removed his hat and spoke with the female hotel clerk behind the front desk. The clerk checked her computer and then wrote something down on a piece of paper and gave it to the officer. The officer thanked her and walked over to the elevators and pushed the call button. Stone got up from his couch and casually walked over to the front lobby doors, while the policeman waited for the elevator. The officer did not notice him. He was focused on the dial above the elevator doors.

Stone looked through the lobby doors to the hotel's driveway and saw an empty police car parked with its engine running outside. Exhaust was billowing out its tailpipe. Moving to one side of the doors, he returned his attention to the lobby and watched as the elevator arrived and the police officer got in. The elevator doors closed. He watched the dial above the elevator hoping that the officer was not going to the seventeenth floor. To his disappointment the elevator stopped on the seventeenth floor—Monika's floor. It was all too coincidental for him. He suspected Skinner had solicited help from the local authorities even though it wasn't necessary. It was a stupid risk for him to take. The police officer would only get in the way. But obviously Skinner was panicking and had gotten extra help. Stone knew he had to act quickly. He did not want Monika to fall into the hands of the Québec City Police. By involving them, Skinner had determined his course of action.

Stone crossed over to the elevators and pressed the call button. As soon as he pressed the button the elevator next to the one the police officer had gotten into, opened. It was empty. He walked in and hurriedly pressed the button for the seventeenth floor anxious for the doors to close. He did not want any other company on the trip to the seventeenth floor.

Once under way Stone pulled out a small, black, metallic tubular device from his jacket pocket. He then removed his revolver from his jacket holster. With the touch of a seasoned professional he screwed the silencer to the muzzle of the revolver extending its barrel about three inches. Placing the revolver under his jacket to conceal it, he checked the dial over the door nervously waiting for the seventeenth floor. He did not look forward to what he knew he had to do but he could not allow any more witnesses to become involved, especially the police who he knew to be on the C2 payroll. He had hoped for a better outcome but now, resolved to his task, he looked forward to a speedy resolution to this unexpected police involvement. This whole operation had become much more intricate than he ever could have anticipated. The longer it was allowed to continue in this direction, the more dangerous it was becoming. Skinner was acting like a fool.

- - - - - - - - - - - - - - - -

Monika sat on the bed trying to decide what she should do. She opened her purse and took out the pieces of paper that contained François Jolliet's and her abductor's phone number. She was confused. She knew she had to phone her abductors sooner or later but wondered if she should call François first. Her instincts told her not to but she needed help now that she had the list. She knew she had to find a way to save James and herself and she couldn't do it on her own. She took her cell phone out from her purse and began to dial her abductor's number but stopped.

"No," she thought. "I'm not going to call. There has to be someone else." She rifled through her purse and found the card that Detective Callot had given her. She would trust him. There were several numbers on the card but she decided to call him at work. She didn't want to waste time trying to track him down. It was most likely he would be at his office. She punched in the number and placed the phone next to her ear. The phone rang.

"Homicide," the young receptionist answered.

"Detective Callot, please." Monika was nervous. She did not know how she was going to explain everything to the detective but she knew she had to and quickly if she was to get his help.

"One moment please." As soon as Monika asked for Detective Callot the receptionist redirected the call.

Jean-Paul Ferisse was standing outside the main entrance of the Ottawa Civic Hospital. It had been a long morning. He had waited at the hospital for word on James' condition, not wanting to return to the station until he had some news. Jean-Paul had spent his time waiting, between the coffee machine in the lobby and the nurses station on the second floor. James had not been brought back to the ICU and several hours had passed. Jean-Paul was weary and needed to go outside, get some fresh air and have a cigarette before returning to the floor. He was drawing his second puff when his phone rang. Regardless of the rules of the hospital he had left his phone on. He was on duty investigating a crime and it was necessary for him to keep in touch.

"Ferisse," he took his phone from his jacket pocket and answered.

Monika was startled. She wondered why Detective Callot had not answered. Perhaps the receptionist had misdirected her call. She did not answer. She held onto her phone and considered her options without saying a word.

"Hello. Hello?" Jean-Paul repeated and getting no response removed the phone from his ear and checked the signal strength. The reception was fine. He put the phone back to his ear. "Hello?"

"I was calling for Detective Callot." Monika decided to talk to Jean-Paul. After all, he was Detective Callot's partner and she needed help.

"Ms. Queller. Is that you?" Jean-Paul recognized her voice. He was surprised to hear from her.

"Yes. I need to talk with Detective Callot. Is he there?" Monika sounded desperate.

"No. He's dead," Jean-Paul said bluntly. He found the words difficult to say. He still couldn't believe his partner was gone.

"Dead? I don't understand." She was taken aback.

"Yes. I'm sorry. He was murdered last night at home." He decided to tell her the truth. Normally he would not have said anything but there was something in Monika's tone that made him change his mind.

"Oh no." This was too much of a coincidence. She knew Jack's death had some connection with the list. "I think I know who's involved," she blurted out.

"What? I don't understand?" Jean-Paul was puzzled. He had no idea what was going on. His heart began to race as he realized he might be able to bring Jack's murderer to justice if what Monika said was true.

"It's all part of what happened to James and

Craig. I need your help. I think they're going to try and kill James. I can't explain it all now but trust me. Can you protect James until I get back?"

Everything was beginning to make sense to her. If she could be certain that James was being protected, she could contact François and get his help in Québec City and maybe everything would work out.

"Who are they? Where are you?" Jean-Paul tested her.

"That's not important now. Can you protect James?" Monika ignored his questions. She needed to be assured James would be safe until her situation in Québec City was settled and she could get back to Ottawa. She knew C2 would act quickly to dispose of James and her once they were confident they could retrieve the list. Being followed to Québec City and the meeting at the basilica were evidence that confirmed her suspicions.

Jean-Paul fell silent while he considered what Monika had said. There was something about her call that persuaded him to go along with her at least for a little while. "Yes. I can. But who's involved and where are you?"

Just as Monika was about to tell him what she knew, there was a knock at her door. She was not expecting any one and she was alarmed by the interruption. "I can't talk now. I'll call you back. Someone's at the door. Be careful."

Jean-Paul tried to speak but Monika disconnected before he had a chance. Putting his phone back into his jacket pocket, he took one last drag on his cigarette and threw it into the street. He would go along with her wishes until he had a better understanding of what was going on. He opened the door behind him and went back into the hospital lobby. If what Monika said was true, then there was no time to waste.

Monika put her phone back into her purse and got up from the bed. Before she answered the door she looked around the room. Seeing the list and the Kraft envelope she picked them up and put them in the side pocket of her purse. Not knowing who was at the door she did not want to take any chances and leave the list out in clear view.

Whoever was outside in the hallway was growing impatient and knocked again. This time the knock was stronger and louder.

"Coming," she called out. If she didn't answer she felt certain whoever was outside would force their way in. She had to answer.

Approaching the room door, Monika prepared herself for whatever might be on the other side. Noticing the security latch on the inside of her door, she slid the chain in place and, opening the door about two inches, peeked into the hallway. Standing impatiently in front of her was a uniformed police officer. She wasn't sure if she should feel safe or more afraid. Adrenaline rushed through her body.

"Are you Monika Queller?" the police officer asked. His English was good but he spoke with a very strong French Canadian accent.

"Yes. How can I help you?" She wondered how the officer knew who she was. There were only two ways this was possible: he was here because of C2 or CSIS. Maybe her tail at the airport had enlisted the aid of the local authorities to track her down or maybe François had sent the officer assuming she had found the list and was trying to protect her. In either scenario she was suspicious of their speedy responses. Someone had very powerful connections to make things happen so rapidly. The timing was too perfect and it unnerved her. She better appreciated why Craig had not been comfortable in trusting just anyone with his discoveries.

"May I come in, mademoiselle?" Monika noted that the police officer was in his early twenties with dark hair and in good physical condition. He had a very stern and official look fixed on his face. He was not asking.

"Yes." Monika closed the door, took the chain out of the security latch and reopened it. She realized there was nothing else she could do. She was trapped. She should have expected this to happen and not remained in her room so long. She had had a false sense of security after losing her C2 tail.

"Thank you, mademoiselle," he said politely.

Leaving the door open, the officer walked into the room. He was just doing his job and following orders.

- - - - - - - - - - - - - - - -

Stone arrived on the seventeenth floor moments after the police officer stepped into Monika's room. Stealthily he exited onto the floor keeping his trigger finger ready on his gun, which he kept concealed beneath his jacket. There was no one else on the floor. He assumed the officer had already found Monika's room and gone in.

Noting the room directions from the plaque on the wall opposite the elevator, Stone headed down the hall toward 1720. As he neared the room he heard a man and woman in conversation. He put his gun out in front of him and kept to one side of the hallway in an effort to conceal his presence as he crept to the room. Stopping beside the doorway he readied himself. The door was opened inward and he could hear their voices.

- - - - - - - - - - - - - - - -

"How can I help, officer?" Monika held the door open and asked the officer as he stepped into her room.

"I'd like you to come with me if you don't mind." He was not asking.

"Go with you where?" Monika asked uneasily. She did not want to go with him but there was no way she could physically get past him.

"I'm not at liberty to say, mademoiselle."

"And if I refuse?" Monika knew this was not the normal police procedure like back home. In Canada, people could not be arrested or detained without just cause and there was certainly no reason for this officer to be requesting her to accompany him.

"I have my orders, mademoiselle. We can do this the easy way or the hard way," he insisted.

"Let me get my coat and things." Monika realized she had to go along with him. She turned and walked into the room to get her things. She did not like his repetitive use of mademoiselle. They both knew he was not genteel and there was no need to keep up the pretense.

"That's all right, mademoiselle. I'll wait here."

- - - - - - - - - - - - - - - -

This was the cue Stone was waiting for. As he heard Monika walk into the room to get her things, he moved in front of the doorway and without a moment's hesitation aimed his gun directly at the police officer's head.

"She won't be going anywhere with you," Stone announced.

Both the police officer and Monika turned to face the intruder. Monika immediately recognized Stone, and fearing for her life, gasped and dropped to the floor hiding behind the bed in hopes of protecting herself from Stone's weapon.

It was a silly place to hide but she was petrified and acted out of instinct.

The officer turned to face Stone and made an attempt to draw his weapon. Stone fired. There was a muted popping sound. A bullet struck the officer in the forehead killing him instantly. He fell against the wall, his eyes wide open in shock and slowly slipped to the ground. Stone kept his gun aimed at the officer. He stepped into the room allowing the door to close and waited a few seconds to be sure he was dead. He then crossed over to where Monika was hiding behind the bed, crouched down and cringing.

"Ms. Queller, I presume. You've given me quite a chase," Stone pointed his gun at her as he introduced himself.

Monika looked up at Stone and though she was afraid, tried not to show it. "Not as good as I would have liked," she replied nervously.

Keeping his gun trained on her, Stone picked up Monika's purse from the bed and went through it. He found the Kraft envelope in the side pocket along with the list. He chuckled. There was a disappointed expression on Monika's face. She saw how Stone was enjoying her situation.

Putting the list in his pocket, he pulled out his cellular phone and dialed Skinner's cell number. Skinner would be pleased with his report. He would not mention the incident with the police officer. Monika was his responsibility and no one was going to intrude on his territory.

- - - - - - - - - - - - - - - -

Skinner and Bonneau were seated in Le Parlementaire. They both had drinks and were waiting to order lunch. It was 12:35 pm. Le Parlementaire was originally a private members restaurant but was now open to the general public, however the vast majority of its patrons were members of the National Assembly, staff and their guests.

The entrance to the restaurant was at the top of the flight of stairs coming up from the main entrance hall of the Parliament buildings. A magnificent stained-glass canopy graced the entrance to the restaurant. The stained glass used a beautiful variety of blues and greens in its design and contained the old coat of arms of Québec which represented the three historical periods in Québec history: the fleurs-de-lis for the early French regime, the British lion for the British era, and maple leaves for Canadian confederation. The Québec motto *Je me souviens* appeared below the representations of the three regimes.

The room inside was large and designed in the Beaux-Arts style. It had an ornate feel of seventeenth century France. One expected to see the restaurant's patrons sitting at their tables in white wigs and the formal attire of courtiers of that period.

The historical ambiance of the restaurant shattered with the sound of Skinner's cell phone ringing in his jacket pocket.

"Excuse me Claude. I should take this," Skinner apologized and pulled his phone from his pocket.

"I understand. Go right ahead." The président was unconcerned. It was a normal occurrence these days.

"Skinner," he answered, trying to keep his voice low in an attempt not to disturb the other patrons or be overheard by the tables close by.

"Sir. I have the list and I have Ms. Queller. What would you like me to do?" Stone was proud of his accomplishment and beamed. He kept his gun pointed at Monika.

"Excellent. Take care of her and pick me up at the National Assembly in an hour. Good work Stone." Skinner disconnected. He was pleased.

"Good news?" Bonneau, seeing Skinner's change of mood, inquired.

"Very. We have the list and Ms. Queller." Skinner was relieved. It had come right down to the wire. If it had been any later he would have had difficulty trying to explain himself to the EXDIR. All that remained to be done was to eliminate any witnesses then everything could get back to normal. Since Stone had Monika and Hackett was in place at the Ottawa Civic, the next steps would be easy. Skinner felt he was now able to relax. After he got the list from Stone he would make his report to the EXDIR.

"Thank God. That was too close for comfort." Bonneau took a sip of his drink. His job and secrets were secure. He was glad Skinner had put everything right.

Skinner was only half listening to Bonneau's comments. He punched in a phone number on his cell phone.

"Hackett." Hackett felt his phone vibrate and answered.

"We have the list and Ms. Queller. Take care of the situation," Skinner spoke briefly.

"Yes Sir." Hackett disconnected. He was happy to get the-go-ahead. He was getting tired and bored sitting around the hospital with nothing to do. Now he could dispose of James and leave.

"To friends who take care of each other." Claude Bonneau lifted his glass to toast, as Skinner finished his conversation and put his phone away. He was grinning.

"Friends." Skinner likewise lifted his glass and joined in the toast, returning Bonneau's sinister smile. All was as it should be. His panic of the past few days receded.

"Bonjour monsieur le président. Monsieur. Êtes-vous prêtes á commander?" The waiter, a mature man wearing a newly pressed long-sleeved white shirt, dark tie and black dress pants, came up to their table to ask for their order. He addressed Bonneau first and then Skinner.

"Yes," Bonneau answered in English. "I think

we're all set."

Chapter 20

Forty-five minutes after speaking with Skinner, Hackett was still waiting on the second floor for James to come back to the ICU. It was almost one o'clock. Other than the nurses and other hospital staff going through their normal daytime routines, no other visitors or civilians had come to the floor or the waiting area. Hackett was completely alone. These were the hours in the hospital when most of the work was done.

Growing impatient, Hackett decided to go and find out what was happening to James. He got up from his seat in the waiting area, adjusted his shoulder holster under his jacket and walked down the hall to the ICU. He was wearing a dark blue polo shirt that matched the color of his parka, dark pants and black, highly polished dress shoes. Though he was dressed too warmly for indoors he could not take off his jacket for fear someone would see his shoulder holster and gun.

Opening the ICU doors he walked in and stopped at the nurses station. Nurse Geena was busy at her desk finishing the morning paperwork. He examined the unit but noted nothing out of the ordinary. The ICU was quiet. He checked James' empty cubicle on the far right side. Perhaps James had not survived. Maybe that was the reason he had not been brought back. If that were the case, it would save him a lot of trouble.

"Good afternoon." Hackett assumed his police detective persona.

Interrupted from her work, Geena turned to see who had greeted her.

"Detective Philips. What brings you around again?" She remembered him. Putting down her paperwork, she twisted 'round in her chair to face him at the counter.

"I came back to see how Mr. Anstey was doing," Hackett said flatly pretending he was there on a routine follow-up.

"Did you see the other detective?" she asked. Geena found something about Detective Philips' abrupt ruggedness attracting.

"Other Detective?" his mind immediately went to the official looking man he had seen during the course of the morning coming in and out of the ICU. Hackett had suspected he was a police officer just by the way he dressed and carried himself and was glad he had been careful, keeping out of sight in the waiting area.

"Detective Ferisse." Again Geena was surprised by Detective Philip's ignorance of the other officers investigating the case.

Noting her surprise, Hackett quickly made up a story. "Oh yes. We work in different divisions. I haven't had a chance to speak with him yet. Is he around?"

"He went out a little while ago for lunch. He should be back soon." She accepted his explanation.

"What about Mr. Anstey? I don't see him in the unit." He had not seen Detective Ferisse since he left the ICU about an hour ago. Though he did not show it, he was nervous the detective might return to the floor at any moment. Hackett did not like to be exposed. He was anxious to find James and complete his mission.

"He was taken to surgery this morning," Geena informed him.

"Is he okay?" Hackett feigned concern.

"Yes. I just heard from them upstairs. It was a difficult surgery but he seems to be holding on. He's a strong man. I don't think most people would've been able to get through what he's gone through." Geena swiveled back and forth in her chair.

"That's good news. When will he be back on the floor?" Hackett was disappointed. Now he would have to do his job and it would keep him there longer than he wanted.

"He's in recovery room 302. They just called to tell us he would be down this afternoon. I hope that's it for him. He's had a pretty rough time." Her skirt had risen up while she moved about in the chair but she didn't adjust it.

"I'll be back later this afternoon then." Hackett was flattered by her flirtatiousness but he did not have the opportunity to take advantage of it. She had given him a useful bit of information. It would be a lot easier to deal with James upstairs in a room than here in ICU.

"When I see Detective Ferisse I'll tell him you were here." She stopped fidgeting and stared at him.

"Thanks. I'll try to catch up with him. Thanks for your help. I'll see you later. Maybe we can get a coffee?" He smiled and winked at her then turned and walked away from the nurses station. He was not worried about Geena saying anything about him to the other detective. He would be long gone from the hospital by then.

"Anytime, Detective," she said under her breath as he left. She was flattered by his offer. She was lonely and did not often meet an available, attractive man.

Hackett made his way out of the ICU to the stairs. Keeping an eye out for the police detective he opened the stairwell door and went up to the third floor. He considered the various scenarios he might encounter there. If he was lucky, the floor would only be busy with hospital staff who would not pay much attention to his presence. If he acted quickly, he could have everything finished within the next ten minutes and no one would be the wiser. After everything James had been through, no one would suspect foul play had anything to do with his death. They would believe he had succumbed to his injuries.

Arriving at the third floor, Hackett opened the stairwell door and cautiously stepped into the corridor. The third floor was similarly laid out to the second. To his right, in the same position as the ICU, was a set of doors that led to the operating rooms. To his left was the long corridor that, like downstairs, ran the length of the wing of the hospital and was lined with rooms every fifteen or twenty feet.

He put his right hand in his pocket and felt the syringe. Other than the occasional nurse or orderly the hallway was empty. He turned left in search of room 302, keeping an eye out for the police detective.

Checking the number on the first room he came to, he ascertained his position. It was room 300. He did not have to go far. 302 would be the next room on his left. He was not at all nervous about what he was going to do. He had done this type of job many times before. Hospitals were very easy places to work since there was a transient population that milled about the building. No attention was given to outsiders wandering the hallways unless the outsider acted in a very strange way or lingered about too long in one place. Not wanting to be regarded as such an outsider, Hackett made his way to James' room.

The door to room 302 was closed. Hackett stopped in front of it, put his hand on the handle and leaned next to the door to listen, hoping no one else was inside the room with James. Not hearing any sound within the room, he twisted the handle and pushed the door slightly ajar. He peeked into the room before completely exposing his presence but all he could see from his position was the interior wall of the room. Taking a quick reconnoiter of the corridor to be sure he had not been noticed, he slipped into the room and stood silently with his back against the door as it closed. He examined the room.

The room was standard for a large teaching hospital like the Ottawa Civic. Directly opposite the door was a large window with drawn cream Venetian blinds overlooking the entrance of the hospital, the parking lot and Carlingview Avenue. It was the size of a university dorm room but far more institutional in its design and feel. With its off-white glossy plaster walls the room appeared sterile. A large rollable hospital bed took up most of the space.

On the wall opposite the bed to the left of the entrance was another doorway that led to the bathroom that was shared between rooms 300 and 302. The door was closed. A bright fluorescent four-foot light fixture illuminated the room from its central position in the high ceiling. James was lying in the bed unconscious. He was so completely wrapped in bandages, it was difficult to identify him but Hackett knew who he was.

Deciding on his course of action, Hackett took the syringe from his pocket and crossed over to the left side of the bed by the window where an IV bag was hanging above James. A tube ran from the bag and under the light green bedspread. Everything was working out as expected.

Grabbing hold of the clear IV tubing, Hackett injected the needle into the shunt valve and emptied the syringe. Within seconds he was finished. He felt relieved. Nobody could help James now. By the time he left the hospital and got into his car in the parking lot the chemical he injected would have entered James' system and its effect would be irreversible.

"Sweet dreams, Mr. Anstey," Hackett said as he removed the syringe and placed it back into his pocket, smiling confidently.

Suddenly, without warning, the bathroom door

flew open.

"Hold it there." Jean-Paul Ferisse broke into the room with his gun held in both hands aimed directly at Hackett. He stopped at the foot of the bed and stared Hackett in the eyes as he turned to see who had barged in on him.

"Back away," Jean-Paul commanded. He flicked his gun and indicated to Hackett to move away from James to the window.

Hackett instantly held his hands up and without commenting slowly backed to the window. He was calm. He was pleased he had managed to complete his job before the detective had burst in on him. There was nothing anyone could do to save James. The chemical was seeping into him. Hackett was far more concerned about what Skinner would do if he had not completed his mission, than being captured by the local authorities.

From the adjoining room beyond the shared bathroom, two uniformed officers came into James' room. They went over to Hackett and taking a firm hold of him, handcuffed him. One of the officers searched through Hackett's jacket and found his gun. He removed the weapon and held it out for Jean-Paul to see. Hackett did not struggle against the officers.

"Dr. Keene," Jean-Paul called into the room behind him. Now that Hackett was securely handcuffed and sandwiched between the two uniformed officers, he relaxed but kept his gun on the prisoner. He was not taking any chances. He knew from his experience that this man was a professional and would have many tricks up his sleeve.

Dr. Keene ran into the room over to James. He pulled back the bedspread and revealed the IV tubing for everyone in the room to see.

"It's okay. It worked." He lifted the tubing to reveal it was not attached to James' arm. It ran instead into a small bag lying next to his arm. "Whatever he injected, it's in here."

Hackett's mouth dropped. It had been a setup. They had expected him and taken precautions to protect James. The chemical he had injected into the IV was dripping into the bag and not James' arm. If James managed to recover from his surgery and wounds there would be a living witness to bring unwanted attention to C2. His failure to eliminate James would seal his doom.

"Take him away," Jean-Paul ordered the officers and holstered his gun. "I'll follow you to the station and interrogate him there."

The two officers manhandled Hackett past the doctor and out of the room. Hackett remained silent and did not struggle. As he brushed by Jean-Paul he gave him a menacing stare. Jean-Paul was not intimidated. Hackett was no longer in control.

"How is he, Doc?" Jean-Paul asked the doctor.

"He's still got a long way to go and he may not

survive his injuries but that goon didn't hurt him." Dr. Keene referred to Hackett's assault.

"Good. How long will you be keeping him here?" Jean-Paul knew it would be easier to maintain protective custody on the third floor than in the ICU but he also wanted whatever was best for James.

"We can keep him here. He's breathing on his own and stable. That would be better for you wouldn't it?" Dr. Keene understood Jean-Paul's concerns.

"It might be better for him too. I'll post an officer to the room. I don't think we'll have any more problems but just in case."

"By the way, is his fiancée back from Québec City?" the doctor was examining James' wrappings as he inquired.

"No. I spoke with her earlier. She should be here soon." Though he had spoken with Monika a while ago, Jean-Paul did not know she was calling from Québec City or when she was coming back but he did not want to tell the doctor. It was better to wait until he had more information and better understood what was going on. He wondered why Monika had gone to Québec City and how she had known that someone would make an attempt on James' life. When Monika returned he had a lot of questions for her.

"I see. It's a pity. I hope she gets back soon. He's been through a lot and..." Dr. Keene did not finish his sentence but clearly conveyed his meaning.

"I know. Thank you doctor. I'll be in touch." There was nothing more Jean-Paul could say or do. He went over to the door, opened it and left. He was determined to extract the answers to some of his questions from his prisoner at the station. He was willing to go beyond the rules and be as rough as necessary. He felt Jack's murder was connected to this case. This budding realization enraged him.

- - - - - - - - - - - - - - - -

Twenty minutes later Jean-Paul was walking down the hall to the interrogation rooms at the police station. This part of the station was like a prison. No one was allowed entry or exit without proper identification. As he arrived at the interrogation room he saw Detective Gerry Robbe standing outside the door. Robbe was a short, stout man in his early fifties. He was a bit of a redneck, having never traveled out of the Ottawa region other than during the annual winter vacation he took with his wife in Pompano Beach, Florida. He always looked as if he had just come from the barbershop. He was wearing a blue conservatively styled sports jacket, white shirt and striped tie, dark gray flannel pants and black leather shoes. He had large feet and his polished shoes stood out.

"Hi Gerry. Did he say anything?" Jean-Paul did

not expect he would.

"No. But look at this." Detective Robbe held out Hackett's wallet. "He has four different identities. Very professionally done. They look like the real thing. This guy is not an amateur. We're waiting on his prints but I don't think were going to be lucky with this guy. How are you doing?" Robbe added this personal question.

"It hasn't really hit home yet." Jean-Paul did not want to go into any greater explanation. He wanted to keep his mind on the case and not the untimely loss of Jack.

"I don't get it. Where would he get this type of work done? This stuff looks like the real thing. He couldn't have had it done in Ottawa. No one's that good. Who are we dealing with? Who is this guy and who is he working for?" Jean-Paul took the wallet and examined each of the pieces of identification. There were credit cards, drivers' licenses, and police identification, all with different names but each containing the photograph of the prisoner. None of the identification revealed Hackett's true identity.

"There's only one way to find out." Gerry opened the interrogation room door. "After you."

Jean-Paul walked into the small ten by ten foot room followed by the Gerry and the sound of his large leather-soled shoes scuffing against the floor. The room was nothing more than a dingy cell. The light from a low wattage four-foot fluorescent ceiling fixture was its only source of illumination. The room had no windows and its walls and ceiling were made of reinforced poured concrete. It was impossible to tell what time of day it might be cooped up in this isolated space. The floor was cold, hard and also make from the same poured unpainted concrete as the walls and ceiling. In the center of the room sat a gray metal table. The prisoner, shackled, was seated behind the table and slumped forward with his face pushed down against the tabletop.

"Time to wake up." Jean-Paul switched into interrogation mode and shouted. There was a bittersweet aroma in the room mixed in with the smell of stale nervous sweat. The prisoner did not react. "I said wake up. Are you deaf?"

"C'mon. You're going to make this harder than it has to be." Frustrated, Robbe crossed to the prisoner and grabbing hold of his collar, lifting him up. The prisoner was limp. There was drool on the table and foaming saliva coming out of his mouth.

Jean-Paul rushed over and put his finger against Hackett's neck feeling for a pulse. "He's dead."

"What? How?" Gerry, though a veteran of the force, was taken aback.

"It looks like some sort of poison. He must have had some hidden. This is unbelievable." Jean-Paul stepped back from the wet mess. Neither he nor Detective Robbe had ever encountered such a dramatic case. This was the sort of thing movies were made of, not real life.

"You'd better call the coroner. Let me know when you get the print report. And run all his ID. I'm going back to the hospital."

Chapter 21

"Get up." Stone waved his gun at Monika, indicating she should get up from the floor.

"Why? You're not going to let me live, so why don't you just take care of it now?" Monika knew her life was of no value now Stone had what he wanted. She looked up at him trying to read the expression upon his face. He seemed distracted.

"I said get up," Stone's voice was not threatening. "I'm not going to kill you." There was a noticeable change in him.

"I don't understand. You've got the list and I'm a threat to you." She slowly got up from the floor and sat on the bed. "What are you going to do?" She was nervous. If he wasn't going to kill her what else did he have in mind?

"I don't know." With his gun still aimed at her, he checked the time on his watch. His watch glass had a crack in it diagonally from eleven to five. The time was 12:40 pm.

Monika's heart raced. This was not going as she had expected. The man before her was not going to kill her, nor was he keeping her alive for sex. There was some other reason he wasn't going to hurt her. He appeared to be in a quandary and was no longer a threatening enemy.

"Can I help?" It seemed like a stupid thing for her to say but before she could stop the words, they came out of her mouth.

"How can you help? You don't understand," Stone chuckled. He didn't see how she could be of any assistance.

"Try me." Her curiosity was aroused. She sensed a change in the man, not understanding its source and softened.

"I'm Michael Stone. I work for the Canadian International Institute in Ottawa. Craig Jeneau was going to bring me in and give me immunity for the list and my testimony." Stone did not mention it had been him who had accidentally killed Craig. Something had gone wrong. Craig was meant to be wearing a bulletproof vest. The bullet hitting him was an accident. There was no point in telling Monika or the authorities it was he who had shot him. He did not know what to do. He was at a loss. He was not going to kill her but he knew once Skinner found out she was alive, he would be suspect. Regardless, it would not be long before Skinner discovered he was the leak. With Jeneau dead there would be no one to protect him from C2, his life was in jeopardy.

"What? I thought you were one of the bad guys." His revelation astounded her.

"That's what I used to think but things happened. It's a long story. I changed. I was going to start over. A new name and a new place. I wanted out but now that's impossible." Stone holstered his gun and remained standing in front of her.

"Why? I don't get it. What's going on?" She wondered what would cause a man like Stone to change his allegiance.

"C2, was set up about thirty years ago by the CIA. It's a secret operation with the sole purpose of creating instability within Canada. We saw an opportunity with the French to create a political situation that would be advantageous to us economically. Over the years we managed to infiltrate key positions in Québec politics. We were responsible for more radical ideas of the separatist movement. We've even managed to plant moles within your police agencies. It took a long time but it's just coming to fruition. The list," he tapped the area of his jacket where he had put the envelope and list, "It's just the tip of the iceberg. The minute C2 discovers what I did, and they will, they'll deal with me quickly and continue on their business as usual. All this will have been a wasted effort." Stone was demoralized. He had put his life and career on the line for nothing. He crossed over to the window and stared out onto the St. Lawrence River. He was not concerned about Monika escaping. There was nowhere for her to go. She would be found no matter where she went.

"I think I can help." No longer worried about Stone killing her, Monika was putting together a plan. François Jolliet had been right. With Stone's information confirming what he had told her at the basilica, she now believed she could trust him and perhaps François could help Stone and herself out of their situation.

"Help? How? They'll kill you, your boyfriend, and anyone else who's a threat to their plans. Including me. The problem is I don't know who we can trust. There are informants everywhere. I'm sure they've planned for this eventuality. They're not going to allow knowledge of C2 to get out under any circumstances no matter what the cost." Stone turned and faced her.

"That's the point. All we have to do is get to someone we can trust and I'm sure your operation will be closed down and hushed up. They won't worry about you or me anymore. Once the Canadian authorities have proof of C2's purpose, I'm sure a deal will be reached. This is not something that either government would want to get out. It would cause a tremendous economic crash not to mention the political fallout. No, both sides will want to keep this quiet. All we have to do is get the list to the right person and I think I know who that right person is."

Monika was pleased with her evaluation of the situation. She was right. Once the Canadian authorities had proof of the covert C2 operation they would use it to their advantage. As long as they could keep it quiet they could use the episode like blackmail to improve their political and economic agendas with the United States. The United States would do anything to protect itself from the level of embarrassment that exposing C2 would bring.

"Who?" Stone was curious. He knew most of C2's agents and wondered if her contact was one of them.

"François Jolliet. He works for CSIS." She gave him François's name.

"I don't know him. He's not one of ours. But I don't see how he can help. I'm picking up Skinner, he's in charge of C2, within the hour at the National Assembly. He'll want the list. Once he gets on the plane to Ottawa, we'll lose our opportunity. It won't be long before he finds out you're alive and puts two and two together." Stone had been assigned to C2 for many years and knew how they operated. Once Skinner got back to Ottawa he would have the upper hand.

"That's okay. François is here in Québec City. I know he'll be able to help. If we work fast we should have enough time." She was hopeful. If she could get hold of François she would be able to set something into motion. She wanted to get even with Stone's boss, Skinner, who she assumed was the man responsible for her abduction, Craig death and James' critical condition. She wanted to put him out of business and give him a taste of the agony she had gone through.

"So they're already onto us. I didn't know it had gone that far. We thought everything was contained, but it wasn't." Stone realized that C2 was no longer a secret. Once Washington knew C2 had been compromised, they would close down the operation and dispose of them. If he wanted to survive his only option was to cooperate with the Canadian authorities and Monika was his link to them.

"I have a number for him." Monika picked up her purse and rifled through it taking out her phone in the process. She soon found the piece of paper François had written his number on.

"Here it is." She held up the piece of paper and showed Stone noting his worried look. "Don't worry. This is going to work out. It has to." She smiled encouragingly. Both their futures depended on François's ability to help them. She punched François's number into her cellular phone and placed it against her ear. The phone rang twice and was answered by a man. Monika recognized his voice.

"François. It's Monika Queller. I need your help."

- - - - - - - - - - - - - - -

"Right on time." Skinner had been standing only a couple of minutes at the driveway entrance to the Président's office of the National Assembly when Stone pulled up in a black Suburban. Skinner walked over to the truck with its black tinted windows, opened the door and got into the middle passenger seat. He was not suspicious of the vehicle. C2 kept it in Québec City for their use whenever they were there. He assumed Stone had picked up the vehicle from the garage on the quai Saint-André in the old harbor where it was parked. It was 1:30 pm.

"Yes, sir." Stone was in the driver's seat and did not turnaround to face Skinner. As soon as the passenger door was closed, he put the truck into drive and made his way out of the parking lot to the street.

"Did you have any problems with Ms. Queller?" Skinner adjusted his overcoat and placed his attaché case more securely on the seat next to him.

"No sir. It's all taken care of." Stone was concentrating on the road and pulled onto the main street. "To the airport, sir?" he inquired, changing the subject.

"Yes. I want to get back to Ottawa quickly. You have the list?" Skinner looked into the rearview mirror and caught Stone's eyes. Stone's look was affirmative which reassured him. He was pleased everything was over.

"Yes, sir. Here it is." Stone took the list from his jacket pocket and handed it to Skinner.

"Good work." Skinner briefly examined the list and, satisfied it was authentic, placed it inside his jacket breast pocket. "We should have nothing to worry about. Hackett's taking care of Anstey and you've done Queller and I have the list.All I want to do is find out how this got out of C2." He tapped his breast pocket indicating the list.

"Yes sir. I can get right on it in Ottawa." Stone wanted to appease Skinner. He knew he would not give up until he had discovered the leak.

"When we find out who it is, we're going to give him a lesson in loyalty he won't forget." Skinner shook his head in disgust at the thought of being betrayed by one of his own.

"Yes sir," Stone agreed, concentrating upon the drive.

The two men fell silent for the remainder of the trip to the airport. It had been a busy couple of days and Skinner welcomed the opportunity to return home and get back to business as usual. Once he got back to Ottawa he would make his report to the EXDIR in Washington D C. He was relieved to have good news for him and be able to redeem himself in his eyes. His position with C2 would be secure for a while longer but it had been a close call. He would personally take care of whoever had leaked the list to Craig Jeneau and caused him so many difficulties. He wondered who it might be? He began going through the list of operatives in his mind trying to determine the most likely candidate.

By 1:50 pm Stone was pulling into the airport. The flight to Ottawa was at 3:00 pm.

"Sir. If you don't mind I'll park in the lot first." Stone checked with Skinner and looked into the rearview mirror to see his reaction.

"That's fine. We have plenty of time." Checking his watch Skinner agreed. He would be returning to Québec City by himself on Saturday for a meeting at the consulate and wanted to know where the truck would be parked.

Stone turned into the parking lot opposite the terminal building to the north of the air traffic control tower. He drove to the third row and pulled into a space. Turning off the car, he opened his door and got out to open Skinner's. Skinner, attaché case in hand, stepped out into the lot. The two men began to walk to the terminal. Stone kept a couple of steps behind.

"Is something wrong?" Skinner wondered why Stone was walking so far behind him, Stone did not answer. Their conversation was interrupted by the abrupt arrival of a gray Suburban and a passenger sedan coming from opposite directions and stopping directly in front of them.

The doors to the Suburban opened and two large men, wearing gray suits, jumped out with their guns drawn. The two men had the same short haircut and gave the impression of being in the military. A third smaller man, casually dressed sporting a goatee, got out from the driver's side of the sedan with his gun drawn and pointed at Skinner. It was François. Monika was sitting in the passenger seat of the sedan watching.

"Hold it there," François rushed over and yelled out.

Before Skinner could react the other two larger men were upon him. He saw Monika in the sedan and instantly realized what was going on. Stone had tricked him. He had been set up. Stone was the leak. The two men from the Suburban grabbed Skinner's arms and handcuff them behind his back as they forced him over to François.

"Hey. What…" Skinner began to protest.

"Shut up." François stuck his gun into Skinner's side and went through his jacket pockets. Finding the list, he pulled it out and waved it in front of him.

"You're under arrest. We have a lot of questions for you before we arrange to have you returned to your friends in Washington. Put him inside."

Skinner was trapped. He had not expected this

sudden turn of events. If it had not been for Stone none of this would be happening.

"So it was you." He struggled to turn and face Stone who was standing off to the side but the two men prevented him from turning and manhandled him into the truck, getting in with him and closing the door, cutting off anymore communication. Skinner sat helplessly between the two men in the rear seat of the Suburban looking out the window.

Now that Skinner was secured in the truck, Monika got out of the sedan and came over to François and Stone. She put her hands in her coat pockets to keep them warm. A light snow was starting to fall. The sky was overcast with heavy dark clouds. A winter storm was brewing. The gray Suburban started to back up. Monika looked over and caught Skinner's eye inside the truck. She silently communicated her satisfaction at his capture knowing full well what would happen to him once he was returned to the US. Skinner would be lucky to live out the next twelve hours.

Skinner was fuming. It was Monika who was responsible for his demise. There was nothing he could do. She had gotten even with him. He continued to stare at her as the truck drove away admonishing himself for being so foolish in underestimating her.

"Thank you both. We couldn't have done this without you." François put his gun away and relaxed. The dangerous part of the plan was over.

It had gone smoothly which was the way he liked things to go.

"What will happen now?" Monika was relieved to see Skinner in custody.

"We'll give Michael a new identity and keep him safe. I don't think they'll try anything now. We know too much. As far as Skinner is concerned, I think he's going on a long one way trip." François confirmed what Monika already suspected. Alive, Skinner was too much of a liability. There was no way he would be allowed to remain alive to tell his side of the story. Of course the US government would deny everything and without any witnesses to corroborate any accusations Stone would be written off as an independent rogue spy. No records would exist to link him to any official agency in the US.

It would be a difficult political situation for the US but they would survivc. Secretly a deal would be made that would favor Canada economically and eventually the two countries would leave the C2 incident behind them. The public would never know a thing.

"He deserves it after what he's done." Monika was angry at Skinner for all the harm he had managed to do. Though she would have to keep everything secret in order to return to her normal life, she was satisfied with the end result. C2 was shut down and Skinner would be terminated.

"We should get you back to Ottawa right away.

I've arranged for a helicopter. It's the least we can do. C'mon. I'll drop you. I've notified the hospital you're coming. You'll be there in an hour."

"Thank you and thank you Michael," she thanked François and Stone. She was anxious to get back to the hospital and be with James.

"No. Thank you. I'm sorry about everything. I hope your fiancé's okay." Stone smiled and shook her hand. He held on for several moments. If it had not been for her help everything would have been impossible. She had given him a chance at a new beginning and for that he was grateful.

"You know what to do?" François interrupted them and asked Stone.

"Yes." Stone clearly understood the arrangements he had made with François before picking up Skinner.

"Then I'll see you soon." François shook Stone's hand.

"Yeah," Stone acknowledged, turned and walked back to his Suburban. In a few hours he would be far from the cold of Québec City in a warmer climate with a new identity, making a fresh start.

"Will he be okay?" Monika asked, once Stone got into his vehicle.

"Yes. We'll take care of him. Don't worry. He's very important to us. Now…let's get you back to Ottawa."

Chapter 22

Jean-Paul was standing next to the rooftop door that led to the hospital stairwell. The view from the hospital's eighth story was magnificent. He could clearly see downtown Ottawa, the Parliament buildings as well as the surrounding suburban area. He watched as the helicopter that was carrying Monika made its approach. The helicopter was of medium size and could carry four passengers. It was painted yellow and had the logo of the Canadian Coast Guard on its side. As it hovered overhead the loud thumping of its rotor caused him to place his hands over his ears. Snow and dust flew up as it lowered and finally touched down on the roof. The side door of the helicopter opened and Monika, keeping her head down and holding her hat on her head against the downdraft, got out. Jean-Paul waved her over. She acknowledged him and, being careful to keep low, crossed over to him. No one else was on the rooftop. It was not often the hospital heliport was used.

"What's going on?" Jean-Paul had to shout above the noise of the helicopter.

"I'll tell you later. How's James?" Monika shouted back not sure if he had heard her. She was still holding on to her hat.

Once she was clear, the helicopter revved its engines causing the downdraft to increase in intensity. The helicopter lifted off. Monika and Jean-Paul protected themselves from the powerful wind and watched as the craft slowly climbed and disappeared into the late afternoon sky. Peace and quiet returned and they were now able to speak normally. Monika took her hand off her hat.

"I'm sorry but he's not good. He's in a private room on the third floor. I'll take you." Jean-Paul decided not to pressure her about all the recent events. There would be plenty of time later to get answers to his questions. When he had found out from nurse Geena that Monika was returning by helicopter, he began to consider a whole new range of questions. This was not a normal occurrence. He realized that there were greater powers than the Ottawa Police Force at work.

"I'd like to see him now," Monika was emotional. She had hoped to hear that James had improved, but it clearly had worsened. She did not want to lose him. She was filled with mixed emotions of fear, anger and helplessness. She held back her tears though she wanted to cry. She needed some sort of release but she knew she had to remain strong for James. She told herself not to give up hope no matter how dismal James' condition appeared.

"This way." Jean-Paul understood the range of emotions he could sense in Monika. After losing his partner he realized how she must feel. He guided her off the rooftop into the stairwell.

They walked down several flights in silence and came to the third floor. Before they exited into the hallway Jean-Paul stopped. Though he didn't want to upset her, he wanted to have a word with her in private before going onto the floor.

"You were right." He put his hand on the door handle and looked at her.

"About what?" She was intrigued and wanted to hear what Jean-Paul meant. She had forgotten their phone conversation.

"Someone tried to kill James but we managed to stop him. How did you know?" He carefully observed her reaction.

"It's pretty complicated and I'm not sure where to start. Trust me. I'll tell you everything I can later. Right now I just want to concentrate on James. All this has kept me away from him at a time when I should have been here and I don't want it to get in the way again. James needs me. Please understand." Monika was not sure what she should say to Jean-Paul and she wasn't ready to speak to him now about everything. She hoped that when the time arrived, François Jolliet would be there to help her.

"Okay. We can do this later. James is this way." He twisted the handle and opened the door escorting her onto the third floor. A uniformed police officer was standing to the left about twenty feet away outside James' room.

Monika became anxious. For some reason she couldn't explain, the sight of the officer alarmed her. She didn't know what to expect. As they approached the police officer, the door to James' room opened and Dr. Keene stepped into the hallway. Monika and Jean-Paul stopped.

"Dr. Keene this is Monika Queller, Mr. Anstey's fiancée," Jean-Paul introduced her. Dr. Keene was still on duty and wearing his operating room scrubs under a white overcoat with his name embroidered on the left breast pocket. He was extremely tired.

"How is he?" Monika was direct and ignored the normal niceties. She braced herself for his answer.

"I wish I could give you better news. I've done all I can. I had to go in and stop his internal bleeding this morning. He lost a lot of blood and is very weak." The doctor was not offended by her directness. He was used this type of reaction under these circumstances. He sympathized with her concern for her fiancé but was not sure what to say. He knew how critical James was but he had seen cases like this survive beyond all odds. No matter how rare the occurrence he did not wish to dash her hopes. She seemed so fragile to him.

"Is he going to live?" Monika was choked up. She sensed the doctor was hedging. She remained strong and fought back her emotions. No matter what the doctor told her she believed in miracles and would not give up on James.

There was an awkward silence while Dr. Keene considered the best way to phrase his answer. "I don't know. He's pretty bad. It's not in my hands anymore. I..."

"Can I see him?" Monika had heard enough. She didn't want to hear what he was trying to say. It was obvious the doctor had done everything he could and felt as helpless as she did.

"Certainly. He's inside." Dr. Keene moved aside to allow her to pass relieved that she had cut him short. He didn't like to give bad news.

"Thank you." Monika stepped in front of the door and put her hand on the handle waiting while she gathered her courage. She did not want James to sense anything bad from her. She wanted to be as positive as she could.

"I'll wait out here with the doctor." Jean-Paul

put his hand on her shoulder to comfort her. He did not believe James would survive. Seeing her devotion for him, he felt sadness for her. It wasn't fair but life was seldom fair.

Monika took a couple of deep breaths, turned the handle, opened the door and walked into the room. As the door closed behind her she saw James in the bed. Even though it was a similar sight as the first time she'd seen him, she was horrified seeing him lying there. He was wrapped in bandages and had an IV dripping into his arm. The tube from his mouth was gone. He was unconscious and breathing in a labored way. There were electrodes attached to his chest and connected to monitors on the other side of the bed.

"Oh James." She brought her hands to her face and hurried over to his bedside taking off her hat and coat, throwing them over the chair next to the bed.

Carefully she sat on the bed, leaned over and kissed him. He did not react. She felt suddenly alone. The sight of him in such poor condition was too emotionally overpowering for her. She was unable to control herself. A dark wave of gloom overtook her. She was unable to speak. She began to pant. Tears welled from her eyes and ran down her cheeks. She wrapped her arms around him and buried her face next to his head. She felt comforted at touching him. She smelled his bittersweet scent and felt the roughness of his skin against hers. She knew there was nothing more that medicine could do for him. She tried to force her energy onto him and will him back. Her heart ached. Though she felt the futility of her actions, she believed in the power of love and focused her thoughts and energy on that power. She silently prayed to God and begged him for a miracle. She lay there a few moments not wanting to let him go but deep inside she was beginning to think that she must.

"Ahh. Monika?" in a long drawn out weak whisper she heard James' voice in her ear. She sat up in disbelief and stared at him.

"James? It's me. I'm here." It was hard for her to talk she was so overcome by her feelings. She blurted her words out between sobs. She wondered if she had really heard his voice or if her mind, being so overwrought, was playing tricks on her. She was caught between despair and joy not knowing what to believe. Everything was beyond her control. Just as she was beginning to accept she had imagined hearing him, she saw his eyelids twitch. She was overjoyed. She had not imagined it.

"James. James. Wake up. Don't leave me," she pleaded and gently shook him.

His eyelids began to flicker more and suddenly popped open. He was staring directly at her.

"Monika?" he did not have much energy and

from his voice she could tell he was in a great deal of discomfort. He lay there disoriented with his eyes half open unable to move or say anything more. He was happy to see her.

"James. I love you." She leaned forward and delicately kissed him. Her tears poured out and dripped on his cheek. James did not speak. He blinked his eyes in communication. He tried to moan a reply but it was too much for him.

"Don't speak, sweetie. Everything is going to be okay. I love you." Monika felt reborn. Her prayer had been answered.

"Doctor. 'Dr. Keene'," she called out smiling and crying joyful tears. She kissed him several more times.

The door to the room opened. The doctor and Jean-Paul hurried in expecting to find the worst.

"He's awake," she sobbed out as she turned to face them, revealing a conscious James.

Jean-Paul and the doctor were moved by the scene before them.

Epilogue

Thursday 10:16 am

"You can't go in there." In Washington DC, Jon Crane's secretary tried to stop two large men from forcing their way unannounced into the EXDIR's office but was unsuccessful. She stood up not sure what she should do.

The two men were CIA agents. After the fiasco of C2 every loose end was being cleaned up. The EXDIR was thc last person on their list.

"Hey! You can't come in here like this." Jon Crane was on the phone and angered by their rude intrusion. He stood up to confront them holding the phone receiver in his hand. His secretary came running in behind them leaving the door to his office wide open.

"I'm sorry sir. I couldn't stop them." Fearful for her job she apologized and remained at the doorway.

"Jon Crane. You're under arrest. You have the right..." one of the agents began to read the EXDIR his rights while the other handcuffed him and hung up the phone. Crane did not struggle.

"I know my rights." The EXDIR knew what this was all about. He had expected something to happen but not so soon.

The two agents escorted him from his office. A small crowd of secretaries and other staff stood nervously gossiping amongst themselves as they watched their boss being carted away, not realizing they would never see him again.

SYNOPSES

MONIKA QUELLER MYSTERY NOVELS™

OBSESSION

A Novel By Best-selling Author:

Terence Munsey

SYNOPSIS

After her family dies, a young woman, Monika Queller, and her friend, James Anstey, are stalked then chased to San Francisco where they stumble upon a secret.

Monika Queller's parents mysteriously die in a car accident. Their bodies are never recovered. Her father was a research scientist at Stanford University. Unable to bear the pain of her loss,

Monika decides to start her life over, away from the reminders of her tragedy. She moves to Los Angeles where she takes a job as an adult education teacher.

Once settled in Los Angeles, strange things begin to happen to Monika. She is stalked, receives prank calls, her car is vandalized, finally her home is broken into and vandalized. She is at a loss to understand and turns to a colleague, James Anstey, for help. Unknown to Monika, James is an undercover CIA agent who has been placed to protect and keep an eye on her. Monika's father was working on top secret experiments and his death is suspicious.

Monika discovers a note from her father, which was hidden in his old briefcase. The note directs her to go back to San Francisco and collect something from a post office box at the university, but she does not know what it is she will find there.

As Monika and James start out on their journey, they find themselves being followed by an unknown pursuer or pursuers. Soon they are being chased. They decide that they must try to get to the university before whoever is after them can catch them—it is their only hope of solving the mystery. Along the trip, Monika and James become romantically involved.

Once at the university they retrieve an envelope from the post office box and are waylaid by their pursuers. James is taken captive, but Monika manages to escape with the aid of Bill Meyers, an FBI agent who also has been following both of them.

Monika discovers that her parents are not dead. A ransom demand is made by James' captors for his safe return—the envelope for James. Working with the San Francisco FBI office chief, Mical Grai, and Bill Meyers, Monika agrees to the exchange. Grai is one of the bad guys. He is after Monika's father's secret research, though Monika and Meyers are not yet aware of this fact.

Further complicating the plot and without Grai knowing, James is rescued by another undercover operative, William, and an exchange meeting is arranged at Fisherman's Wharf. William's undercover operation suspects Grai and is hoping to set him up—he wants to expose and arrest Grai.

At the exchange Grai panics once he realizes that he has been set up. He takes Monika and tries to escape capture. Grai manages to get to his car and with Monika, attempts a get-away. Unfortunately the attempt is foiled when Monika struggles with Grai inside the car; a struggle that causes the car to crash and sink into the harbor.

Monika awakens in the hospital. She was rescued from the harbor, but does not remember anything after crashing into the dark cold water other than being trapped with Grai in his car and then passing out.

Now awake and recovered the mystery is

revealed to her. Grai is dead. Monika's parents are alive and by her hospital bed. The story ends as Monika is reunited with James, with whom she has fallen in love.

EMERALD CITY

A NOVEL BY BEST-SELLING AUTHOR:

TERENCE MUNSEY

SYNOPSIS

A gripping thriller involving subterfuge, and international intrigue, set in the most sophisticated city of the world.

The story opens with a brutal murder of a courier, Ted Ambrose, in the first class lounge at Toronto International Airport. It is a professional hit. The bag that Ted is transporting is handcuffed to his wrist and the killer is forced to hack-off

Ted's wrist to get the bag.

Two weeks later, Monika Queller, our heroine, is on her way to Toronto to participate in the Harborfront Writer's Festival. While at the festival she encounters the son of the murdered courier, Andrew Ambrose, who convinces her to help him to prove the involvement of ABM COMPUTERS in his father's murder.

ABM has developed a new chip technology that allows them to access all the data on any of their new computers that contain the chip. By offering free internet access and voice mail capabilities on their computers, ABM encourages owners of their computers to leave their machines permanently connected to the phone lines and switched on. Through their new product registration lists, ABM is able to gain all the information needed in order to gain access to the data on any of their new computers. The result is ABM's ability to acquire all sorts of privileged information from a variety of international sources, including governments, businesses and those who use ABM's new computers and have registered their warrantee information.

Someone working for ABM, Bob Rosen, tried to sell the new technology to a competitor and used Ted Ambrose to deliver the chip. Like Ted, he is also murdered, and the sale prevented. ABM's secret is kept secure.

Monika and Andrew, stumble onto this information while searching for evidence to prove ABM's involvement in Andrew's father's murder. As a result they become targets, and ABM tries to stop them from revealing what they have discovered. ABM catches Andrew, but Monika escapes.

Monika manages to notify her boyfriend, James Anstey, a CIA operative working in Los Angeles, via an internet message while she tries to hide from ABM.

James comes to Toronto in an attempt to save Monika from ABM, but is unable to locate her. Eventually he manages to trace her movements and with the aid of the local authorities, manages to find her just in time at the top of the CN Tower, where ABM CEO Arthur Kazinski, is attempting to throw her off the tower. A scuffle ensues. James fights with Kazinski. Shots are fired and Kazinski falls off the tower to his death, 1100 feet below.

Monika is saved by James and later, Andrew is found tied-up and unharmed in ABM's Toronto warehouse. ABM's activities are exposed. James and Monika are reunited. This adventure has made them realize how much they need and love each other.

DIVE MASTER

A Novel By Best-selling Author:

Terence Munsey

SYNOPSIS

While on vacation, Monika Queller stumbles upon a body and is thrust into a murder-mystery whodunit set along Florida's Gold Coast, from Pompano Beach to Key West, delving into the world of power, politics and cloning…

Monika is to join her fiancé, James Anstey, at the end of the week in Key West, where he is going to take her to meet his parents for the first time. Deciding she wants a few days to explore Florida on her own, she arrives in Miami on a Saturday, rents a car and heads a few miles north to Pompano Beach, planning to work her way down through the Keys and meet James on the following Saturday as they'd agreed. In the meantime, her first stop is the beach.

While on the beach in Pompano, Monika stumbles upon a dead body in the water. She is horrified. The police are called, but the man's body cannot be identified right away. Monika doesn't realize that the dead man is a clone of Dive Master Jesse Ehrlich, that was meant to be disposed of in the ocean and is part of a plot to kidnap the President of the United States.

The kidnapping is being planned by a large computer software company called Microtech and a small group within the military and security forces of the United States. William Fence, CEO of Microtech, along with Major Britin a liaison officer for the military, Cedric Hemings, a Secret Service agent attached to the White House and Dr. Vernon Pearl, are all co conspirators.

In conjunction with the military, Microtech has secretly developed a new method to clone and download all memories and personality of a person. These memories can be uploaded into the clone, creating an almost perfect duplicate that is undetectable to anyone. Moreover, Microtech is able to modify the personality through the upload to make the clone replacement unknowingly do their bidding. The dead body in Pompano was a trial version of the Dive Master to be used in Microtech's scheme. The President is set to attend a ceremony at Fort Jefferson, seventy-eight miles off the coast of Key West. It is there during a dive, that the plot is to unfold.

Monika continues her trip after the experience in Pompano and goes to Key Largo where she hopes to dive at Coral Reef Park. While there, she hires a guide only to discover that he is the exact twin of the dead body she found in the water at Pompano. Monika has discovered a main player in Microtech's conspiracy without realizing it.

The conspirators, who are alerted to Monika's finding of the dead clone in Pompano and the duplicate in Key Largo, chase and capture her. They cannot afford to let her run loose and jeopardize their plans. She is imprisoned in an old abandoned naval base on Key West. While imprisoned, she comes upon the real Jesse Ehrlich who is incarcerated in the cell opposite hers.

Together they unravel the plot against the President. Escaping their imprisonment, Monika tries to contact James but is only able to leave him a message. She and Jesse realize they are now the only ones who can save the President.

Pretending to be part of the media covering the Presidential visit, Monika and Jesse make their way to Fort Jefferson. Once there, they run into a problem and make a startling discovery.

LA

A Novel By Best-selling Author:

Terence Munsey

SYNOPSIS

Monika Queller finds herself entangled in a web of glamour and sin, plunging her into a whirlwind suspense adventure from the fantasy world of Hollywood to the tropical paradise of Puerto Vallarta, where she must solve the crime or die...

Lupita Anez, an employee of Rupert Wels Productions in Hollywood, discovers something and threatens to expose Rupert Wels, a successful movie and television producer and celebrity. As a result, she is raped and murdered by Rupert Wels' chauffeur, Bobby Jurgansen, in order to silence her threat. In the process she loses a silver seahorse earring engraved with her initials. The seahorse is the symbol of Lupita's home town—Puerto Vallarta.

Monika has sold film rights of one of her books to Rupert Wels Productions not knowing about Wels' seedier side and is invited to be his guest for a couple of days in Puerto Vallarta to oversee the filming. She is driven to LAX in Wels' limousine and finds a seahorse earring hidden in the carpet, not realizing that it belonged to Lupita Anez.

In Puerto Vallarta Monika stays at Andréez Vallarta, a five star resort where she discovers it is run by Wels' Mexican partner, Miguel Andréez. Monika shows the earring to Miguel Andréez, who secretly identifies it as belonging to Lupita and understands the danger it presents.—He helped to get Lupita the job in Los Angeles using forged immigration papers. He worries that the engraved earring can be linked eventually to Wels and himself. This is something that he cannot allow to happen.

Wels and Andréez are ruthless and operate on the illicit side of the Hollywood show business world. The trail of their crimes reaches high up into the entertainment industry. Through Wels' top rated television show, Who Wants To Be

Rich, they have managed, amongst other things, to launder money for organized crime in return for certain favors.

Concerned about being exposed, Wels and Andréez attempt to kill Monika while she visits Mexico by throwing her into the Ameca River high in the Sierra Madre mountains behind Puerto Vallarta en route to the movie set. Believing they are successful, she is reported as missing to the local authorities who go through the motions of conducting a search bringing no results. The local authorities are controlled by Miguel Andréez.

Monika manages to survive the horrific experience of the river and a waterfall and is rescued by a local indian, Hernando. With Hernando's help she finds her way back to Puerto Vallarta and eventually Los Angeles.

Meanwhile Monika's fiancé, James Anstey, along with his friend LAPD Homicide Detective John Atero, have flown to Puerto Vallarta to try and find Monika, but they are unsuccessful. To his delight James discovers that Monika is alive and has mysteriously returned home.

In Los Angeles Wels is expecting Andréez for the annual movie awards. He also discovers that Monika has survived and sends Bobby Jurgansen to kill her. A cat and mouse game ensues.

James and John return to Los Angeles and are able to apprehend Bobby Jurgansen before he can kill Monika. They make him talk. He tells them everything about Wels and Andréez.

The story continues with an ingenious plan to entrap Wels and Andréez during the televised awards ceremony, where a spine tingling drama at the Los Angeles Auditorium culminates in a spectacular twist of fate.

RETRIBUTION

A Novel By Best-selling Author:

Terence Munsey

SYNOPSIS

Monika Queller's latest murder-mystery whodunit, Retribution, unfolds in the politically charged streets and legislatures of Ottawa and Québec City. Craig Jeneau, an RCMP officer, uncovers a disturbing international plot. His wariness of the local authorities leads him to secretly contact Monika's fiancé, James Anstey, who is a CIA agent based in Los Angeles. They meet in

Ottawa at the Empire Grille but before they can follow up on their hunches, they are ambushed on the street behind the bar and shot. Craig is mortally wounded and James is left barely clinging to life. Monika rushes from Los Angeles to James' Ottawa hospital bed, where she discovers a secret that leads her to Québec City. But is she prepared for what she finds?

Monika Queller is notified of James' condition by Detective Jack Callot of the Ottawa police who picks her up at the Ottawa airport. Unaware they are being followed, he drops her at the Ottawa Civic hospital. Jeneau found a list that has the potential to expose the Canadian International Institute, C2, a front for a covert CIA operation to create political and economic instability in Canada by infiltrating Québec politics and promoting French Canadian separatism.

After spending some time with James, Monika goes to her hotel, where she is given an envelope by the front desk clerk. When she returns to the hospital she opens the envelope to find an encrypted message.

Having seen her with the envelope, Monika's C2 tail follows her to the hospital where he drugs and abducts her, and then takes her to his superiors at the C2 office near the parliament buildings. Detective Callot is murdered and Monika is kept blindfolded while she is interrogated at C2. She is given forty-eight hours to find and return the list, which contains the names of C2's Québec-based operatives, or she and James will be killed.

Monika's unknown abductors return her to the hospital where she begins to decipher the coded message. She finally determines that the encrypted message reveals that the list is hidden in a room at the Château Frontenac in Québec City. Without telling anyone, she leaves for Québec City hoping to retrieve the list and save herself and James within the time limit. Monika is followed by a C2 and a CSIS, Canadian Security and Information Service, agent (who has been keeping tabs on her and the C2 operative since Craig Jeneau's murder).

As she arrives in Québec City, Monika realizes she is being tailed by C2's operative and successfully loses him. At the Château Frontenac, she decides to collect her thoughts and wait for check-in time at the hotel bar. In the bar, thc bartender hands her a note that tells her she must go to the Basilique Notre-Dame if she values her life.

Monika goes in search of the basilica and enters the confessional where she meets François Jolliet, the CSIS agent. Jolliet tells her everything he knows and asks for her help in finding the list. Although Monika is not sure if she can trust him, she agrees.

Monika returns to the hotel, checks into her room and searches until she finds the list, only to be confronted by her C2 tail. Just when she thinks all is lost, she discovers her tail is responsible for leaking the list to Craig Jeneau and is willing to help her. They devise a successful plan, along with François Jolliet, to capture the head of C2 and put an end to his operation.

Monika's retribution is complete, but it is hollow since she discovers, upon her return to the hospital in Ottawa, that James has taken a turn for the worst and lies at death's door.

Terence Munsey lives in Richmond Hill, Ontario, Canada. He holds an M.A. from Stanford University and writes mystery, fantasy, science fiction and HOW TO books.

Visit the website: www.MunseyMusic.com

Read these books by TERENCE MUNSEY:

The FLIGHT of the STONEMAN'S SON
The KEEPER of THREE
LABYRINTHS of LIGHT
MARKS of STONE
THEY of OLD
OBSESSION
EMERALD CITY
DIVE MASTER
LA
RETRIBUTION
TATOO
HOW TO: BE A PUBLISHED AUTHOR